Night Wonder

Night Wonder

Linda Kelly

Night Wonder

Abbott Press books may be ordered through booksellers or by contacting:

Abbott Press
1663 Liberty Drive
Bloomington, IN 47403
www.abbottpress.com
Phone: 1-866-697-5310

ISBN: 978-1-4582-0054-9 (sc)
ISBN: 978-1-4582-0053-2 (e)

Library of Congress Control Number: 2011916292

Printed in the United States of America

Abbott Press rev. date: 9/26/2011

Prologue

In the tiny South African country of Katari, Dr. Michael Lugano, assistant minister of health, closed the manila folder on his desk with a sigh. The file, stamped, "Case Closed" in bold, black letters, would be placed in the dead records office along with the effects of ten women slain by "The Katari Ripper," the brutal serial killer who had terrorized the nation. Rumors had been spread throughout Africa that the great leader of Katari, President Mozamba, had possessed the right magic to stop the murders.

Closing his briefcase and picking up his medical bag, Dr. Lugano strode wearily out of the government building and climbed into his jeep. After removing his white lab coat and hastily loosening his tie, he headed out of town. The doctor carefully flashed his badge and papers at the each of the checkpoints leading to the border. When the dirt roads changed into the beaten paths of tribal herds, he turned to the right and climbed steadily up the Hill of the Ghosts. The villagers believed these verdant ridges were home to spirits of the dead and therefore, sacred.

Dr. Lugano, who respected the superstitions of the herdsmen, fingered the talisman of feathers, beads, and lion claws on the leather strap around his neck. When a tall medicine man dressed in a brightly hued, feathered tunic and white face paint stopped him at the base of the third hill, the doctor bowed his head in respect, showing him the charm.

The medicine man raised his arm and shouted a special incantation as he drove away.

Sweat poured down Lugano's face as the late afternoon sun continued to beat down on the open jeep. At the base of a vertical escarpment, he stopped, turned off the engine, and started off on foot. Hastily removing his binoculars from its case, he scanned the trees and rocks until he found what he was looking for: the mouth of a small cave nearly hidden by thorny brambles. Taking a drink from his canteen, he climbed slowly up the mountain, carefully scanning the area.

The Hill of Ghosts, was not just a holy place, it was home to a pride of mountain lions that fiercely guarded their territory. The only human the feral animals feared was the man the doctor had come to see.

Before going any farther, Lugano removed a hand mirror from its leather pouch. Catching the sun's reflection, he moved the mirror back and forth until the beam could be seen from the entrance to the cavern. When a flash of reflected light signaled in return, he knew it was safe to proceed.

Hiking up the side of the cliff was agonizingly slow and treacherous, but his sturdy walking stick, given to him by a tribal chieftain years ago, kept him from falling during his precarious ascent. Once near the apex, he wiped the sweat from his worry-lined face and took a long drink from the canteen. Pushing the brambles aside with gloved hands, he entered the dark recesses of the cave. It took several minutes for his eyes to adjust as he continued down the low, narrow tunnel to the right. His mouth creased into a grimace as he moved deeper and deeper into blackness, his back aching from its uncomfortable stooped position.

Finally, the tunnel opened into a larger cavern, illuminated by the small flame of a kerosene lamp. The man he sought sat in the gloom, surrounded by a sentient pride of lions reclining near his feet.

"It's about time," the man's deep baritone echoed from the shadows.

Dr. Lugano waited nervously as the vigilant animals stared at him suspiciously with large yellow eyes. The hulking man rose and moved into the light. His dirty, disheveled clothes hung on his body in shreds. His ghostly white face, lined with deep creases, was enveloped by matted, wild hair. The beard on his chin and jaws had grown so long and shaggy that he resembled the mythical Yeti of Tibet.

Seeing the disturbed look on Lugano's face, the tall man asked, "What did you expect? I've been living in the jungle for months. I ran out of supplies weeks ago. Fortunately, my feline comrades provided me with the first taste of their kill. Not what I prefer, but one has to eat."

"If you hadn't insisted on taking unacceptable nourishment, the authorities wouldn't be hunting you down like a wild animal," Lugano replied angrily.

"Please don't bore me with your lopsided morality," the man replied sharply. "Did you book passage for me or not?"

"The Mercado leaves port in two days," Lugano answered stiffly. "Here is the name of the man I want you to see when you get to the States." The doctor handed the glowering man a business card saying, "If you want to live, you'll do what he asks."

"I've always wanted to visit the States," the man stated sarcastically.

"I don't know why I'm helping you," Lugano commented wearily.

"Blood is still thicker than water, I guess," the pale man replied with a slight grin.

"Not after tonight," Lugano retorted. "If you don't keep your promise, I'll take care of you myself."

"I believe you would," The man concurred. "You better go now. My feline friends are getting restless and hungry."

Lugano left hastily, rushing down the mountain, fleeing from the low moans of jungle cats on the prowl. Sliding awkwardly down the last hill, the doctor ran to his jeep and got in. As he glanced in his rear view mirror, the fiery sun was setting beyond the ridges.

Dust and dirt kicked up behind the jeep as he pressed down the accelerator demanding more speed from the engine. He had to get back to the office before the electricity was shut down for the night. There was an urgent phone call he had to make. His heart stopped beating wildly when he arrived at the final checkpoint into Katari.

Four weeks later, in a city in the mid-western United States, a gaunt figure moved with purpose through a shadowy, rain-slick back alley in the Central West End, rifling through dumpsters and upending trashcans. The cold November wind whipped through the narrow passageway with a low-pitched moaning sound. Disturbed by the commotion, an alley cat nearby screeched angrily as his prey streaked away, its long rat tail flying as it frantically scrambled into a jagged crack and disappeared into a hole in the brick wall.

As the lone dumpster diver continued scavenging, he paused momentarily, to gaze down the alley toward the busy street, distracted by the sounds of chicly dressed couples as they hastily entered their favorite shops, restaurants, and pubs. These ordinary people thrived in the "normal" world, now lost to the shabbily dressed man who watched them wistfully. As he moved furtively toward the glow of the multicolored holiday lights, his dirty, bearded face was briefly cast in luminous relief. His limpid gray eyes darted back and forth nervously in contrast to his calm exterior.

After briefly scanning the busy avenue, the man suddenly whirled away, seeking the anonymity of the shadows once again. Scrounging around for a cigarette butt, he tripped over something soft and unmoving in an oily puddle of water. He gasped recoiling at the sight of a young woman's motionless body sprawled near his feet. Her eyes were opened wide, an expression of surprise forever frozen on her tawny young face. Ripped shreds of fabric, once her clothing, barely covered her body.

With one gloved hand, the trembling man touched the flawless skin of the young woman's cheek. Acutely aware of possible danger, the wary man grunted and turned sharply. Moving swiftly in a complete circle, his intense eyes searched the gangways, back yards, and basements surrounding the area. Fearful the killer was lurking in the shadows, he carefully scanned the ledges, balconies, and fire escapes above his head.

Seeing no one, the agitated man hung his head and crouched near the girl's body. The tune of a requiem hymn from St. Ignatius' church played in his confused mind. He quietly sang the Latin words over and over, wanting to pay his respects, yet unsure of what the words meant:

"Dies ere dies ela, solvet sacum, in fa fila, Tuva me rum spargen so num."

Salty moisture rolled down his cheeks. He quickly wiped his face, surprised at his tears. Seeing the dead girl had pierced the steely armor of his usual reserve. He looked away briefly, trying to regain control. The deceased woman had been a friend of his.

Reaching out tentatively with a trembling hand, the man carefully slipped the expensive gold jewelry from the dead girl's fingers and wrists. Ever so gently, he removed the dangling diamonds from her pierced ears, but he was reticent to touch the tiny gold cross and chain around her slender neck. Although saddened by her brutal death, his survival dictated that anything she had of value was now his.

Stuffing the unexpected treasure in the pocket of his stained raincoat, the nervous derelict turned away. Hurrying down the alley, he swiftly climbed over a chain link fence barricading his exit. He flipped open the dead girl's cell phone and dialed 911. After he alerted the police, he rapidly traversed the busy street, dumping the phone in a chained-down trash receptacle in Forest Park. Pulling up his collar against the brisk night air, he melted into the darkness and vanished from view.

Above the macabre scene, several lights came on in a third-floor apartment. A young minister, unable to sleep, paced restlessly in his rooms, carrying a leather-bound book in his hands. His lips were moving, but the familiar words he read provided little comfort. Sensing something from outside, he threw on a black jacket, opened the window in his office, and climbed onto the landing of his rickety fire escape.

Above him, the firmament was dotted with gray cumulus clouds that would shortly bring the rainstorm that had been predicted on the nightly news. A myriad of stars stood out against a velvety purple sky, winking down at the earth below. To the troubled young minister, they seemed like cold, blinking eyes, unsympathetic spectators to the human dramas played out below.

Glancing downward, something unusual caught the preacher's eyes. At first it appeared that a storefront mannequin had been carelessly discarded in the alley. He gasped when he realized it was a woman's body that lay on the rain-streaked pavement below. Jumping nimbly over the landing, he climbed down the metal ladder to the pavement and knelt beside the woman.

Suddenly recognizing the dead woman, the startled man mouthed the words, "Oh No!" With two slender fingers he touched her neck. Although her skin was slightly warm, he could feel no pulse. For a final test, he leaned his right ear near the girl's mouth, hoping to feel a touch of exhaled breath from her parted lips. Mercifully, the poor woman was now beyond the troubles of this world and all that led to her demise.

At the sound of running feet, the sorrowful man glanced worriedly down the dimly lit alley. He caught a glimpse of a coattail flapping behind a familiar homeless man whose long, unkempt hair whipped behind him. Before he could call out his name, the fleeing man had bounded over the fence with surprising agility and bolted across Kingshighway Boulevard. Once in Forest Park, he leaped over a row of woody hedges and disappeared into the darkness.

Turning back to the murder victim, the minister noticed the absence of jewelry on her body, save a gold chain and cross pendant. Using a cotton handkerchief from his pocket, he checked the dead girl's purse; the wallet inside was empty of cash, yet her I.D. and credit cards were untouched. Two white tickets with bold red lettering caught his eye. Removing them carefully, he turned them toward the bright bulb of a streetlight nearby, his eyebrows arched in recognition of the venue named on them. Looking around, he quickly slipped the tickets into his pocket.

Leaning back on his haunches, the grieving man sighed and lifted his hands upward in prayer as tears streamed down his strained face dropping silently to the ground. A police siren in the distance broke his concentration. Melting into the shadows, the preacher waited patiently, willing himself to avert his eyes from the young woman's pitiful body, which lay in front of him under a thin blanket of soggy newspapers. He noted with interest that the bold headline on one of the pages read, "Central West End Ripper Strikes Again." The paper was dated, November 1, three weeks earlier.

Chapter 1

Theodore Falcon observed the packed audience for the Midnight Supper Club's special event from the very last row. Friday, the 13th marked a special occasion for the organization's highly connected members. The club, boasting a secret membership equaling that of the Masons, would meet a "real" vampire for the first time.

The club members' obsession with the undead, previously based on myth, had been no deterrent to their animated arguments about the "rules for being a vampire." Certain assumptions: immortality, animal transformation, and fear of sunlight, were accepted as facts.

The famous movie actor, who had played a riveting vampire in a frightening film of the 1990s, waited in anticipation with his young wife at a front-row table. Having read all the literature and researched his character extensively, he considered himself an authority on vampires.

Club representatives from England, France, Spain, Serbia, Russia, Egypt, and other nations comprised most of the VIP section. Curiously, Transylvania, the historic home of the vampire, had declined the invitation. The United States was by far the lead nation in its adulation, if not outright idolatry, of all things concerning the infamous creatures of the night.

Suddenly, the house lights dimmed and people hurried to their seats. An exceedingly pallid middle-aged man with slick, black hair going gray at the temples, wearing a flowing black cape over an elegantly tailored tuxedo, and a white pleated dress shirt with a scarlet cummerbund, walked briskly to the microphone on the velvet-curtained stage. Bowing low to the audience, he spoke in a cultured baritone voice, announcing:

"Good evening. I'm Rascal Gold, Esquire, emcee for this auspicious occasion. I know you are waiting anxiously to meet our guest speaker." With a dramatic flourish of his arm, he continued, "Without further ado, I introduce Theodore Falcon, vampire!"

The audience looked puzzled, because if anyone looked like a vampire it was Rascal Gold. Their disappointment did not ebb when the main attraction rose from his seat in the back row and casually made his way toward the stage.

Falcon hopped up on the stage and took a seat on the bar stool in front of the audience. Not at all what they expected, he stood about five foot ten, was slight of build, and wore a brown leather bomber jacket, gray T-shirt, black jeans, and gray snakeskin cowboy boots. The smallish man's more rugged features—thick hair, heavy eyebrows, full reddish-brown mustache, pug nose, and wide mouth, did nothing to dampen the boyish look of his round face. In fact, Falcon looked more like a mascot for the Fighting Irish than a vicious predator. But there was nothing amusing about his intense ebony eyes. They were unusually large and so uniformly black that the iris and the pupil appeared as one. In the direct beam of the spotlight, they appeared as flat golden discs, giving him the eerie look of a wild animal caught in a vehicle's headlights.

"Thanks for the intro Mr. Gold," Falcon said in a slight British accent.

"I bet you thought old Rascal here was the real vampire," Falcon began with a grin. "Sorry to disappoint you mates. It's just me."

Taking a drink from the glass of red wine on the table next to his perch, he continued, "For the record, most of what you know about vampires is a bold-faced lie and complete fabrication!"

The audience was visibly perturbed by this revelation and showed their puzzlement with caustic whispers. When the confused chattering ebbed, Falcon continued.

"First off, Vampires are not walking corpses. They are living, breathing beings. How do you suppose they are able to live among ordinary folks like yourselves and go unnoticed, hey? They live solitary lives, spending most of it remaining inconspicuous. If vampires were to go around jumping out of coffins and hissing, 'I want to bite your neck' in an Eastern European accent to every good-looking babe that came along, they would have become extinct long ago. That nonsense came from books, legends, and old films. Vampires are cunning, clever, and evasive-hence, their extreme longevity." Clearing his throat Falcon said, "For all you know the person sitting next to you could be a bloody vampire."

This statement brought an immediate reaction. Patrons began eyeing their tablemates suspiciously and chattering nervously among themselves. Falcon waved his arms to get their attention and added, "Don't worry ladies and gents, they aren't out to kill you. They don't go around gnawing away at people's jugulars in a crowded room. That's a stupid myth perpetuated by scary stories meant to frighten children. My ancestors might have hunted in packs out of desperation, but they paid dearly for their indiscretions by getting beheaded, impaled, or burned at the stake. Those who escaped lived in seclusion, raided animal dens for food in the winter, and avoided town folk like the plague. Any impulsive male vampire who molested a farmer's daughter got stuck with a pitchfork."

Falcon stood up, took the microphone off the stand, and resumed with, "But enough about the bloody past. I'm sure you have lots of questions."

"How do we know that you're a real vampire?" a platinum-blonde starlet poured into a slinky black sheath asked.

"You have my word," Falcon answered.

"We demand proof!" a bespectacled older gentleman with a thick head of silver hair and an unlit pipe in his hand demanded. "Anyone can say they're a vampire."

"You're name wouldn't be Van Helsing would it?" Falcon asked pointedly.

"I wasted my money on this table!" a rotund gentleman exclaimed, rising from his chair and shaking his fist at the speaker.

"What's the matter, bloke? The steak's no good?" Falcon asked. "You'll have to take that up with Mr. Gold."

Over the audience's outburst of laughter, a huge fellow whose bulging muscles strained in an ill-fitting suit jacket, stood up and shouted, "I ought to come up there and beat the living daylights out of you!"

"You'll have to go to the end of that long line old chap," Falcon retorted.

Seeing that the crowd was getting out of hand, the handsome actor who had played the quintessential vampire bounded on the stage and shielded Falcon with his body. Flashing his perfect white teeth, he expounded, "I believe you, Falcon. But these good people need proof."

Falcon moved away from the actor's protection and replied, "I see that you believe what I'm saying without question. Your faith moves me deeply, but there will be no ostentatious displays of power tonight."

After the audience had quieted down and the actor had returned to his seat next to his wife, a matronly woman, wearing a loud black-and-white checked jacket stood up and asked in a trembling voice, "Mr. Falcon, just how old are you?"

"You wouldn't like it if I asked *you* that question," Falcon replied with a slight smirk.

After the audience's hearty laughter quickly dissipated the edgy atmosphere that had permeated the club, Falcon smiled at the woman and explained, "In my estimation, I am nearly three hundred years old. My earliest recollection is of my family leaving England on a merchant vessel, the HMS Eleanor, bound for America. My father was taken on as the ship's physician with my brother as his assistant and my mother as his nurse. I was appointed cabin boy to Captain Wellington for the duration of the trip. To the best of my knowledge, that was the year 1712.

Falcon took a long drink, gazed at the audience and continued his narrative. "We disembarked in New York and traveled over land to West Virginia where my father was pressed into service as the company doctor on Paul Robertson's tobacco plantation. Father took care of a large population of indentured servants and African slaves. We were given a modest house, all the food we needed, and the promise of our freedom in five years." He paused, then relayed,

"We stayed on for twenty-five, until the locals began to notice that we didn't age like normal folks. Rumors of witchcraft and black magic spread like wildfire. On All Hallows Eve, in 1737, my family and I escaped into the forest making winter camp with a tribe of Native Americans. After gaining the trust of the Osage, we were able to leave on our own accord. My parents hired a boat and we traveled via the Mississippi to St. Louis where my father opened his first medical practice."

"Why do vampires live so long?" a dark-skinned beauty with large brown eyes and long African braids inquired.

Falcon answered with a question, "Why does any being live to a certain age? It's the way we're made—our physiology and genetics. A cleric once told me that vampires live for centuries because God wants to give them enough time to repent their two great sins: killing people and drinking human blood."

"Do you drink human blood?" a short, pudgy man wearing a St. Louis Cardinals baseball cap asked, his bold brown eyes peering through wire-rimmed glasses.

"Well, now-a-days it's more like having a cocktail or perhaps a transfusion," Falcon explained. "Draining blood from folks, like you see in the movies, is never advisable; they die, you get caught. Even Native American tribes knew how to handle the Pale Spirits as they called vampires. A clean shot with an arrow right through the heart would do the trick. Swoosh, and they were dead, whether a vampire or an intruding settler."

"How did you and your family survive all those months in the wilderness?" a pale woman with short, maroon hair and dark-violet eyes asked interestedly.

"My parents were smarter than the so-called, rogue vampires," Falcon returned. "Making a vow to never kill any living creature, we trapped animals, consuming only what we needed, leaving them alive. We never hunted down and subdued wild game, like you see in films. Deer are stronger than you think. A doe is stronger than a man, and a buck could trample you and gore you with his antlers. Small game were our food of choice; rabbits, beaver, and raccoons."

"Have you ever fed on a human?" a man in a minister's collar asked pointedly.

"Only to save my life, Reverend," Falcon answered soberly.

Scanning the audience, Falcon noted varied reactions to this statement. Some people had satisfied smirks on their faces, others wore horrified expressions. Most were leaning forward, eager to hear the details. Restless, he shifted his weight on the bar stool, briefly bowed his head, and looked up at the audience as he recounted his autobiography in the expressive tone of a master storyteller:

"The winter of 1738 was the harshest in history for the Midwest. We were living with an Osage Indian tribe in the Ozarks during a terrible famine; even the stored grains in secret caches were empty. The chief decided that he and the strongest members of the tribe would feast on the last bit of meat left and then travel south to find game. Because my family members were outsiders, we had no choice but to stay behind with the elderly, women, children, and the sick. There was only one way to keep them alive until the braves returned with food. My father gave them a nightly sleeping draught in their broth of hot water, wild onions, and turnips. While they slept, we fed on their blood, draining several ounces of our own into their cooking pots. We used wild beet juice to disguise the color and herbs to hide the taste. The Osage never knew what they were drinking with their vegetable soup, but our mingled blood saved their lives and ours.

When the braves returned and saw that everyone had survived the winter, the chief attributed the miracle to the great power of my father's medicine. He was awarded membership in the tribe and thereafter called Pale Healer.

Having been granted permission to continue our journey, we were given gifts of horses, food, and supplies. My father was so traumatized about drinking human blood that he refuses to talk about that part of our history to this day."

Seeing the audience's puzzled expression, Falcon explained, "My father had a strict code about extracting blood from people. He considered it immoral, an abomination."

"So you're a moral blood-sucking vampire!" a smirking man in jeans and a polo shirt protested disgustedly.

"Disappointed?" Falcon asked. "You know you ought to put a cap on that rage. You're a bit scary." Addressing the audience, he added an aside with an ironic smile, "I wouldn't want to be on the receiving end of his road rage out on the streets."

Staring intensely out at the audience he continued. "A vampire can't be too careful." he remarked. "You see, there's a crowd outside that has cannily guessed what's going on in here. They're angry and scared. Some people are holding torches, well, candles really, for a prayer vigil. There's a passel of blokes outside carrying sharp pointed stakes, just in case I'm a real vampire. To top it off, the news media is milling about, eager to take an award-winning video of any one of the VIP's in the audience tonight."

Feigning displeasure, Rascal Gold grabbed the microphone from Falcon and hastily announced, "I'm sure there are more questions for Mr. Falcon. Let's take a break and listen to the energetic sounds of our guest band, Schizophrenia, singing their latest hit song by the same name."

The heavy-metal rock band broke into music as the lead singer, Cue-T, belted out;

> "Schizophrenia, this country's got a wicked kind of mania. We'd better wake up and change our ways, or I guarantee they'll be hell to pay."

After a loud burst of earsplitting guitars and pounding drums, he continued:

> "Poor and middle class can't pay the rent. Their houses are foreclosed they're living in tents. Crooked brokers wrecked their American Dream-Made off with their retirement on a Ponzi scheme. Schizophrenia, this country's got a wicked kind of mania . . . ."

Falcon heard the faint sounds of the chorus as he slipped out the back way and hurried down the dark alley. It was embarrassing how melodramatic he could be sometime. To be sure, the audience would be incensed when he failed to return, but that was the point. Gold had suggested this contrived exit, which would require the audience return the next week. His vampire presentation was a good payday for Gold. The mortgage on the old St. Louis Arts building, that housed the dining room where the Midnight Supper Club met, did not come cheaply.

Falcon replayed the events of the evening in his mind as he rushed by the busy streets in a blur. Ordinaries, regular humans, didn't want to know the truth about the small community of vampires that lived secret lives in their cities. Instead, they craved a carnival show with colorful lights, death defying acts, and a mind-boggling display of extraordinary powers. Supper Club members preferred to hold onto the myths surrounding vampires that could terrify and awe them at the same time. Perhaps they would understand that consuming blood was a necessity for a vampire's survival, but he doubted they could accept the truth; that some vampires preferred taking blood directly from humans. That would bring in the question of choice. Without the element of choice, vampires could be sympathized with, perhaps even be forgiven, for their unnatural ways.

Vampires living in the past had required taking the blood of Ordinaries to live. By the twentieth century, blood was readily available, for a price. No invasive contact with a sentient being or animal was necessary to nourish oneself. Free will had been given to all God's children, vampire and Ordinary alike. It was how these choices were made that distinguished the Freebloods, vampires with a strict code, from the Keepers, rogue vampires who believed their natural state was to reign over all other beings on earth.

Falcon entered his apartment and poured himself a glass of his essential nutrients from a stainless steel carafe. His unique drink was a mixture of 5% dark-red wine(preferably Merlot), pureed pomegranates and blackberries, assorted spices, and a packet of freshly thawed flash-frozen plasma. He opened the small freezer under his wet bar, grabbed an packet of B positive, and placed it in the refrigerator in a dark canvas lunch bag. Being the owner of the second largest blood bank in Missouri seemed justified because he was able to supply himself and other vampires with much-needed nourishment. He reasoned, that if others thought he was a ghoul, so be it. This was survival for a twenty-first-century vampire.

Chapter 2

Falcon pondered the history of his family as he walked the dark streets. He and a remnant of other vampires living across the globe were conscientious Freebloods, although their ancestors hadn't been so enlightened. Years of being hunted down and killed by Ordinaries had taught them an important lesson: survival meant secrecy. Abstaining from humans, they took their nourishment from animals. As time progressed, they became farmers, buying land and herding large animals into corrals and barns, living in peaceful coexistence with the people around them.

Something threatened the present harmony between vampires and Ordinaries; a serial killer was preying on young women in the area. Whenever there were unexplained killings, the local authorities made a massive search and invaded the privacy of citizens. Their intensive investigations could expose his people to danger. If the existence of a vampire nation was exposed, the resultant upheaval could destroy them.

Falcon was concerned that a different kind of vampire had invaded his city. Believing they were superior to every living being on earth, a small itinerate group of rogue vampires fed on whatever species they chose. This ancient vampire clan saw no reason not to graze freely on the prolific population of Ordinaries. Keepers, as they called themselves, felt that they were the last bastions of the natural, vampire state. Completely self-absorbed, they didn't consider the ethical ramifications of their actions. In their minds, Ordinaries were cattle and therefore, disposable.

From his top floor apartment, Falcon gazed at the city skyline. In the distance, the St. Louis Arch pierced the night sky, its metallic legs gleaming below an enormous, harvest moon. The Old Courthouse and The Cathedral were reflected in the mirrored glass of the tall downtown skyscrapers. Beyond these sentient structures, the Mississippi River's dark, satiny currents flowed like quicksilver in the moonlight.

Directly below Falcon's building, the Central West End was a glittering panorama of bright streetlights, multicolored holiday lights, and the nonstop streak of headlights from vehicles whizzing up and down the busy avenues. In the midst of this dry, bustling city was the green oasis of Forest Park, Falcon's favorite haunt.

The graceful spires of St. Ignatius Catholic Church, a glowing monument to the spiritual side of humanity, pierced the dark-violet sky. "Faith," Falcon whispered aloud, pondering man's fundamental belief in a Creator and what it meant today: hope for a better life, good works, concern for the poor, and the desire to purify oneself, were the same aspirations that embracing one God had given the peoples of the ancient world.

Despite the violent actions of their past, faith had subdued the baser side of Falcon's Freeblood ancestors. Furthermore, he believed that transforming faith still flourished, in such places as: St. Ignatius Church, The Redeemer Mission, and Abraham Temple. He saw these charismatic houses of worship as three glowing beacons of hope in the city.

The Central West End Ripper's terrorism threatened the physical and spiritual health of vampires and Ordinaries alike. With a killer lurching about in the shadows, hope for peace this holiday season was floundering. The mayor and other city officials were on the news daily, urging citizens to be observant and report anything that looked suspicious. Falcon fully intended to initiate his own investigation. His friend and Freeblood contact at City Hall, Eli Tobias, was keeping him apprised of the situation.

Profilers described the Central West End Ripper as; a white male in his forties, educated, familiar with anatomy, compulsively specific about his victims, socially acceptable, and able to blend in with society.

According to forensic evidence, the Ripper killed methodically, leaving no human DNA or fingerprints on the slashed body of his victims. The Rippers fiendish acts were executed with determined, paranormal skill. Falcon contemplated that only a special team of enforcers would be able to find and apprehend this elusive killer.

Falcon believed that vampires could play a unique part in finding the Ripper. Their physiology worked more efficiently than that of Ordinaries. Consuming blood sent the flow of important nutrients directly to tissues and organs, including the heart, increasing their endurance. If wounded, a vampire would heal rapidly. A broken bone would not merely knit, but become stronger. Penetrating night vision and accelerated speed made them efficient hunters. With the help of a unique group of Freeblood vampires, Falcon believed that The Central West End Ripper that plagued the city could be stopped.

Still unable to find peace, Falcon donned his black, great coat, hurriedly taking the elevator to the ground floor. He prowled the streets each night hoping to catch the Ripper before the police found him. Many of the killer's habits were much like his own: both were nocturnal, kept a low profile, and blended in well with Ordinaries.

A cool breeze buffeted Falcon's coat as he traversed the Dogtown neighborhood. He was struck by the quietude of the area which was unusual at this time of the year. No joyous holiday music filled the air with the melody of bells and flutes. The Christmas season, usually Falcon's favorite time of year, was marred by the untimely deaths of three young women. Earlier today, the city's mandatory curfew had begun. Fearing to linger in the streets, people rushed to their cars and locked their doors. By ten o'clock the streets were vacant, except for police officers patrolling the sidewalks, alleys, and breezeways. Falcon hid in the shadows as they passed, making his way to Forest Park.

Strolling deeper into the park, his breath condensing into a white mist, Falcon streaked by paved walking paths, enjoying the sound of the crisp fall leaves crunching under his quick steps. He was in his element, enveloped in cool darkness, watching the bowed branches of the tall trees reaching toward him like friendly arms. Many of these monuments to longevity were the same trees he had strolled by decades before. The crackling of the dry leaves under his feet reminded him of the many autumns spent on the family farm as a child. As he moved along the path, the sudden cry of a hoot owl dispelled the peaceful ambience of the park. Like the plaintive cry of a child, it reminded him that there would be no peace until the Ripper was found.

Falcon spied a figure running ahead of him, a stealthy looking character dressed in a black, hooded jacket and sweatpants. The stranger didn't move like a runner, but furtively, like a man who was following someone. The man's head turned from side to side, his eyes scanning the area to see if anyone else was around.

Falcon quickly moved back into the shadows and followed silently from a distance. He soon realized that the stealthy figure was in pursuit of someone already on the path. Feeling protective, Falcon loped ahead to find the stalker's intended victim. Taking a shortcut across the grass, he outdistanced both runners, and hid in the darkness to watch the impending drama unfold.

A young woman in a dark jogging outfit ran effortlessly down the trail with the grace and speed of a gazelle. Long strands of dark red hair escaped her knit cap and streamed down her narrow shoulders and back like flickering flames. Sensing she was being pursued, the woman twisted around to see who was following her.

As her profile turned his way, Falcon sighed. His vampire eyes scanned every detail of her face. Her high, tawny forehead was smooth, while her wide oval eyes were the color of a dark-violet night, peering beneath smoky-colored lashes and elegantly arched brows. Caught in the glow of the harvest moon overhead, the expression on her lovely face was at once wild and intelligent. Her full lips opened to gulp in oxygen as she quickened her evasive pace. Rather than becoming frantic, she remained cool and calculating as she fled from the man now struggling to catch up with her.

Falcon waited at his vantage point ahead of the scene, his heart thumping wildly in his chest. He would make sure that she came to no harm, but he was reticent to interfere. The man could be someone she knew, Falcon thought, a brother, or a playful lover. One could never be sure of the games people played after dark.

To Falcon's surprise, the girl gradually slowed her pace, appearing to tire. Her assailant was only a few feet behind when she suddenly turned on him. With one lunge she felled her attacker, planted two feet firmly on his chest, easily holding the squirming man down. Like a tigress defending her cubs, the girl pulled back her right arm, bringing it swiftly forward to strike, long nails glinting in the lamplight.

Before the woman could lower her arm and slash the mugger's throat, Falcon intervened. As he pulled the startled woman's arm away, the man broke free, sprang to his feet, and fled. Falcon left the woman on the grass and flew to intercept the hooded man. Grabbing the attacker by the seat of his pants, Falcon gave him one swift kick, sending the surprised assailant flying a hundred feet into a prickly hawthorn bush. The entangled man struggled violently a few moments, finally freed himself from the bush, and darted away, glancing back nervously.

Outraged at being deprived of her revenge against the stalker, the woman lunged angrily at Falcon, who instantly stepped aside. In one swift movement he caught her before she fell to the ground. When she attempted to retaliate, Falcon pinned her arms to her sides and sat her down on a wooden park bench.

"Calm down and I'll let you go," he said. When the disgruntled woman looked up at him with an angry stare, Falcon added, "Killing that pervert would have been the biggest mistake of your life."

Struggling to break free, the woman retorted through clenched teeth, "Let me go! That creep deserves to have his throat cut!"

"I grant you that he deserves a sound thrashing," Falcon returned. "Get control of yourself. Do you really want that Ordinary's blood on your hands?"

"Who do you think you are?" the woman answered, eyes flashing. "I was going to be that thug's next victim!"

"He would have been *your* victim if I hadn't stopped you," Falcon replied levelly.

"No one would miss that worthless piece of trash!" The woman retorted, rising to her feet and facing him indolently.

Amused by the woman's vehement stare and jutting chin, Falcon picked up her hat and handed it to her, explaining, "If you kill one of them, you'll have the whole town of Ordinaries down on our heads. When they discover what we are, they'll hunt us down and kill us like rabid dogs."

The woman looked at him with irritation, answering, "You have got to be kidding. I don't intend to be caught!"

"This time," Falcon corrected. "The next time you could lose your cool with an inconsiderate driver who cuts you off, or a surly store clerk. You have to control your rage if you want to live a full lifespan."

"Now, that's what I'm talking about," the girl commented, staring at him as if he were completely insane. "Lifespan," she pointed out, "is so—retro. Nobody talks like that anymore."

Falcon returned her bold, but interested stare, which started his heart pounding again like a teenager's.

Lowering her eyes, the woman spoke in a matter-of-fact tone saying, "I suppose you expect me to thank you for saving me, but I can handle myself." Thinking better of her attitude, she quickly added, "Well, I can see you are older, and probably still bound by the Code of Chivalry."

Falcon laughed lightly and replied, "You're about five centuries off, and I should remind you that rudeness is unacceptable in any era. I have just witnessed that you can take care of yourself, and I pity any Ordinary or Freeblood who trifles with you, Miss . . . . ?"

"Giselle Montreau," the woman said with a slight smile.

"You *can* smile," Falcon replied. "You should do that more often, it lights up your face." Falcon gave an exaggeratedly low bow while flourishing one arm and proclaiming, "Theodore Falcon, ancient, Freeblood vampire, and rescuer of otherwise very capable girl vampires in minimal distress."

"I'm not a girl. I'm almost twenty-five," Giselle retorted.

"You meant one hundred twenty-five," Falcon corrected with a grin. "But I know the rule. A woman never reveals her true age, and it's much more frustrating for a female vampire than an Ordinary."

"I'm a liberated woman," she explained.

"Now who's retro?" Falcon asked. "That's a comment straight out of the seventies. Liberated from what, may I ask? To my knowledge, and I am quite mature, Freeblood females have never been enslaved or treated as second class anything. You've been reading too much Ordinary history."

"Whatever. Anyway, why were you following me?" she asked.

"I was actually following the stalker," Falcon answered, motioning for her to walk with him. "Considering the curfew in this town because of the Ripper, I was curious when I saw that cretin chasing you. When I saw how slow he moved, I was pretty sure he wasn't the killer. When I saw you, I thought you were either the Ripper or a vampire. I was hoping for the latter."

Giselle strolled beside Falcon, saying, "You could have allowed me just one little swing at that disgusting mongrel."

"That mongrel, however loathsome, has a brain," Falcon explained. "A somewhat feeble and demented brain, I'll grant you, but if you had sliced his throat, I would have tried to save him, leaving my saliva behind. I would have been forced to drop him off at the Barnes ER. The doctors would have been dumbfounded that he hadn't bled to death. They would have analyzed the substance that sealed the wound and discovered that, unbeknownst to all mankind, an alien race was living among them, roaming the streets, possibly killing people. I won't be responsible for the erosion and ultimate breakdown of society that bit of knowledge would cause. The authorities would have no choice but to hunt us down and . . ."

"Kill us like rabid dogs," Giselle finished.

"Exactly," Falcon replied, taking her arm. "We should get out of here before the police patrols arrest us for breaking the curfew. We could continue this discussion at my apartment."

"What makes you think I'd want to hang out with an old blood sucker like you?" Giselle taunted playfully.

"For one thing, I'm not that old," Falcon explained. "And since you are one of the few vampires living in this city, you're probably hungry for a friend who is not your own reflection in the mirror, a faceless name in a boring chat room, or a blood relative."

Back at his apartment, Falcon poured sparkling wine into two tall, fluted crystal glasses while Giselle was enjoying the panoramic view of the St. Louis skyline. She sipped her wine and walked tentatively through the balcony greenhouse feeling as if she had been transported to a tiny piece of a tropical jungle. A café table and two chairs sat next to the small garden fountain.

"It's so peaceful here," Giselle observed. "It's hard to believe that a killer is out there in the streets, probably stalking another young woman right now."

"If the Ripper follows his usual pattern you may be correct," Falcon remarked. "He has been targeting one woman a week."

"The wine is good," Giselle replied accepting another glass of wine he offered her. After sniffing the wine's bouquet, she took a sip and commented, "There's a Falcon on the label. Is this your family vintage?"

"Yes," Falcon answered, pouring himself a glass of wine.

"Used in the Falcon family elixir?" Giselle asked.

"Along with the obvious," Falcon returned.

"Where's your family's vineyard? Napa Valley?" the girl asked

"Actually much closer, The Two Brothers Winery in southwestern Missouri in the foothills of the Ozarks, just outside a little town called, St. James," Falcon explained.

"I guess every family has a different formula for their elixir," Giselle commented. "The Montreau recipe was originally from Europe. My father got me started on a new recipe about two years ago. He claims it's an improvement on the old one, but he's so secretive even I don't know the formula."

"One day we won't need filtered blood," Falcon mused, "Vampire scientists will discover a synthetic alternative, and we'll be free of blood bondage."

"What a lovely thought," Giselle said. "That's been the focus of my father's research for the last twenty years." She looked at Falcon and commented, "I hope the Ripper is caught soon. These killings have every woman I know, vampire or Ordinary, very nervous."

"Eventually, the Ripper will slip up," Falcon said. "One of the reasons I walk the streets is to find the killer. My hope is to come upon him before he does a disappearing act."

"No trace of him was ever found at the scene of the crimes; no DNA, no fingerprints, nothing," Giselle commented. "I heard that the slash marks he made weren't human."

"The marks were made by the claws of a lion," Falcon stated. "According to my contact, forensics showed they were from a deceased animal."

Giselle finished her wine and rose from her saying, "I would love to continue this discussion, but it's getting late. I have to go."

"Are you sure you wouldn't like to stay for dinner?" Falcon asked.

"Some other time," Giselle responded, walking with him back to the living room. Looking over at Falcon with a smile she explained, "My parents are expecting me in half an hour. My family is kind of old-fashioned. They insist on dressing up for dinner. I live a few miles away in the Ash Apartments. Would you like to walk me home?"

"Absolutely," Falcon said. "I know your building. It has excellent turn of the century architecture. The Ash was one of the first buildings I looked at twenty years ago before I bought this one."

Once on the street, the couple streaked by in a blur, speeding arm in arm, melting into the shadows, breathing the cool night air, and energized with the promise of a blossoming friendship.

Chapter 3

After saying goodbye to Giselle at the Ash Apartments, Falcon returned home and logged onto his PC for the local news. The St. Louis Today website report was startling, the front page headline read:

Local Socialite Latest CWE Ripper's Victim

"Police and authorities are in a quandary over the discovery of the body of Valerie Chouteau, twenty-eight, daughter of Pierre Chouteau, the prominent real estate tycoon. The young woman's mutilated body was found in a Central West End alley. The Chief of Police is waiting for the autopsy results to say for certain that this brutal crime was the work of the serial killer known as: The Central West End Ripper."

The article gave a rundown on the massive manhunt the authorities had organized. It went on to explain the latest curfew times, the placement of ten extra patrol cars and additional foot patrols in the area. Pulling up his coded e-mail account, Falcon sent a message to his contact in the police department. Almost immediately a "You've Got Mail" message popped up and he eagerly read the details of the murder.

He was surprised to discover that Valerie Chouteau was murdered in the alley behind his cousin Colin's building. Colin owned the three-story apartment, which housed his coffee shop, Java Heaven. Along with donations, the proceeds of the restaurant funded the food bank and soup kitchen for his storefront "Redeemer Church and Ministry." Falcon noted that the most recent murder scene contained several discrepancies from the other three cases: several pieces of jewelry had been removed, and the body had been covered with newspaper.

Falcon threw on his coat and hat and took the elevator to the street. Within a few minutes, vampire speed, he had traversed the six blocks to his cousin's building. Falcon had sent Colin a text message to let him know he was on the way. When he rapped on the door, his cousin peered through the window before releasing two dead bolts, and using his key to open the door from the inside. He waved at Falcon, his dark eyes scanning the street as he let him in.

Sitting at the kitchen table, Falcon handed Colin a brown bag containing a bottle of elixir. Colin took the bag with trembling hands and poured himself a drink. Falcon shook his head when his cousin offered him a drink. Colin took a few sips and said, "Thanks man. We were almost out."

Falcon looked at him with compassion saying, "No problem. I'll have my distributor Nino drop a case by this week when he makes his rounds." Reaching into his pocket for his pack of cigarettes Falcon asked, "How's Nicole?"

"Her best friend was killed," Colin replied. "She's taking it really hard."

"I didn't know that she and Valerie Chouteau were friends," Falcon responded sadly.

"Valerie was murdered right in our alley," Colin said, his voice cracking.

"I know," Falcon stated. "I've been scouring the neighborhood night after night, but I haven't seen anything."

Seeing Colin eye his cigarette, he asked, "Would you like a smoke?"

"Yeah, I need one," Colin admitted. "Let's hang out on the fire escape balcony. Nicole doesn't want me to smoke at all, let alone in the apartment."

After sitting down on two lawn chairs, Falcon handed Colin a cigarette and watched him light it with trembling hands. He lit his own, took a long drag, blew out a curl of gray smoke and commented, "You don't look so good. Are you doing okay?"

Colin bowed his head in the darkness answering with, "I saw her Teddy. I came out here for a smoke, looked down, and there she was."

"I'm sorry, that must have been really rough," Falcon replied.

"Valerie volunteered at our soup kitchen the night she was murdered," Colin explained. "I walked to her car about nine-thirty. I couldn't believe it when I saw her body only a few hours later."

"How long were Valerie and Nicole friends?" Falcon asked.

"Over a year," Colin replied. "Nicole gave Valerie private cooking lessons last year, as a thank you gift for her family's generous donation to our mission. When the class ended they hung out together all the time. They were close, like sisters."

"I can imagine how you felt seeing her dead like that," Falcon said.

Colin turned and looked at his cousin saying, "I've prayed over people on their deathbed. At funeral visitations, I know what to say to comfort the family, but when I saw that vibrant young woman slashed and killed so mercilessly, I fell to my knees, unable to speak."

Falcon lit another cigarette for his cousin and said, "When I was a kid, sometimes I was unable to talk about my feelings. I didn't even know how to pray about them. Somehow mom always knew when I was going through a hard time. One particular time she took me aside and said, "Even when we can't speak, God hears the words of our heart." Falcon stared helplessly up into the night sky, not knowing what else to say to comfort Colin.

"Thanks, Falcon," Colin replied, stubbing out his cigarette. "I love Aunt Clara. She took me aside a couple of times, too, and imparted some of her gems of wisdom." In an unsteady voice, he added, "You know, something else has bothered me ever since that night."

"What?" Falcon asked. The two men were so enveloped in darkness that only the fiery red tips of their cigarettes betrayed their presence.

"Valerie's body was still warm," Colin offered in a whisper. "The killer must have been right out there in the darkness, hiding." He blew out smoke and continued, "I was so angry, I prayed that I would see him. That really worried me."

"Why?" Falcon asked, his brows knitting in concern.

"Such a rage rose up in me, I was ready to forget my vows and kill him," Colin explained. "I guess I've been kidding myself thinking I've finally conquered my aggressive feelings," Colin relayed. "If I had found the Ripper in the shadows, I would have torn him apart with my bare hands! Forget handing him over to the police."

"No way!" Falcon replied firmly. "You're not that person anymore, Colin. I could do it, in a heartbeat, but not you."

"Maybe, maybe not," Colin answered doubtfully. "My personal demons are still inside me. I've been holding them at bay all these years. Remember, I'm a half-breed."

"That's exactly why you won't let yourself lose control," Falcon retorted. "You're a Freeblood hybrid. Besides, your faith is stronger than that." Gazing into the darkness, he asked, "Did you call the police?"

"No. While I was praying, I heard the sirens and hid," Colin answered.

"Has anyone questioned you yet?" Falcon asked.

"No. They'll probably be around tomorrow," Colin answered. "We were at a church conference in Springfield. Nicole and I left after we closed down the mission for the night. I didn't tell her anything. I just helped her pack the car, and we took off."

"You were right to protect Nicole," Falcon commented. "Just tell the police the time you left and that should be enough."

"I guess I should have come forward right away," Colin conceded, "but I really didn't see anything. If we had called 911, Nicole would have had to identify Valerie's body. It would have been a nightmare for her." Colin cleared his throat and added, "How could a woman be brutally killed right outside my home without me hearing anything?"

"According to the report I saw about the murder, Valerie may have been killed somewhere else and dropped in this alley later," Falcon replied. "You wouldn't go to the window every time a car cut through the alley. You know this city. People use the alleys like streets."

"Could the killer be a rogue?" Colin asked tentatively.

"It's a possibility," Falcon said. "If a Keeper killed Valerie, he could have done it right in the alley. He would have drugged her first, drained her blood, and slashed her unconscious body, making it look like the work of a demented killer. Tobias' report indicated there was very little blood at the scene. It fits the pattern of the other murders."

"A serial killer might drug a victim to transport them, but don't they usually want them awake when they torture and kill them?" Colin asked.

"That's pretty accurate," Falcon agreed. "According to the cases I've researched. Jack the Ripper with a heart, doesn't fit the profile. Sooner or later, they get careless and leave clues behind, usually DNA. This killer is compulsively methodical."

Colin shifted in his chair, stating, "I saw Damien running away from the scene."

"Damien wouldn't hurt a fly," Falcon replied, shaking his head. "The man is mentally ill, I'll give you that, and he probably stole Valerie's jewelry. I know a few shady characters in town who would give him cash for all that gold. Old Damien would use it to rent a house somewhere for a homeless lady friend with kids, but he's not a killer. Out on the streets they compare him to Robin Hood."

"Damien's sticky fingers did make things more complicated," Colin agreed.

"If the police are any kind of detectives at all, they'll figure out someone else visited the crime scene right after the murder," Falcon insisted.

"I bet Damien covered Valerie's body with the newspaper," Colin said. "She was one of the few people that could carry on a conversation with Damien," Colin commented.

"I just hope that crazy fool didn't leave any fingerprints behind, or the cops will arrest the wrong person," Falcon stated.

"He would certainly be a convenient person of interest for them," Colin stated, "until the next victim was killed."

"Or, it could be the perfect opportunity for the killer to move on to another city, case closed, perpetrator found, and the Ripper gets off Scott-free," Falcon suggested.

"I hope that doesn't happen," Colin said. "If the Ripper is a vampire, then a vampire could stop him," he added. Peering at his cousin in the darkness he declared, "Falcon, you could do it."

"Me?" Falcon asked. "What makes you think I can stop the Ripper?"

"You love this city like I do. You wouldn't stand by and let a killer destroy the peace in this town," Colin insisted.

Falcon rose from his chair with, "I want the Ripper caught as much as you, but what you're asking may be out of my league." Seeing Colin's crestfallen look he hastily added, "I'll need help from other Freebloods to catch the Ripper."

"Count me in," Colin replied. Jabbing at Falcon's arm he added, "By the way, I found these in Valerie's purse."

Falcon gave a start at the sight of the two tickets to the Midnight Supper Club that Colin handed to him. "Secrets," he whispered more to himself than his cousin. "Valerie must have been on her way to my presentation," he suggested. "If the cops had gotten a hold of these, a whole lot of unwanted questions would have been asked. Our cover could have been blown sky high."

"I was meant to find them," Colin said quietly.

Falcon gave his cousin a wry smile as they took the stairs to the street below. To Colin, there were no coincidences; everything that happened was part of The Plan, as he called it. Falcon didn't usually agree with his cousin about divine intervention, but he was willing to consider the possibility.

"Why is it so important that you give lectures to Ordinaries?" Colin asked as they stood together on the sidewalk.

"Because," Falcon said, pausing under the streetlight, "if and when the proverbial dung hits the fan, we're going to need friends in high places, lots of friends, who don't want to see us get our butts kicked to hell and back."

Standing in the glow of the lighted window, Colin and Falcon looked more like brothers than cousins. They were the same height and slim of build, with sandy colored hair and had the same round boyish face. However, Colin wore his hair long and had a full beard, a mustache, a facial piercing, and a sleeve tattoo of Bible verses. Falcon was a skeptic, Colin a believer. While Falcon was cynical, Colin was hopeful. Colin had faith, Falcon wasn't sure that God was all that involved in the lives of his creations. But in spite of their differences, they always found some common ground.

Falcon mused that it would take more than he and his courageous cousin to apprehend the Ripper. He made a mental list of Freebloods he could recruit to help with his covert manhunt. He didn't discount the help of Ordinaries. They could be valuable allies. Inspired by Colin's faith in him, Falcon planned his next move as he streaked home eluding the heavy street patrols.

Chapter 4

Dawn was breaking when Falcon arrived home. The sun, a giant reddish-orange sphere hanging on the horizon, burst forth brightly. Shielding his eyes, Falcon climbed tiredly up the stairs to his loft, stretched out on his bed, and quickly sent a message to Giselle, arranging to see her the following evening.

It was twilight when Falcon stirred contentedly from a full day's sleep. After a warm shower, he pulled on his robe and went to his desk. Tobias had left a message giving him the name of a contact in the Federal Building who had information about a similar Ripper case in South Africa. Falcon sent the agent a quick e-mail, "Where can we meet?"

"SubZero—tomorrow—1:00 pm," was the agent's quick reply.

Falcon replied with "I'll be there," and signed off. SubZero was a popular bar and grill on Euclid, usually crowded with business types having a power lunch. He carefully set his clock for noon. Only the high-pitched sound of his special alarm clock could awaken him at midday.

While he hoped the agent had several good leads for him to follow, he relied heavily on Tobias and the Metro Police Department to give him the latest information about the Ripper. Falcon wasn't convinced the police were as inept as everyone thought. Last August, they had captured the South City Rapist, Bill Wilkes, in three weeks.

There was a colorful e-mail from Rascal Gold, with a slue of compliments praising his staged escape from the club. Twice the number of members bought tickets for the next week's event. Falcon suggested that he tell the ticket holders that he was called away on an emergency. After all, rock stars cancelled concerts all the time for such reasons. Gold liked the idea. His next message was more informative,

"EZ the Great will open Friday, the 20th. I hear he's taking his Bonaparte Magic Act to Vegas this summer. Lucky we got him."

Falcon smiled crookedly at Gold's last message. An illusionist would be the perfect person to open for his presentation. After all, the whole show would be a contrived prestidigitation.

He decided to dress early and take a walk in the park. He wanted to visit Damien and ask him a few questions about the night of the murder. Pulling on his black overcoat, 1940's style hat, and black leather gloves, he stepped out into the crisp, November air breathing in its cool freshness. He moved speedily until he arrived at the entrance to Forest Park. Within a few seconds, he had crossed Kingshighway, outrunning rush-hour travelers speeding to their various destinations.

Falcon pulled his collar up against the brisk wind, rapidly darting in and out of the shadows, carefully checking the hidden alcoves where a homeless person might spend the night. When Falcon disturbed one such a haven under a walking bridge, a grizzly, bearded man jumped up and begged for cash.

"Come on pal, you barged in my home," the shabbily dressed vagrant stated. "The least you can do is help me out."

"Sure buddy, if you help me out first," Falcon agreed.

"Now, how can an old man like me help an obviously cultured gentleman like yourself?" he asked, slurring his words.

"Where did you get you're PhD. old man, Washington U.?" Falcon asked. "I'll spot you for a bottle and a warm meal at a soup kitchen, if you tell me where Dumpster D is tonight."

"Whose asking?" the old man replied guardedly, "the CEO of City Waste?"

"Don't be smart, it's Falcon, Theodore Falcon," the vampire replied. "I own the Nightwing Arms Apartments, the place where you slept all last winter when it got below 40 degrees."

The old man scratched his bewhiskered chin and stared at Falcon then slapped his knee, saying, "Yeah, I recognize you now sonny. Woo! You clean up nice. The name's Beauregard, my friends call me Beau."

Falcon handed the old man a bottle of cheap, red wine and continued, "Now, about Damien."

"Haven't seen him," Beau returned tersely. Suddenly, Falcon grabbed the bottle back, spilling a few swallows. The old man protested, "Say, you don't have to be so pushy. Give an old man time to think."

"Come on, I don't have all night," Falcon demanded firmly.

"Okay, okay already," he replied. "What day is this?"

"Thursday," Falcon answered impatiently.

"Well, then D is taking his nightly constitution over by the boat docks," the homeless man returned. "He'll be staying dry in one of the rentals."

"Here's your bottle old man, now get up," Falcon ordered.

"Why?" Beau replied his voice rising. "You ain't taking me off to the clink are ya?"

"No I'm putting you in a cab and sending you to my cousin's soup kitchen," Falcon replied taking the man by his collar and hoisting him up. "You'll get a good meal and sleep in a nice warm bed for a change. If you're polite, preacher Colin might give you a job, and you can keep you're bed."

"Well that's mighty nice of him," Beau said nervously. "Why would anyone want to go through all that trouble for the likes of me?"

"I've asked myself that many times," Falcon commented, "Just take my word for it, Colin practices what he preaches."

Falcon hailed a cab and gave him a twenty to take him to Java Heaven. The old man grinned, finishing off his bottle as the cab pulled away. Shaking his head, Falcon took a deep breath and raced to the boat docks. Moonlight glittered on the dark waters of the lagoon, the boats swaying gently, bumping the wooden dock. The tarp, covering one of the canoes hidden in the shadow of the flat roof of the rental office, had a nearly imperceptible bulge under it. With his paranormal hearing, Falcon could detect Damien's breathing before he lifted the tarp.

Damien shot up in the darkness, but Falcon held him on the ground before he could sprint away, "Damien, hold still, it's, Falcon. I just want to ask you a few questions man."

"What do you want with me?" Damien pleaded pitifully. "I didn't do anything! I didn't kill Valerie. The Ripper got there before me!"

"I know. I know," Falcon said sitting next to the man on the wooden dock. "You see the thing is, if you left any fingerprints or DNA the police will arrest you."

"You mean, for the murder of all those young girls?" Damien asked.

"They're anxious to make an arrest Damien, and you're the closest thing they have for a suspect right now," Falcon explained.

"I didn't touch anything," Damien told him with trembling lips. "I just covered Valerie with newspaper. It wasn't right, her lying there like that."

"It's a funny thing," Falcon said. "Valerie's cash and jewelry were taken, but her license and credit cards were still in her purse."

"Don't know about that," Damien said, lowering his eyes and shifting his position.

"Damien, I don't care about the jewelry. Valerie doesn't need it anymore, and if someone were to fence it to help some homeless family live better, well, it's none of my business," Falcon confided in a quiet matter-of-fact tone.

His resolve faltering, the confused man looked over at Falcon in the darkness, asking in a pleading voice, "What should I do?"

Falcon helped Damien to his feet and offered, "Well, you could check yourself into Renfield. I have friends there. If the police question you, they'll find out that you checked in before the murder took place. That is, if you left no evidence."

"It was cold that night," Damien remembered. "My mind is fuzzy, but I remember wearing gloves. I never took them off," he finished, with moist eyes.

Falcon looked over at Damien and said, "It's going to be okay. Come on. I'll ride with you to the hospital."

"Thanks Falcon," Damien said, walking briskly alongside his friend.

An hour later, Falcon was back in town and on his way to Giselle's place, in his 2000, midnight-blue Thunderbird, having lost his desire to prowl the city streets on foot. Giselle was at the door when he arrived, smiling and relieved to see him.

"I'm sorry," Falcon apologized. "I had to get an old friend out of a jam."

He relayed the story of Damien's troubles as they walked to the dining room table. The smoky, glass top table was carefully set with candles and gleaming china of an elegant Calla Lily design. The wine glasses were dark crimson, almost black. On the center of the table was a sculpture of prancing crystal stallions.

Like many old apartment buildings in the city, Giselle's apartment had twelve-foot ceilings and arched doorways. The floor to ceiling windows were draped elegantly with white brocade, layered over black chintz, to block out the sunlight. Realistic portraits of big cats in the wild, by a familiar, local artist, Lenoir, graced the cream-colored walls.

"I like the animal paintings," Falcon commented.

"The pastel tiger on the far wall is my work," Giselle commented, smiling.

"It's my favorite," Falcon said walking over to take a closer look. "His eyes follow you everywhere."

"You mean her eyes. She's a Tigress," she corrected. Reaching for Falcon's hand, she announced, "Please have a seat. It's time for dinner."

Giselle's black velvet dress, designed in a style reminiscent of the forties, moved softly as she walked into the kitchen to get dinner. She returned with two well-presented plates of aromatic foods. Falcon's plate held a few slices of rare Porterhouse steak covered with thin slices of grilled Portobello mushrooms in wine sauce. A serving of arugula with pine nuts and cranberries garnished the meal. Giselle's plate held half of a five ounce filet mignon with the same Arugula garnish. A silver gravy boat held extra au jus and wine sauce to add to the steaks. Cut crystal bowls held dark berries to clear the palate. They touched their wine glasses and made a toast to each other.

"This is delicious, and just how I like it, rare," Falcon complimented. In between bites of mouth-watering steak, he added, "The seasoning is really tasty."

"My mother is a wise woman," Giselle returned. "She encourages me to get a Masters Degree, urges me to cultivate a career, and promptly takes me to the kitchen and teaches me another recipe." Smiling over at Falcon she commented, "Oh, by the way, my father wants to meet you after your presentation."

"I look forward to it," Falcon said. "I would love to discuss some of your father's work with him."

"I'm pretty sure he wants to discuss the Ripper," Giselle explained. "He rarely talks of anything else these days."

"All the more reason for us to meet as soon as possible," Falcon replied. "I want to hear what he has to say about him."

"Then we'll drive over after your lecture," Giselle agreed. "My parents don't live too far from the club. They own a huge white elephant on Lindell."

"I'm glad you mentioned the presentation," Falcon stated. "How many tickets should I reserve for your family?"

"There'll be five of us," Giselle said, "myself, of course, my parents, and a visiting doctor from Africa, and Dr. Sidney Hayden"

"Dr. Sidney Hayden, administrator for Renfield Rehab, and a dozen other cutting edge research centers in the country?" Falcon asked.

"The same," Giselle answered. "Dad and Sidney have known each other since before I was born. They met at a conference in London. In case you're wondering, Dr. Hayden is a Freeblood."

"I knew there was something different about Dr. Hayden," Falcon observed. "I've always admired your father's philosophical essays too. Speaking of work, you're a psychologist right?"

"I will be, after I finish my clinical rotation," Giselle replied

"What have you read about serial killers?" he asked.

"I've read a few definitive works about them," Giselle answered. "Is this about the Ripper?"

"I'm putting together a team to find him," Falcon explained. "What can you tell me about him?"

"As you probably guessed," Giselle began, "he uses similar techniques as Jack the Ripper. He kills young women who walk alone at night. He's skillful with his claw-like weapon and never leaves evidence behind."

"Specifically, how would you profile him?" Falcon asked.

"I would say he's somewhere in his forties, educated, resourceful, and probably likeable," she informed him. "He exudes an aura of confidence, or great wealth, although this could be a superficial front. He must be somewhat charismatic, considering he's able to attract women nearly half his age."

"Does he work alone?" Falcon inquired, as Giselle poured the after dinner coffee.

"It's hard to say," Giselle said. "Most serial killers are compulsive and work alone on their victims. They wouldn't want a witness for the terrible things they do. Their actions, however horrible they may seem to us, serve to release tension that builds up inside of them. However, it's not unheard of for a serial killer to have a partner who helps them acquire their victims and cleans up the mess later."

"That coincides with my research," Falcon commented, putting his fork down. "Why would any sane person help the Ripper?"

"I think the key word here is *sane*," Giselle stated. "The accomplice of a serial killer is usually emotionally disturbed too. There has to be some payoff. It could be money, or participation in a shared perversion. In another scenario, the accomplice is coerced into complying with the killer, in other words, cooperate or die."

"Could the Ripper be a Keeper?" Falcon asked, helping her clear the dishes from the table.

"My father and I discussed that possibility last week," Giselle commented. "A Keeper would certainly murder without remorse. Such a killer would be the hardest kind to capture."

"We have to stop him," Falcon stated emphatically.

"We're probably the only ones who can," Giselle concurred, as they walked into the living room to sit by the fire. "A team of Ordinaries alone would be no match for a Keeper's cunning."

Dessert was a thin slice of dark chocolate tart, which they ate sitting in the two white overstuffed wingback chairs that flanked the fireplace. Falcon stoked the fire, feeling far removed from events outside in the cozy confines of Giselle's apartment.

"Dark chocolate is my weakness," Falcon said letting a smooth morsel melt on his tongue.

Giselle laughed lightly and said, "That's supposed to be a woman's line."

"There are two things a vampire craves in this world," Falcon commented, "blood and chocolate."

"I could add a third thing with an even more powerful draw," She offered, her dark eyes gazing at him softly.

Falcon gazed back at her, asking, "What would that be?"

"Love's first kiss," Giselle returned.

Falcon set down his dessert dish as Giselle rose, sat on the arm of his chair, and wrapped her arms around his neck. He turned his face upwards, meeting her lips with his own.

The room, the fireplace, and the universe returned after a long, long, while. Giselle's eyes were two gold coins in the firelight. Falcon burned that picture into his memory to resurrect on lonely nights when they were apart.

"I wasn't sure you were ready for that," Falcon stated. "We've only known each other a few weeks."

"You had me at week one," Giselle said, her eyes dancing. "When you rescued me from my angry impulses the night we met, I couldn't take my eyes off you. No one has ever taken control of me like that, not even my parents. My heart was beating so loudly, I thought you might hear it."

"So that's why you were making all those sarcastic remarks," Falcon said with a grin. "Where do we go from here?" he added quietly.

"No need to rush," Giselle answered softly. "Let's take our time and enjoy each day. Right now, we have to stop the Ripper."

"Thank you for that," Falcon said relieved. "About a billion plans were racing through my mind, most of them covering what you might want." Holding her gently, he explained, "I've been alone for many years, and I've never fallen in love with a Freeblood woman before. In all this time, finding true love has eluded me."

"I've had close friends before, but not like this," Giselle agreed. "I never imagined a relationship could last, until now."

Later, when the fired all but died down, Giselle and Falcon cleared the table and cleaned the dishes together. They talked about their hopes and dreams for the future, and how to make sense of all the tragedy around them. It was nearly dawn when Falcon kissed Giselle goodbye, walked to his car, and drowsily headed home.

Chapter 5

Falcon hesitated as he stood in the doorway of his apartment. Looking up, he noticed the transom which he always locked, was ajar. With senses alert, he peered into the darkness and walked in. He had taken only a few steps when someone flew at him from the shadows and knocked him across the sofa. Using his feet as ramrods, he pushed the attacker over his head, hearing the intruder's body thud on the hardwood floor behind him.

Falcon sprang to his feet, racing around the couch. He was poised to attack, until he recognized the baritone voice of his brother, Zeke who was shaking with laughter on the floor.

"I'm relieved that city life hasn't made you soft, little brother," Zeke commented.

"I can always count on your surprise visits to keep me in shape," Falcon returned sarcastically. Helping Zeke to his feet, he asked, "You got my e-mails. What do you want?"

"Don't be that way," Zeke returned with mock offense. "Do I have to have an ulterior motive to see my little brother?"

"In a word, yes, and stop the little brother garbage, it's getting on my nerves," Falcon answered, pouring two glasses of elixir. "Do you know what time it is?" Not waiting for a reply Falcon continued, "Its, almost dawn, and I'm beat. Out with it, will you?"

"I'm doing a gig at the Midnight Supper Club tomorrow, and I want you to scope it out for me," Zeke replied, taking the offered drink.

Falcon sipped his drink saying, "It's legitimate. The Supper Club is a world wide organization of Ordinaries obsessed with vampires."

"Get out of town!" Zeke exclaimed. "I'm opening for some crazy guy who says he's a real vampire. Anyone I know?" he asked with a grin.

"It's no deep, dark secret, Gold must have told you," Falcon replied, refilling his brother's quickly drained glass.

"He doesn't know I'm your brother?" Zeke asked.

"I didn't feel the need to tell him, and you're show name is E.Z. Bonaparte," Falcon returned, yawning. "Besides, it's none of his business."

"Burning the midnight oil?" Zeke asked.

"I was with a lady," Falcon replied guardedly.

"Making friends are we?" his brother commented, pressing him on the shoulder with his fist. He stared at Falcon sideways asking, "Ordinary or Freeblood?"

"She's a Freeblood," Falcon returned, "intelligent, feisty, and actually, quite beautiful."

"Falcon in love," Zeke stated. "Mom and dad are going to split a gasket."

"I haven't told them yet," Falcon replied. "I would appreciate it, if you didn't tell them either."

"Your secret is safe with me," His brother said, motioning for another drink. "This stuff is pretty good bro. It almost takes my guilty thirst away," Zeke commented. Draining the glass he added, "Almost, that's the key word."

Seeing his brother's hand tremble when he reached for another refill, Falcon commented, "That two-week stint at Renfield Rehab didn't do much good did it?"

"My partner Gorky has a big mouth," Zeke returned. "I tried to stay off the stuff, but I got thirsty, and the girl's were so willing."

"It's wrong!" Falcon stated angrily. "Mom and dad didn't raise us to be blood suckers!"

"We were good little soldiers growing up, weren't we?" Zeke asked, shaking his head. "It took with you. Me, I just wanted the wild life."

"Your wild life could ruin everything for our whole family," Falcon stated, rising to his feet.

"Don't act so self-righteous," Zeke returned angrily. "Don't knock it until you've tried it."

"Doesn't your conscience ever bother you, going against everything our family believes in?" Falcon asked in exasperation.

"The trouble is," Zeke returned with a wry smile, "I don't have an over inflated, holier-than-thou conscience like you." Seeing his brother's pained expression he added, "Look, I don't hurt the girls. I drug them and drink a little of their hemoglobin. They have a good time with a Rock Magician, I'm not thirsty anymore, and I don't get caught."

"Yet!" Falcon retorted. "You haven't been caught, yet. One day you're going to go too far, and someone will die."

"No chance of that," Zeke replied arrogantly.

"How do you know that?" his brother questioned, glaring at him. "You're an addict. If you go too far and kill an Ordinary, you're no better than a "Keeper."

"Take it back, now!" Zeke said, taking a swing at his brother.

Before two swift punches landed on his jaw, Falcon ducked away and rose to his feet. When Zeke lunged at him again, Falcon bent backwards and eluded his brother's fist. They both ended up on the floor gasping for air.

Zeke got to his feet, straightened his rumpled shirt, and said. "All right, I got the point. I know you didn't mean what you said."

"I guess I've got other things on my mind at the moment," Falcon said gruffly, rising to his feet unsteadily.

"No doubt," Zeke replied refilling his drink. "The Central West End Ripper is all over the news. The whole country is watching the show."

"Four girls have been brutally killed," Falcon reminded him. "Colin and Nicole knew the last victim, Valerie Chouteau."

"What are we going to do about it then?" Zeke asked.

"Are you offering to help?" Falcon asked in return.

"Just let me know what I can do," he affirmed.

"Put on a good show tomorrow night," Falcon stated. "Keep your eyes and ears open for anything at the club that might help us find the Ripper."

"Do you think the he has ties to the club?" Zeke asked.

"It's the one place he could show his face in this town," Falcon said. "There'll be a lot of strangers in the West End, Friday. The Ripper could blend in like a chameleon."

"Since this drink of yours keeps the edge off my thirst, maybe I'll stick around until my Vegas show," Zeke commented, draining his second glass of elixir.

"I'll ship you a case wherever your performances are, just leave me a copy of your schedule," Falcon offered.

"Thanks. Is it okay if I crash here?" Zeke asked. "I could go back to the hotel, but there's probably an underage groupie waiting for me in my room."

"Don't be a jackass," Falcon answered quickly. "You know where the guest room is."

"I could find it blind-folded," Zeke replied, picking up the bottle. He turned to look at his brother saying, "See you in the evening."

"Sleep well," Falcon replied. Giving his brother a thumbs-up sign he added, "Someday, we'll find a drink that will kill that thirst of yours."

"That'll be the day," Zeke replied, walking into the guest room.

The next evening Falcon arose to the delightful odor of bacon frying and aroma of very strong coffee. Throwing on his robe as if it were Christmas, he flew down the stairs and into the kitchen.

Zeke was at the stove mastering two frying pans. The griddle pan contained slices of half-cooked maple flavored bacon, the frying pan held melted butter. All that was needed were the eggs to cook, over-easy.

Zeke grinned at Falcon's expression of sheer joy and poured his brother a cup of black coffee, saying, "Take a load off. When was the last time you had a good breakfast? From the looks of you it's been a while."

"Last New Year's Eve when mom insisted we have a family meal," Falcon answered, eyeing the food hungrily.

In a few minutes the two brothers sat at the tall kitchen table, each with a plate containing an egg-over easy, a slice of nearly raw bacon, and a half-slice of wheat toast with fresh butter, melting and spilling over the sides.

"I take it you slept well," Falcon commented, lifting his egg-filled fork.

Zeke finished chewing the slice of bacon he had crammed into this mouth, saying, "That vintage of yours worked wonders. After I finished the bottle, the craving went away, and I slept all day."

"Don't forget to leave a copy of your itinerary with me before you leave town," Falcon reminded him.

"This lady of yours, will I get to meet her?" Zeke asked curiously.

"Possibly, she's coming to the Supper Club Friday," Falcon replied.

"I have a lady out in L.A.," Zeke offered, seeing his bother's surprised looked he quickly added, "Can you believe it, she wants to settle down, have a couple of kids with me, of all people."

"Does she know what she's getting into?" Falcon asked carefully.

"No," Zeke replied shoving a forkful of eggs into his mouth. After chewing the morsels, he explained, "Babs is an Ordinary. I met her in Vegas two years ago when she was a showgirl."

"Babs?" Falcon asked with a wry smile. "I take it that's her show name?"

"Barbara Anne is her first name," His brother replied, sounding sorry he had shared personal information with Falcon.

"I'm happy for you," Falcon said. Seeing his brother's look of relief, he added, "I mean, it'll be difficult, but you deserve to have someone in your life. Now that I've found Giselle, I realize that no matter how it graces us, love is as essential to life as blood."

"Such deep thoughts," Zeke commented. Pouring more coffee in Falcon's mug, he asked, "What you said last night, about finding a drink that could cure me, is it possible?"

"There is a group of vampire chemists working on the solution to that problem right here in St. Louis," Falcon offered. "Half of an addiction is up here," he pointed to his head, then elaborated, "After the physical need has been quieted or eradicated, the mind still relies on the substance to function."

"A necessity becomes a preference?" Zeke asked.

"Correct," Falcon nodded. "Because of scientific advances, no vampire alive has to drink blood from humans, or animals. It's readily available, fresh, filtered, and imbued with nutrients."

"Like your stash under the wet bar," Zeke pointed out.

Falcon rose, took the two empty plates, rinsed them, and put them in the dishwasher saying, "Let's go to the greenhouse and have a smoke." He carried a coffee carafe and two cups out to the greenhouse table. Taking his pack of cigarettes from the pocket of his robe, he handed one to Zeke.

"I'll be honest with you," Zeke began, "No matter how many times I check myself in for rehab, within days, the thirst for fresh warm blood returns, stronger than ever."

"Dad told me that a small percentage of us have a predisposition for that addiction," Falcon returned. "He calls it Keeper's Disease."

"That's just great," Zeke returned with a shrug. "I don't want this hanging over my relationship. I can't put it off anymore, if I don't do right and marry Babs, she'll move on."

"Giselle's father is Dr. Montreau, the famous vampire psychiatrist," Falcon commented. "Maybe he'll have some answers. We could discuss it with him sometime."

"That would be awesome," Zeke commented. "Thanks for letting me crash. Sorry, I've got to go. I have get to the Club and rehearse. By the way, my latest act is awesome."

"Tell me about it," Falcon replied, walking with him to the door.

Chapter 6

Falcon's alarm, a bright light that pierced his eyelids to the beat of a high-pitched whistle, brought him to wakefulness with a start. Remembering this was the day he had an appointment with the FBI contact, he groaned wearily and jumped into the shower.

Because walking by day could be dangerous, Falcon dried his face with a soft towel and put in his special tinted, light-dimming contact lenses, making him appear as a hazel-eyed Ordinary. He carefully applied a SPF 60+ Sunscreen cream with skin tinting melanin. Not only would his face be protected from UV light, his complexion would have a warm sun-drenched color. Vampires usually wore color when they mingled with Ordinaries, otherwise their unusually, pale skin would attract the wrong kind of attention.

Falcon wore a long-sleeved royal blue shirt, black chinos, dress shoes, and his wool all-weather coat. Placing his felt hat on his short curls, he waited outside for the cab he had called. When the red and white cab pulled up he got into the back seat and told the driver to drop him off at SubZero.

He removed his hat and coat and walked up to the bar. Standing next to him, a tall African American man in a gray, wool suit asked, "Frank White?"

"Yes, I take it your Robert Malone?" Falcon inquired shaking his hand. "Sorry about the gloves, got a bad case of frost bite."

"Eli mentioned you were investigating the Central West End Ripper murders," agent Malone commented. "I suppose you can't tell me who you're working for."

"Sorry," Falcon replied then explained, "Let's just say my client wishes to remain anonymous. Believe me, it's someone just as anxious as the FBI to get the killer off the streets."

Malone paused while the waitress took their drink orders then said, "Here's what I know. Dr. Michael Lugano is in town. He recently worked with the government of Katari in South Africa to apprehend the Katari Ripper."

Agent Malone got up from his bar stool and motioned for Falcon to follow him to a small table in a secluded corner of the restaurant. After the waitress took their lunch orders, he stated, "The Ripper murders began in Khayelitsha, the largest shanty town in South Africa. They were almost identical to the ones committed recently in Katari." the FBI agent continued. "Ten young women employed in various after hours occupations, were murdered in a space of ten weeks. Their bodies were discovered in basement stairwells and alleys. Not a shred of evidence was found, no fingerprints, no DNA, nothing."

"How much blood was found at the scenes?" Falcon asked quietly.

"Not much, which led the police to believe they were killed elsewhere, and their bodies dumped later," Agent Malone explained. Taking a drink of water he continued, "The bodies were placed in the same position—on their backs, with their heads turned slightly to the left."

"Were there any strange markings anywhere on the body?" Falcon asked.

"Other than the four-inch slash marks on their left sides, none was reported," Malone answered.

Falcon nodded, he knew the Ordinary investigators wouldn't find the Keeper's marks. They weren't looking in the right place. The mutilating slashes on the bodies would distract them from searching for the tiny punctures made by a vampire's incisors.

"What was the time line for the murders, and were any communications left from the killer?" Falcon asked.

"The last murder ended about six weeks ago," the agent confirmed. "The killer never communicated with anyone. Dr. Lugano and the local police must have been frustrated with the lack of evidence. The government now claims the case is solved, reporting that the Ripper was killed trying to escape custody. No doubt it was a political solution to make ten unsolved murders go away."

"Lack of communication from such a killer is unusual," Falcon commented. "Most serial killers want recognition. Sometimes they take a trophy from their victims, or leave some clue about their next move. While the act of murder becomes a compulsion, the need for recognition becomes equally important."

"The murders started here about four weeks ago," Malone explained. "It could be the same perpetrator. The time frame is about right, if you figure a week to book passage on a merchant ship heading for the states, some down time to set up shop here, and then boom, the rampage begins."

"Why not travel on a cruise ship?" Falcon inquired.

"He would be too visible, and there were no cruise ships in port. Seasonal storms had already docked private craft," Malone stated.

"What about the airlines?" Falcon asked.

"There was a serious rebel incursion that month, and the airlines were shut down. Army squadrons guarded the airport for weeks," Malone responded. "The only possible way out of the country would have been by merchant vessel."

"Was there any evidence the women were drugged before they were slashed?" Falcon requested.

Malone paused while the waitress set their lunch plates down and took another drink order. Once she walked away, he asked, "How did you know? They were drugged, with a rather outdated type of chemical, chloroform."

"Which would fit the Jack the Ripper profile," Falcon commented. He took two bites of his beef and a swallow of water before adding, "Our killer copies him, but doesn't kill for the same reason."

"How's that?" Malone asked, leaning forward with interest.

"His motives are different," Falcon explained. "Jack the Ripper wanted to rid the streets of prostitutes, theoretically, because they brought shame and disease among the upper class. He had a compulsion to kill women he considered parasites on society."

"Some say the Ripper had connections with the royal family," the agent added. Looking at Falcon levelly he asked, "How is this guy different?"

"The Central West End Ripper is not motivated by passion," Falcon theorized. "He's motivated by the act itself, a quick kill with ample blood letting, and an easy escape."

"You mean he wants their blood?" Malone asked, looking at Falcon doubtfully.

"I know it sounds bazaar," Falcon answered quickly. "There are documented cases of psychopaths believing they're vampires. If you check the amount of blood missing from each of the women, you will probably find that it was about 5 pints."

"I don't have to check," the agent replied, pushing away his plate. "About 5 pints of blood were missing from each girl, but hardly any was found under their bodies."

"Were there any other clues or coincidences that you can think of that could help us find the killer." Falcon inquired.

"Interpol checked all the merchant ships that left the harbor the week the killings stopped," Malone stated. "There was only one common item on the bill of ladings. The ships carried hundreds of crates of wine, bound for the United States."

"Wine," Falcon repeated, his mind spinning.

"A few hundred cases of wine isn't much to go on," Malone commented with a sigh.

Checking his watch, Agent Malone motioned for the waitress. She came over immediately, and he paid his lunch bill. As he got up to leave he said, "Let me know if I can help in any way, and by the way, we never met."

"I'll contact you through our mutual friend," Falcon agreed watching the man's tall figure as he left the pub. In other circumstances they might have become friends, but secrecy had to be respected, on both sides.

Falcon considered the wine connection an interesting, but ironic clue. There was a true obsession in a vampire's need for blood and wine. Wine was considered the elixir of the gods in Greek and Roman mythology, substance for holy rites in the Catholic Church, and a daily drink in many parts of the world. Invariably, where there was wine in abundance, there were vampires. Southwestern Missouri wasn't Napa Valley, but if a vampire wanted to remain inconspicuous, it was the place to frequent. He wouldn't be surprised to discover that the Ripper had visited a number of towns in that vicinity, including the Two Brothers Vineyard, owned by his family.

After the meeting with Robert Malone, Falcon hailed a cab and headed back to his apartment. It was nearly 3:00 pm and he needed to catch up on his sleep. In four hours he had to prepare for his second stint at the Midnight Supper Club, and he wanted to go over his notes. This time, he would give them a show they wouldn't forget.

Chapter 7

Falcon's sharp, irritating alarm interrupted his nap. It took a long lukewarm shower to bring him to wakefulness. He scrubbed his weary body to increase circulation, drying off with a soft white towel. His wet hair, which was already too wiry, sprang into curly cues as he dried his unruly locks and stepped into the bedroom. In the back of his closet was his costume for the presentation, a white silk shirt with a crimson tie, worn under a black tuxedo jacket with satin trim on the lapels. His slacks were tapered with a pressed crease. Only the absence of a flowing cape departed from what was deemed by the public as the traditional vampire attire.

As he drove to the club, his heart thumped loudly at the thought of seeing Giselle again and meeting her parents. He had read several of Dr. Edmond Montreau's essays on prolonging life. They were written for the Ordinary, "Journal of Psychiatry", but if you read between the lines, Montreau's ideas applied to vampires as well. In the article, he stated that living an authentic and ethical life was directly related to longevity. Dishonest, self-absorbed people were more likely to develop life-shortening illnesses, like heart disease and high blood pressure. He was the first clinical Psychiatrist to assert that being a moral person was essential to health and longevity. He boldly asserted that honesty was as important as nutrition for physical and mental well being. Moreover, Dr. Montreau stated that faith, with an emphasis on helping others, could be an integral part of that equation.

Such profound words, Falcon thought, from a man whose entire life was a charade. In today's world, vampires had to develop a dual personality; behaving like an Ordinary in public, and revealing their authentic self in private. This dual personality was so reflexive that most vampires were oblivious to the hypocrisy of their actions. Survival dictated their contrary behavior, a survival based on a history of unattractive alternatives.

Falcon parked his car several blocks away and walked with his face hidden in the folds of his hooded trench coat. He crossed the street swiftly, avoiding the milling crowd by entering the side door of the club.

As he walked into his dressing room, Rascal Gold walked up to him commenting excitedly, "Good, you're early! We have to go over your presentation. Our idea worked. Your faux catastrophe last week had all the members atwitter!"

"Here's a copy of my notes," Falcon said, handing Gold the papers. "Now loosen your knickers before you get chafed."

Gold read over the notes, his frown at Falcon's comment quickly turning into a grin. He slapped Falcon on the back and said, "This is amazing. Can you really do that? We'll have the audience eating out of our hands after this."

"And I know where your hands will be Gold, old pal, right in their wallets," Falcon replied, checking his appearance in the full-length mirror.

"Absolutely, how else can I keep this joint running?" he asked.

After Gold left, Zeke entered the dressing room, closed and locked the door behind him and said, "I overheard something today that might help us."

"Go on. I'm listening," Falcon responded, sitting across from him.

"I happened to walk by Gold's office and heard him talking to someone," Zeke relayed.

"Did you see who it was?" Falcon asked.

"No. I didn't want them to see me," Zeke answered. "Gold was talking to a man with a deep baritone voice, very cultured and refined. He asked Gold to hook him up with someone in the club. I'm sure I heard the man say that he was interested in investing a large amount of money with a local wine merchant."

"Thanks," Falcon said. "The man must be a friend of Gold's, or a VIP member of the club."

"Is it any help?" Zeke asked.

"Possibly," Falcon stated. "My FBI contact informed me that the Katari Ripper could have come to this country on a merchant vessel carrying a shipment of wine."

"Do you think the man talking to Gold was the Ripper?" Zeke asked.

"I don't know," Falcon stated. "It could have been a coincidence. Gold has connections with a lot of local entrepreneurs."

"E.Z. you're on!" Gold shouted from the hall.

"That's my cue," Zeke said, glancing over at his brother.

"Break a leg," Falcon stated, smiling. He knew his brother would put on a good show. There were no mirrors involved in his magic act, just natural, vampire ability. Zeke was a consummate entertainer. With his star-quality looks, stunning magic tricks, Rock music, and dazzling light displays, the audience would be mesmerized.

Falcon watched in the wings as Zeke seemed to elevate above the stage. All eyes were riveted on him, especially the women, whose delicate hands covered their mouths in surprise, or held their cell phones forward to take pictures. He quickly went through his repertoire of magic tricks, each one more surprising than the other. Suddenly, he vanished in a puff of smoke and reappeared in the back of the club. Zeke strolled between the tables, kissing the offered hands of many a lovely young guest. Back on stage, he prepared for the finale.

As a smoky mist enveloped the stage and spilled out into the audience, E.Z. appeared in the middle of it. He pursed his mouth and blew. When the mist whirled into a thin funnel-shaped twister, he swiftly took it into his mouth. The audience gasped as he swallowed the entire mini-twister whole. To their astonishment, the funnel was regurgitated as a giant flame, bursting eight feet into the air. The audience rose to their feet with a deafening applause. Zeke slowly levitated above the stage, swallowing the flame as he moved upward. By the time he landed silently on the floor and took a bow, the audience was shouting, clapping, and whistling their approval.

Zeke bowed several times and exited stage left.

The lights went out and a spotlight shone on the microphone, as Rascal Gold glided back onto the stage. He bowed low to the audience and said excitedly, "E.Z. the Great! Doesn't he make it look easy? Bravo!"

The audience was given a ten-minute break and dispersed noisily to meet with friends and share their impressions of the entertainment. Zeke sought out Falcon and suggested, "The man Gold was talking to could be in the audience."

"Too bad we don't know what he looks like," Falcon stated.

As the house lights blinked off and on, and the patrons hurried back to their seats, Gold came up to Falcon in the wings and stated, "EZ will be a hard act to follow."

"I think I'll manage to wow them," Falcon returned. "Who was the gent with the deep voice you were talking to earlier today?"

"I've been working on the books all day," Gold said, looking away absently. "The only person I talked to was EZ when he came in to rehearse."

The house lights dimmed, and the spotlight focused on the middle of the stage. Gold waited patiently until the audience quieted down. He announced in a booming voice, "And now, the one you've been waiting for, Theodore Falcon, vampire!"

This time Falcon streaked swiftly to center stage in a dazzling blur. The audience grew quiet as he sat on the stool in front of them. Taking the microphone in his hand he began with,

"Thank you for graciously returning this evening. A family crisis preempted my second set last week." Gazing out at the audience he continued, "Vampires are not immortals, as folklore dictates. Like all living beings, they have a life span. People assume their immortal because no one has lived long enough to witness their natural death."

Falcon took a drink from his crystal glass, cleared his throat and said, "Don't let our mortality fool you. We don't need your sympathy, just your blood."

At this remark Falcon had the audience's undivided attention. Out of the corner of his eye he could see his brother watching him from the wings with a wry smile on his shadowed face.

"Some of us are very civilized and obtain nourishment by purchasing our special drink from a blood bank," he continued. "Other vampires go to the Red Cross, not to give blood, but to take it. Twenty-first century vampires thrive because they keep their identity a well-guarded secret. We are not the monsters of myths and folklore, but as in any human culture, some of us are good, and others are evil. It's all a matter of choice. Because of our need for blood, our survival instinct is more developed than that of Ordinaries; we live in constant danger of being exposed. Your culture possesses certain traits that help you survive, such as; highly developed intelligence, language, agriculture, and organized government. We too have traits that help us to survive. Many of them are more highly developed than yours."

Falcon rose from his stool and offered, "Let me demonstrate. The first trait that a vampire excels in is speed." The moment he mouthed the word, he raced by in a blur, and in the next instant, he was speaking from the back of the room. "Back here my friends."

The audience twisted around, surprised to see Falcon standing in the back of the club. Strolling jauntily back to the stage he added, "The fastest human runner on earth runs a four-minute mile. Any aged vampire can easily run a two-minute mile." He settled back on the stool and continued, "Our second trait is agility."

Falcon leaped into the air somersaulting three times and landing softly on the stage floor. Racing across the floor of the stage, he hit the wall, walked sideways up the wall, executed a back flip, and landed gracefully on his feet.

In the next moment, he motioned for an assistant to join him on stage saying, "I've asked E.Z. The Great's manager, Gorky, to aid me in the demonstration of the next vampire trait; advanced reflex action."

Gorky bowed to the audience. Raising a lightweight javelin he threw it directly at Falcon. As the audience gasped, Falcon suddenly bent backwards. The javelin whizzed by him harmlessly, sticking into the thick corkboard mounted on the wall behind him. The javelin throw was repeated three more times. To the audience's amazement, Falcon reached out and caught the projectile on the final throw.

The audience's response was highlighted with shrieks of elation and thunderous hand clapping. Falcon gave a slight bow and announced, "My final demonstration will require that everyone remain seated at all times. If you have a weak heart or any type of nervous condition, please excuse yourselves now. I will give you a few moments."

When no one moved, Falcon positioned himself at center stage. A few moments later he lowered his head. His eyes, two black orbs in the middle of a brightly lit face, stared intently into the crowd. The spotlight shrunk, until the only thing illuminated was a sphere of light on Falcon's unmoving continence. With his heightened vampire hearing, Falcon easily detected individual heartbeats of club members.

"My final power," Falcon spoke in a quiet voice, "is, control of atmospheric electricity."

Holding out one clenched hand, Falcon pointed his index finger at the crowd. Instantly, a bolt of static electricity arced into the audience, separated into tiny filaments, and struck a number of random guests. Club members, zapped with a static shock, flinched in unison.

In seconds, the demonstration was over, and Falcon was bowing as the awestruck audience expressed their approval with a standing ovation. Waiters rushed over with water and smelling salts, in case any overwhelmed guests were on the verge of fainting.

When the houselights came on, the audience rose en masse and applauded for several minutes. As Falcon waved to the crowd, he spotted Giselle and her parents. They were grinning and applauding like the rest of the satisfied audience.

He hurried back to his dressing room as the guests filed out. His brother, who was sitting on the tiny dressing room couch sipping a glass of elixir said, "Great show. You had them right in your hands."

Suddenly Rascal Gold burst into the room clapping his hands, "You two were awesome! I tell you, this event will finally put me on the map. St. Louis will become the main headquarters for the Midnight Supper Club!"

"I'm glad you finally hit it big Gold, but don't count on a repeat performance," Falcon replied. "This is a one time deal, not a circus act."

"Don't worry Gold," Zeke interjected. "I'll come back as often as you like."

Gold looked at Zeke, then back at Falcon, and threw up his hands in exasperation. Glancing at his wristwatch, he turned abruptly, and left. Both brothers chuckled together, with Zeke observing, "Rascal is something else,"

"That's the truth," Falcon agreed. "I just haven't figured out what." Falcon shook his head and added, "By the way, thanks for the orb. It made a nice finish."

"No problem," Zeke acknowledged. "After all, the opening act can't outdo the main attraction, especially when it's your own brother."

When Giselle stepped into the dressing room with a welcoming smile, Falcon rose and accepted her embrace and lingering kiss.

"Wonderful show," She complimented breathlessly. "My father and his colleagues were quite impressed. Mother is absolutely awed by your talents. She probably has us married with five children in that over-imaginative, matchmaker brain of hers."

"Hello," Zeke spoke up quietly.

"Oh, you have company," Giselle replied softly, looking from Falcon to Zeke.

"Giselle, this is my brother, Ezekiel," Falcon announced.

"I would have never guessed you were related," Giselle stated, "Of course, EZ Bonaparte is your stage name."

"Let that be our little secret," Zeke said rising politely. "Anonymity is our family's stock and trade."

"And that of every Freeblood family I know," Giselle agreed. She turned toward Falcon saying, "We're not expected at my parents until 2:00. Let's have a celebration drink at my apartment."

"Sounds good to me," Falcon answered getting his coat. He took her offered arm and they walked out of the club, Zeke following close behind.

Giselle turned toward Zeke and asked, "Would you like to join us?"

"Why not, it's a party," Zeke agreed heartily.

The trio left the club the back way and took a short cut through the alley. With Giselle between them, the brothers scanned the shadows for strangers. Once on the street, they got into the Thunderbird and Falcon drove to the Ash apartments.

Zeke asked from the back seat, "How did my obscurely shy brother find you?"

"We ran into each other in Forest Park," Giselle replied cheerfully. "Falcon saved me from a very determined mugger."

"It was more like I saved the mugger from her," Falcon observed.

"I think you got lucky bro, "Zeke stated, "The club members sure cleared out fast tonight," he mused, gazing out the window at the empty streets.

"It's the curfew," Falcon responded. "Didn't you see the police patrols in front of the building?"

"Sure," Zeke replied, "I thought that was to keep the press away."

"The police were also there to escort guests to their cars," Falcon explained.

"The Ripper has sure put a damper on the night life in this town," Zeke observed.

"I hope they catch him soon," Giselle commented. "I know I'll breathe a little easier, when he's behind bars."

Riding to her apartment Giselle looked at the two brothers. She finally saw their resemblance, in their eyes and in the slight dimple on their chins. Zeke was over six feet tall and gangly, while Falcon was shorter, slim, and wiry. Falcon's unruly curls were sandy-brown and close cropped. Zeke's hair was white blonde, straight, and shoulder-length, giving him the rock star appearance that enhanced his career as a magician.

The two brothers seemed to have different personalities. As they chatted, Giselle enjoyed Zeke's cheerful, joking manner. His personality was fun loving, and he didn't appear to take life too seriously. Falcon however, was droll, charmingly shy, and more reserved than Zeke.

Once the trio was seated comfortably in her apartment, Giselle poured the sparkling wine into three fluted glasses. They toasted to the success of the evening. After they chatted about the show and less serious topics, Giselle finally broached the grim topic that had been on her mind most of the evening, stating, "We need to talk about the Ripper."

"My contact at City Hall and I are working on a few leads," Falcon stated. "There may be a connection between our Ripper and the Katari Ripper out of Africa."

"Did they find *him*?" Giselle asked interestedly.

"No," Falcon answered, "According to the agent I spoke to, he disappeared without a trace and the murders ended."

"Did the agent say how he escaped?" Zeke inquired.

"The only possible way he could have gotten out of the country was by ship," Falcon explained. "Several cargo ships, docked at Katari Harbor, left within days of each other, all carrying shipments of wine, bound for Spain, England and the United States."

"Do you think the Central West End Ripper and the Katari Ripper is the same person?" Giselle asked.

"It's seems plausible," Falcon stated. "What are the chances of there being two Jack the Ripper copycats"

"Well, it's a start," Zeke commented. "At least we know how he got here. Where did the merchant ship dock in the United States?"

"A ship called The Mercado landed in New York Harbor six weeks ago," Falcon explained.

"Let's review the clues we have so far," Giselle suggested, after refreshing their drinks.

"Our serial killer came from Africa, and may have boarded a merchant ship carrying a cargo of wine to the United States," Falcon began.

"He targets young women," Zeke added, "slashing them like Jack the Ripper."

"He kills one woman a week," Giselle added.

"As we stated earlier the absence of any clues, even DNA points to the probability we are dealing with an obsessively careful Keeper vampire," Falcon suggested.

"Don't forget about the man I heard talking to Mr. Gold before my performance," Zeke broke in. "He wanted Gold to introduce him to a local merchant in the wine business."

"That could be a clue," Giselle said.

"I asked Gold about the visitor," Falcon informed them. "He said he was alone until Zeke arrived to rehearse."

"He's lying," Zeke retorted. "I know what I heard."

"I think you might be right about Gold's visitor being connected to the murders," Falcon responded.

"I'm afraid we'll have to continue this discussion another time. Falcon and I are dining with my parents in twenty minutes," Giselle broke in. "You're welcomed to join us," she added smiling a Zeke.

"Thanks for the invite," Zeke said, "but I'll have to take a rain check. I'm beat. Falcon can drop me off at his place."

When they stopped at the Nightwing Arms, Falcon got out of the car and rode the elevator with his Zeke. By the time Falcon rejoined Giselle, his brother had crashed on the sofa nursing a tall glass of elixir.

When Falcon took Giselle into his arms and kissed her, she smiled and asked softly, "I'm dying to know. How did you do that last trick?"

"I'm hurt that you of all people would call my demonstration of power a trick," he returned. "My brother's the magician, not me."

"Falcon," Giselle demanded.

"Zeke lent me his orb," Falcon replied, grinning.

"His orb?" Giselle asked.

"It's actually called a MSEC-Miniature Static Electricity Collector," Falcon answered then explained, "It operates like a stun gun, but instead of holding a charge, it collects static electricity present in the room. The static is released as random bursts of harmless current, the same thing you feel on a cold morning when you walk across the carpet and then touch something metal."

"Clever," Giselle complimented. "You certainly earned the respect of the audience with that performance."

"I want more than their respect," Falcon. "I need their devotion and loyalty."

"Why in the world would you want that?" Giselle asked.

"Oh don't worry, I'm not a narcissistic maniac," Falcon reassured her. "If our vampire nature is ever made public, we'll need the help of influential Ordinaries on our side."

"If the Ripper is caught by the police and examined, we'll all be rounded up," Giselle stated sadly. "We have to make it our main priority to find the Ripper before the authorities do," Giselle insisted emphatically. "I couldn't stand living in one of those dusty old catacombs under some crumbling, ancient ruin in Europe."

"What do you mean, we?" Falcon asked. Placing two fingers under Giselle's chin and gazing steadily into her dark eyes, he ordered, "Giselle, stay out of this. A Keeper can be a threat even to another vampire."

"I can handle myself," Giselle replied, eyes flashing.

"I know that," Falcon stated with exasperation.

As he drew Giselle toward him, she relaxed as he encircled her in his arms. He was unable to keep his voice from cracking as he said, "Giselle, don't you see how dangerous this is for you?"

Giselle moved away and stared at him stubbornly stating, "The best way to catch the Ripper is to offer him bait he can't refuse."

"Giselle you're not suggesting that you should be that bait are you?" Falcon asked. "He would certainly recognize that you are not an Ordinary like the other victims."

"By the time he discovers that, it will be too late," Giselle replied. "We'll call it Plan B. It may be the only way to beat him at his own game."

With a stricken look Falcon gazed back at her. He knew Giselle was a very tenacious woman. When she made up her mind, there was no stopping her. He would make it his main priority to find the Ripper before Plan B was necessary.

Chapter 8

After Giselle made her startling comment to Falcon, the couple rode to her parent's home in silence. Finally, Giselle put her hand on Falcon's cheek and said, "Of course, I would be backed up with adequate protection."

"I didn't mean to act like a complete chauvinist," Falcon said sighing. "The thought of you being in danger makes my blood run cold."

They arrived at the Montreau's stately mansion on Lindell and parked in the circle drive. Falcon held Giselle's hand, feeling a nervous excitement in the pit of his stomach. He was relieved when it was the family butler who answered the door and invited them in.

"Miss Giselle, it's good to see you," The butler greeted them with a smile.

"Paul has been with my family since before I was born," Giselle explained, giving the austere white-haired man her arm. "I'm afraid I played awful tricks on him as a child," She commented, gazing at the old man kindly.

"A large toad swimming in a tureen of cold cucumber soup comes to mind," Paul said, the lines around his eyes crinkling.

"Paul, this is my friend, Theodore Falcon," Giselle said.

"I'm honored to meet you Mr. Falcon," Paul stated shaking his hand. "Mr. And Mrs. Montreau relayed the complete story about your presentation at the club tonight. I must admit it sounded astonishing."

"It really wasn't," Falcon returned. "I'm just a clever vampire with a few tricks up my sleeve."

"Your parents and their guests are in the drawing room," Paul informed Giselle. "I was just about to serve the wine."

Falcon was impressed with the antique beauty of the stately home. The ceilings were easily twelve feet high, painted pale ivory with intricately carved crown molding. An elegant crystal chandelier protruded from a small oval inset in the ceiling, painted with smiling cherubs, flying among puffy blue-gray clouds. The living room was arraigned with an elegant French couch flanked by two large wingback chairs. Two stunning Tiffany lamps, with colorful, stained-glass shades graced the end tables and softened the room with pale light. A vibrant, blazing fire in the immense, stone fireplace warmed the chilly room.

Three men rose as Falcon and Giselle entered the room while Giselle's mother, an exquisite older copy of her daughter, remained seated.

"Mr. Falcon," Paul announced, "Mrs. Yvonne, and Dr. Richard Montreau."

After shaking hands with the men, Falcon gave a slight bow and kissed Mrs. Montreau's hand lightly, saying, "I'm honored to meet you." Addressing Dr. Montreau he said, "Sir, I've read your treatise on 'Character, Faith, and Mental Health'. It intrigued me with its genuine truths about human nature and the search for a peaceful life." Giselle's father was tall and stately with wavy, black hair gray at the temples, a thin brown mustache and goatee.

Dr. Montreau turned toward his other two guests and introduced them saying, "These are my esteemed colleagues and friends, Dr. Sidney Hayden and Dr. Michael Lugano."

Falcon tried not to react in surprise at the familiar name he had heard in his meeting with his FBI contact, Robert

Malone. He nodded to Lugano, not realizing that he had squeezed Giselle's hand reflexively upon hearing his name. Giselle looked up at him questioningly. Falcon leaned over and whispered, "I'll tell you later."

"My father told me that you're from Central Africa," Giselle commented. "I've never seen the continent, but have always been intrigued by it."

"If one were to take out the equation of human strife," Dr. Lugano replied, "it would be a most majestic country. It seems where mankind builds his habitats, nature gets dealt a vicious blow."

Paul announced that dinner was served, and they filed into the large dining room. The long narrow cherry wood table was adorned with a delicate lace tablecloth. At its center lay an enormous gleaming sterling silver bowl filled with Calla Lilies, flanked by two silver candelabra. Soft candlelight, the room's only illumination, provided a warm intimate atmosphere for the gathering. The table settings were of fine china with a grape vine motif, and silver utensils. Etched crystal, wine goblets sparkled and glittered at each place, reflecting the flickering candles. Steaming hot soup containing thin slices of rare roast beef, mushrooms, leeks, and barley was served first from a porcelain tureen painted with brightly hued cloisonné birds.

After finishing the soup, Falcon gazed across the table at Dr. Lugano saying, "Time Magazine had an excellent article about your new president, Mozamba. He's taking on a difficult problem with his war on disease in Katari."

"Public health is an issue that is close to the president's heart," Dr. Lugano agreed. "Diseases such as typhus and malaria, all but extinct in your country, are rampant in mine. Africa has the same social diseases that your country has stabilized, while, ours have grown to epidemic proportions.

HIV is decimating the population of our young adults, while children and the elderly struggle to maintain the family. It is crucial that Katari brings forth a supreme effort to save its people."

"Speaking of dangers to public health, how did President Mozamba react to the Khayelitsha Ripper?" Falcon asked.

"I'm impressed to hear you have international contacts Mr. Falcon," Lugano replied, "President Mozamba met with the city police commissioners of South Africa and mandated that all their resources should be focused on finding the killer. When the Ripper struck in Katari, the police were ordered to handle him with extreme prejudice."

After taking a sip of water, Dr. Lugano continued. "The president is well loved by the people. He has succeeded in establishing order and peace. He courageously implemented his war against crime by enlisting the aid of the people. With their help in reporting crimes, perpetrators are found and swiftly dealt with. He has consulted with major police forces in Europe and this country to modernize education and training of officers to insure they are more effective in their investigations. They are now trained to go out into the communities and interview witnesses on a more personal basis. These new methods have lowered the crime rate by nearly 20% in the last year."

"Very impressive statistics," Falcon replied. "That is much higher than most western cities can boast. Have you considered the possibility that the Katari Ripper murders were a cover-up for a more insidious crime?"

"Dr. Lugano believes that the Katari Ripper was a vampire." Dr. Montreau offered.

"Was?" Falcon asked. "I take it the killings have stopped."

"The authorities stopped him eight weeks ago," Lugano answered, reaching for his wine goblet.

"To what do attribute your success?" Falcon asked pointedly.

"Our team worked tirelessly and our efforts were rewarded," Dr. Lugano answered guardedly.

"It must be seen as a great victory for President Mozamba," Giselle commented.

"A great victory for all of us," Lugano returned with a smile. "I have had the honor of being appointed the assistant to the minister of health, Onri Umboto. Our close contacts with the medical and investigative authorities around the globe provide a great resource for improving the health of our people.

"To say the killings have ended, isn't that an over-simplification of the facts?" Falcon asked insistently.

Paul served the butter-dipped lobster tails with baskets of warm crusty French bread that were eagerly passed around the table. Falcon took a morsel of lobster and dipped it in garlic butter sauce, waiting patiently for the doctor to respond to his question.

"To answer your pertinent question Mr. Falcon, you are correct, ten young girls were brutally slashed, one each week, then it was over," Dr. Lugano explained. "What little trace we had of the killer, disappeared with him. Of course the president used the cessation of murder to his political advantage. He suggested the Ripper had been killed, and the media took it from there. In truth, no physical evidence was ever found to confirm that assumption."

"Perhaps the Ripper left the country," Falcon stated. He saw a slight expression of surprise on Lugano's smooth brown face, which he quickly covered with a mask of calm. "The time frame would be correct," Falcon continued. "A clever vampire can hide anywhere, especially if he is a Keeper who lives by his cunning. He could have found a merchant vessel, either arranged passage with a bribe, or stowed away in a cargo hold, hibernating for the weeks it took to come to the United States. It would be easy for him to set up a false identity here, and begin preying on American women."

"A well-informed deduction," Dr. Lugano admitted. "It seems unlikely that there would be two identical Rippers working in our countries. Unfortunately Katari has downplayed the Ripper's existence to the rest of the world."

"Michael, your expertise as a profiler is well-known in the field of Abnormal Psychology, as well as Criminology," Dr. Hayden offered. "In your opinion, are these two killers the same person?"

"That possibility is what motivated my visit to your country," Dr. Lugano acknowledged. "Keepers are rarer than Freebloods in the world today. They have been systematically exterminated by Ordinaries for centuries because of their aberrant behavior. In my latest estimation, only a few hundred Keepers exist in the entire world. It is unrealistic to believe that two of them were acting independently, continents apart, within weeks of each other."

Giselle offered, "If all you are saying is true, why not provide an irresistible bait for him; a young woman who fits his specific type."

Dr. Lugano nodded, "You have presented a plausible solution to finding the killer. It is imperative that we apprehend the perpetrator and study his behavior, before our anonymity is compromised."

"Don't you mean before more lives are put at risk?" Falcon asked dryly.

"Of course, Mr. Falcon, you are correct," Dr. Lugano agreed readily. "Our immediate concern is to save lives. Miss

Giselle has presented an interesting solution, but it would be very dangerous for the young woman used as bait."

"It's out of the question that we allow any young woman to risk her life." Falcon stated, emphatically.

"Of course, Mr. Falcon," Dr. Lugano said. "Such a plan would only be used as a last resort, when all else failed."

"If we were to entertain such an idea," Dr. Montreau responded. "The young woman would have to be carefully selected, trained, and protected," he suggested, looking at Giselle.

"Absolutely," Dr. Lugano agreed. "My dear Giselle, please do not suggest that you put yourself in danger. No one in this room would agree to that."

"Please hear her out gentlemen," Yvonne Montreau requested.

"I agree that baiting the killer should be implemented only if all else fails," Giselle explained. "I am well-educated in psychology, vampire and Ordinary. I did my clinical rotation at Barnes Hospital and studied a year under Klaus Buchner, the author of 'The Psychology of the Serial Killer'."

"I agree that you are well qualified my dear," Giselle's father acknowledged. "Let's hope that we can find this Keeper without resorting to such a plan."

Paul returned to serve the main course; rare prime rib with peppercorns, roasted seasoned potatoes, sautéed Portobello mushrooms in wine sauce, and rosemary asparagus. Yvonne diplomatically turned the conversation to the upcoming Thanksgiving Holiday and other lighter topics during the delightful repast. The others responded readily in sharing their plans, happy to discuss something less disturbing.

After dinner, the group retired to the drawing room for coffee and dessert. Giselle took a seat at the piano and played several classical pieces. Falcon gazed fondly at her as she lost herself in the music, the passionate emotions evoked by the melodies evident on her young face. The realization that people he loved, and other innocent people in the city were in grave danger, even tonight, hit Falcon in the stomach like a well-placed punch. While this peaceful group sat listening to the strains of "Moonlight Sonata," a killer, possibly in the throes of a mindless, hungry rage, was hiding in the shadows, waiting to strike. With such a monster at large, no one was safe.

After Giselle completed her music and everyone applauded in appreciation, Dr. Montreau announced, "I want to share something remarkable about our latest research." When all eyes turned toward him expectantly he continued, "Dr. Hayden and I have discovered a formula that will replace our need for blood plasma."

Giselle, the first to react, leaned forward saying, "Father, how exciting. Please explain." She gripped Falcon's hand, and he responded by quickly covering it with his own.

"Sidney, will you do the honors?" Dr. Montreau asked, turning to his friend.

"Of course," Dr. Hayden replied. "As you know, our physiology is based on the consumption of blood. Without it our lifespan would be cut 75% and we would be too weak to exercise our minds and physical bodies. My colleagues and I have created Alpha-T, synthetic plasma containing all the nutrients, minerals, and elements, contained in organic blood."

"Imagine," Dr. Montreau interjected, "never having to drink the blood of animals or Ordinaries ever again."

"From our initial studies on vampire bats," Dr. Hayden explained, "Alpha-T not only nourished the bats, but it decreased their desire for blood. After feeding on our formula for two years, test bats have nearly weaned themselves from it. In our latest case study, tagged bats, reintroduced into the wild, fed on animals only 1% of the time."

"How did Alpha-T affect their life span?" Falcon asked.

"The bats we used that were, five to six years old, lived to age 8." Dr. Hayden answered. "Their normal span is nine or ten years. According to our research, a bat's lifespan was cut short by about 2 years."

"Using the formula we would still enjoy 80% of our normal longevity," Falcon deduced. "When can I start the program?"

"Steady now Theodore," Dr. Montreau cautioned. "At the moment, we have five Freeblood test subjects, none of which is a male vampire in their prime."

"All the more reason to use me as your guinea pig," Falcon insisted. "Are the five test subjects thriving?"

"You're looking at them," Montreau stated. "Sidney and I were the first. We've been using the formula for about seven years, my wife, six, Giselle, two, and Dr. Lugano, a year."

Falcon looked over at Giselle then back at Dr. Hayden asking, "What are you waiting for? I know many Freebloods who would be more than willing to participate in your trials; my parents, brother, and cousins, to name a few."

"Please help Falcon," Giselle spoke up, touching her father's arm.

"Theodore, don't admonish my daughter for not telling you," Montreau insisted. "We were all sworn to secrecy. I'm at fault here. I introduced a new elixir to her without telling her its contents. It worked for her mother, and I knew it would work for her."

Turning back to Falcon Dr. Montreau added, "You must know how the scientific world is. Such a discovery has to be kept secret." Seeing the melting plea in his daughter's eyes, he sighed and relinquished, "I fully intended to add you and your family to the trials, because I know you are putting together a team to find the psychotic Keeper who threatens our very existence. I must test him before I use the treatment on any male Freeblood vampire in their prime."

Dr. Hayden broke in with, "If we can cure the Ripper's need for blood, we can transform him from vicious predator to a civilized Freeblood."

"I hate to dispel your wishful thinking," Yvonne Montreau interjected. "You're all forgetting something. Drinking blood from humans hasn't been a necessity for Freebloods or Keepers in over a hundred years. Keepers prefer to prey on humans. How will this formula or any other elixir stop that?"

"Keepers in our program will go through an intensive, medical trial. Test subjects will be strictly monitored in a secure hospital facility. We will administer continuing doses of Alpha-T, combined with behavior modification, hypnosis, and counseling," Dr. Montreau explained.

Dr. Lugano's eyes glittered stonily when he commented, "Think what this will mean for all of us. No more guilt and shame because we live on Ordinaries like parasites. The ethical and moral ramifications will change our people forever. We will become an integral part of the human race. Keepers will no longer be our enemies. Our two nations can unite as they were meant to do."

"Being human means having free will," Falcon pointed out. "Not even a Keeper should be forced to use Alpha-T against their will. You'll have no problem getting Freebloods to volunteer." Seeing the others ready to object, Falcon hastily continued with, "I don't disagree that the formula be tested on the Ripper, but I doubt if any Keeper will willingly participate in such a trial. It's anathema for a Keeper to be considered equal to any being. It goes against their nature.

It took thousands of years for their way of life to develop. A magic elixir alone will not cure their aggressive behavior."

"If they want to live, they will submit," Lugano stated coldly.

A shudder ran through Falcon. Believing that Michael Lugano was an overzealous fanatic he suggested, "Let's see how it works on the Ripper before we start converting the whole Keeper nation. It should be a matter of choice, not compulsion."

"The Ripper is a cold-blooded killer," Giselle protested. "He gave up his right of choice when he killed the first girl. It was totally unnecessary for his survival. I agree with Dr. Lugano. He must submit or be stopped."

"Giselle," Falcon pleaded. "I agree the Ripper should be punished, but if we force all Keepers to use Alpha-T we are no better than they. Don't you see? Our ancestors were Keepers before they were Freebloods."

"I agree with Theodore's rational viewpoint," Dr. Monreau spoke up. "It is unethical to force the elixir on any vampire other than the Ripper. Remember, my theory is hypothetical until we capture the Ripper and try the formula. We don't know the side effects of Alpha-T on male Keeper vampires."

"Falcon, remember what you said to me the night we first met?" Giselle asked.

"I said that one day we'll be free from blood bondage," Falcon answered.

"We have to give it a chance," Giselle persisted. "We have every thing to gain from this test. If Ordinary law catches up with the Ripper, his medical examination would expose all of us to danger. After the Keeper's test trials are completed, he'll face the Freeblood courts anyway."

"We will give him two choices," Dr. Lugano suggested, "Agree to the test and live, or refuse the test, and be remanded to the Freeblood court."

"The problem can't be solved tonight," Dr. Hayden said. "The Ripper must be captured first."

"It's getting late," Falcon announced, rising from his seat. "I have commitments tomorrow evening." Nodding to the Montreaus he added, "I'm pleased to have met you and your wife."

"Come back anytime," Yvonne Montreau responded, smiling. "Perhaps we can discuss less provocative things, when the Ripper is apprehended."

"Yes," Dr. Montreau agreed, shaking Falcon's extended hand. "I'll be in touch with you."

As Falcon and Giselle walked along the brick pathway, he told her about his meeting with agent Malone. He relayed the information the agent gave him about Dr. Lugano.

"I'm relieved the bureau is keeping him under surveillance." Giselle commented. Touching his arm she added, "Falcon, I think Dr. Lugano is sincere about his desire to catch the Ripper. Don't be too hard on him. Look at it from his point of view. He witnessed the damage the killer inflicted on his own people."

"I suppose he has a right to be over-zealous about catching him," Falcon agreed.

"Perhaps Dr. Lugano feels guilty the Ripper got away," Giselle suggested. "He seems to take the brunt the responsibility for the killer's escape."

"Michael Lugano is intelligent and tenacious, but he couldn't control the Ripper's movements," Falcon stated. "The Ripper knew when to quit and relocated while he had the chance."

"I'll be glad when this whole nightmare is over, and we can live in peace," Giselle stated softly.

"I'll do my best to make sure that happens, soon," Falcon replied, putting his arm around her.

Chapter 9

Giselle watched Falcon drive briskly away, confident that he would easily beat the rising sun. She was impressed by his tenacious pursuit of the Ripper, and comforted by their growing friendship. Riding on a wave of love's awakening, Giselle stepped lightly into the kitchen to brew a cup of chamomile tea.

A few minutes later, as Giselle sat at her dresser brushing her hair, she heard a quiet knock at the door. Assuming it was Falcon, she eagerly opened the door. When she saw who stood in the hallway instead, the smile on her face abruptly faded.

"Well, are you going to let me in?" the visitor asked, an amused look on his face. "It's beastly cold in this hall."

"Come in," Giselle answered listlessly, stepping aside.

"Let me have a look at you dear girl," the towering man stated. Gazing at her with piercing black eyes he commented, "The last time I saw you, you were a child. My, my, you certainly have blossomed into a ravishing young woman."

Wrapping her velour robe more tightly around her, she watched as the arrogant man strolled over to the coffee table and poured a glass of wine from the crystal decanter.

"It's been a long time since Cannes," Giselle commented.

"Not so long, my dear," he corrected. "After all, a decade is but the blink of an eye to our kind. Surely you remember our special walk in the Villa Du Creve Coeur gardens after the festival?"

"I could never forget that night," Giselle responded. "Attending the Cannes Film Festival and ball was a graduation gift from my parents."

"I remember standing with your lovely mother and astute father discussing the politics of amnesty, when you walked into the room," he reminisced. "As I recall, it was the stroke of midnight. You were wearing an elegant gown of emerald green. Your hair fell like a crimson waterfall down your back. I couldn't keep my eyes off of you. It was only out of respect to your parents that I curbed an overwhelming impulse to pick you up and whisk you away."

"How could I forget," Giselle responded sarcastically. Glancing at him momentarily, she wondered what had happened that could have changed the man sitting in front of her from the dashing charismatic adventurer of her youth, into the conceited, self-indulgent, stranger that guzzled her wine. His eyes were more-deep set than she recalled. There were gray streaks in his long wavy hair and his mouth was deeply lined into a permanent frown.

"We walked nearly an hour through those moonlit gardens," the man continued, ignoring her remark. "Remember how the night blooming Jasmine and Deadly Night Shade blossoms caught your eyes?"

"You put a sprig of Jasmine in my hair," Giselle recalled in a monotone.

"I picked you up and stood you on a wooden bench," the man relayed wistfully. "I wanted to give you your first kiss, but that vicious hound from hell sprang from the bushes and jumped on me."

"My father trained Lancelot to protect me," Giselle explained. "He didn't harm you. He merely stopped your inappropriate advances."

"You didn't seem to mind those advances," he stated, rising to his feet.

"I was young and innocent," Giselle returned. "I was flattered that a mature man of the world would be interested in someone like me, but I was also terrified. I can assure you, your advances would have gone no further than a kiss, in spite of my impulsive behavior that night."

"Yes, I vaguely remember something about a purity code, or some such nonsense," he returned.

"A vow of chastity," Giselle corrected him. "I promised to remain pure for my future husband."

"There is something very unnatural about a woman cloistering herself from life, especially when she is dauntingly beautiful like you," he admonished.

"Get to the point of this visit, it's nearly sunrise, and I'm tired," Giselle demanded, moving closer to the door.

"Can't old friends meet after a long separation and rehash old times?" he asked, his eyes narrowing into slits.

"We were never friends," Giselle stated. "I was nearly your victim."

"Don't be ridiculous!" the man exclaimed, moving toward her. "I wanted to make you my queen, and lay the world at your feet."

"It wouldn't have worked," Giselle said flatly. "I don't think I would have liked stumbling over the specters of all the women you left in your wake."

"People can change," he said softly.

"People yes," Giselle stated. "*You* will never change."

"I'm hurt that you would speak of me in such an unkind manner," he responded, an ugly grimace stiffening his lips.

"I think you should leave now," Giselle insisted. "I'm not a gullible teenager of sixteen anymore. I don't want to hurt you."

The dark haired man halted his movement, laughed heartily, and said, "Such courage from one still so young!"

"I'm not afraid of you," Giselle stated firmly.

"I must admit," Raven replied, towering over her. "I was very taken with you when I saw you running through the trees like a young huntress. My pleasure turned to distaste though, when I saw you applauding that miserable showman boyfriend of yours at the club." His eyes, two, black pits, stared steadily into hers.

"Don't waste your energy," Giselle warned between clenched teeth. "Your vampire tricks won't work with me. I'm not easily swayed like the other misguided women in your life must have been."

"No, I imagine you can handle yourself," Raven agreed. "I don't want to conquer you my dear. I want you to come to me willingly."

"Why would I do that?" Giselle asked coldly.

"It's too unfathomable!" he retorted. "You prefer the company of that misguided intellectual you've been toying with."

"Please go!" Giselle ordered coldly, opening the door.

Raven backed away slightly, an incredulous look in his eyes. "By the gods, you're in love with him!" he exclaimed. "If only I had gotten here first, I might be the one who put that hungry look in your eyes."

"I won't allow you to twist my emotions into the lowest common denominator!" Giselle retorted. Pointing to the door, she ordered, "Get out, before I cleave your throat from ear to ear!"

Like a charging bull, he was suddenly upon her, reaching for her with pale hands. Giselle evaded the hulking man, leaping gracefully into the air, landing lightly on the lane table by the door. Moving swiftly, she wrapped one arm around his neck, and poised two, long, red nails at his jugular.

"Now, will you leave?" she asked.

"I will see to it that he leaves!" a deep voice from the hall reiterated.

Startled by the cultured voice of Dr. Lugano, Giselle released the man and dropped down from the table, asking, "Dr. Lugano, what are you doing here?"

"I've been searching for my troubled friend for weeks," Lugano replied, moving in front of the doorway. "Forgive me for following him to your apartment."

"Must you stalk me to the ends of the earth?" the man asked in an irritated tone.

"And beyond, if I have to," Dr. Lugano stated. "Let's go."

"Very well," he replied. He turned toward Giselle saying, "Farewell. If you insistent on fraternizing beneath your station, who am I to get in your way."

Dr. Lugano bowed slightly, saying, "I'll make sure that he doesn't bother you again."

Giselle watched from the front window as the two men walked briskly away, melting into the early morning mist. Quickly closing the drapes against the light, she walked shakily into her bedroom. She lay under her comforter until the trembling finally ebbed. For some time, sleep eluded her, and she tossed restlessly. She shuddered in the darkness feeling as if she had narrowly escaped the jaws of a hungry lion.

After leaving Giselle's apartment, Michael Lugano drove his companion to the Forest Park, stopping near the entrance to the Zoo. Pulling the lock off the front gates, he warily escorted him through the park. When they arrived at the Big Cat Country, they scaled the fence. Leaping over the empty moat, they landed near a rock formation inside the habitat.

"I see you still prefer the company of wild animals," Lugano observed. "You always did love the jungle." Standing just inside the lion's den he continued. "Listen to me, brother. When I agreed to help you escape on the Mercado Queen, you promised me you would see Dr. Montreau as soon as you arrived in America."

"I changed my mind," the man replied tersely.

"You are a stupid man," Lugano retorted. "I should have killed you when I found you hibernating in the mountain lion's den in the hills of Katari."

"Would you break our mother's heart?" his brother asked.

"Wake up!" Lugano returned, exasperated. "Your stubborn insistence on clinging to the past will get you killed."

"You sicken me!" the hulking man spat out. "You want to change the natural order of things. We are at the top of the food chain. Everything else is food. You are a disgrace to the family name."

"That is your opinion," Lugano stated. "Nevertheless, the fact remains, if we refuse to evolve, we will be exterminated. Because of our unnecessary predation, there are only a handful of us left. We have become an endangered species."

"You sold out didn't you?" his brother asked. "You're taking Montreau's treatments aren't you?"

"Yes. I want to live to see my great grandchildren," Lugano answered. "Our way of life is over, and it mocks God who gave us free will."

"I don't believe in God," Raven replied. "*I* control my life."

Lugano sighed and turned to his brother in the darkness. He raised his arm to strike with the ancient dagger he held in his hand.

"Like Cain you would kill your own brother?" the man asked.

"You are no longer my brother," Lugano returned sadly. The blade fell swiftly, hitting its mark. His brother grunted, fell to the ground, and lay motionless. Lugano dropped the knife with a gasp, and slowly backed away. Hearing agitated animal sounds, he tried to flee the den, but the male lion moved quickly and closed the distance between them. Dr. Lugano tried to veer away, but with one swipe of his powerful paw, the lion knocked him flat. The big cat pinned him down with two front paws, cracking his ribs. With extreme difficulty, he twisted free and pushed at the lion's chest with all the vampire strength he had left. The animal flew across the den, hit his head on a rocky protrusion, and lay stunned.

Lugano rose unsteadily from the dirt and raced to the moat, leaping across to the sixteen-foot retaining wall. He climbed down, stumbled to his car, and drove to Dr. Montreau's home. When the butler answered the door, he collapsed on the tiled floor of the foyer gasping the words, "I killed my brother!" as the doctor rushed over to help him.

Chapter 10

Falcon entered his apartment, tossing his coat on the desk chair. His mind was in turmoil, rehashing the serious discussion at the Montreaus. The debate about the Ripper and Alpha-T had left him pensive and exhausted. Suddenly a "you got mail" reminder sounded on his computer, he clicked on the message icon and read the memo: "you will get a call."

Frowning at the oblique secrecy of the message, he started to check the other messages, flinching when the phone rang a few seconds later. Answering quickly, he recognized the voice of Father Francis on the other end.

"I haven't seen you at confession, Theodore," Father Francis admonished. "We have a special session tomorrow night at eight."

"What's this really about?" Falcon asked.

"Just be there," the priest insisted.

"Okay Father," Falcon said, as the line went dead.

Frustrated, Falcon got up from his chair and paced furiously around the room. His irritation propelled him to the liquor cabinet for a strong, cocktail of elixir and brandy.

Contemplating his situation, Falcon realized he wasn't angry with Father Francis. He was enraged at the Ripper for ruining his peace, and interfering with his budding relationship with Giselle. Moreover, the killer had picked his city to ravage, threatening the peace of his neighborhood, and taking four lives. Falcon realized that if he didn't lose his vengeful state of mind, the Ripper would never make it to Dr. Montreau's clinic. The authorities would find him torn to bits in an alley, the same way he had left his victims.

He felt badly that he had been so self-righteous with Giselle about ethics. Deep down, he agreed with her. Extermination of all Keepers had crossed his mind. He wanted to feel shame, but all he felt was determination to end the Ripper's killing spree.

Falcon slept restlessly the next day. He awakened groggy and still tired. He had to gulp down three cups of coffee before he could get ready for the evening. Once dressed, he decided to walk to his meeting with Father Francis, hoping the night air would clear his mind.

It was nearly eight when he arrived at St. Ignatius Church. The cool mid-November breezes had finally eased his earlier tension. Father Francis was nowhere in sight as he dipped two fingers in holy water, and made the sign of the cross. He walked quietly toward the statue of St. Ignatius, gazed at the saint briefly, moving on until he stood in front of an ethereal sculpture of God the Father. Lighting a candle, he kneeled, saying a prayer for strength and protection. It would take divine intervention to find the most evasive vampire in history.

When he walked back toward the confessionals, he noticed that he was the only visitor in the church. He approached the third confessional with the glowing green ready light, and entered. As he lowered himself on the kneeler, he heard a familiar voice on the other side of the screen.

"Is there anything you want to say, before I get to the main purpose of this visit?" Father Francis asked quietly.

"Father, you know I don't believe in confession," Falcon answered. "I never quite understood that part of the faith. In my opinion, one shouldn't need a middleman when it comes to God. I prefer going straight to the source. Anyway, your penance is wasted on me."

"Theodore, we are all sinners," Father Frances reminded him.

"True, but that's between me, and God," Falcon replied.

"As you wish," the priest relented. Speaking in a whisper, he continued, "I have a name for you. I acquired it during my weekly ministry at Jefferson Barracks."

Falcon took the piece of paper the priest slipped through the grating of the confessional. He was about to leave, when the priest insisted, "Please enlist the aid of this remarkable man. He's been through a lot, and his world has been shaken. He'll be a courageous ally in finding the Ripper, and this important work will renew his faith."

"Thanks Father. I need all the help I can get," Falcon agreed.

"Visit me again, and bring that lovely girl of yours," Father Frances stated, moving back into the shadows.

Falcon rose from the confessional, unfolding the note the priest had passed to him. Albert Ramos was the name written in Father Frances' bold script. Falcon took the paper over to the prayer station, thinking, "Father Frances must be on cloud nine. He loves a mystery, and we have the mother of all mysteries on our hands right now."

He considered Father Francis' words as he left the church. For a young man, barely in his prime, Father Frances possessed the wisdom of a much older person. He had turned St. Ignatius from a church with a mere fifty, loyal neighborhood parishioners, into a religious center of the city. His unconventional sermons about contemporary issues, and fiery oratories about discipleship in the community, filled Sunday Mass to capacity. His dream was to create an ecumenical place of worship. Father Francis had established a goal-oriented youth ministry whose members regularly volunteered in neighborhood outreach services. He frequently urged Catholic Church leaders to donate funds to any organization that helped the needy. It was rumored that the charismatic priest had the ear of a member of the church's hierarchy in Rome who turned his wishes into reality.

In spite of Father Francis' reputation, attendance at Saturday evening mass was dwindling because of the Central West End Ripper. Parishioners were hesitant to attend church functions after dark. It was in the Church's best interest to help the authorities find the killer. Falcon had heard the riveting sermon Father Francis had made about that subject weeks ago, when the body of the first young woman was found.

"It is our duty to bring evil out of the darkness and into the light," he had instructed. "Be aware of your surroundings. Remember what you hear and see as you move about in the city. Do be your brother's keeper. Don't hesitate to use the number on the screen to contact the police about anything strange, anything that sets a light bulb off in your heads. Don't be afraid, the call is anonymous. When evil preys on a community, it is our responsibility as Christians to become involved, and, of course, cooperate with the police in their endeavors to end this brutality."

Falcon arrived at Jefferson Barracks shortly after evening visiting hours were over, but was admitted when he flashed his detective badge at the information desk. Eli had appointed him an unofficial detective on the Ripper case using the cover, Frank White. He was ushered into a visitor's room to wait for Lance Corporal Ramos. Falcon studied the room and building with interest. The hospital was kept neat and clean, but the furniture was old and worn. He had read that the south city Barracks was one of the better V.A. hospitals in the country. He made a mental note to contact the many volunteers who solicited private funds for its upkeep.

He was momentarily taken aback when Alberto Ramos entered the room. He wheeled into the room using an old-fashioned wheel chair. Both of his legs had been amputated below the knee. Falcon shook his hand, impressed by his upper body strength.

"What can I do for you?" Ramos asked casually.

"Father Francis sent me," Falcon replied. Seeing Ramos's obvious relief he continued, "He seemed to think you might be willing to help me."

"Padre sent you?" Ramos asked. "That's good enough for me. I couldn't have made it without him," Ramos added. "I was so depressed when I woke up in the hospital, I wanted to kill myself. When he came for that first visit, he bawled me out for giving up. He says, "You survived Iraq, saved thousands of soldiers lives, and now that you're back home, you want to end it all? You don't have the right to do that. You're here for a purpose."

Falcon laughed with Ramos, commenting, "Sounds like Father Francis all right."

Ramos looked away a moment, then turned back to Falcon, admitting, "It gets to all of us in here. Father Francis said that to get over this war, I have to be a soldier in a different kind of war. He says: good against evil. I tried to tell him he was full of . . . well, you know," Ramos stated. "After a few more visits, I forgot about what I couldn't do, and concentrated on what I could do. Somehow, Padre got the funds to get me new legs: the latest prosthetics; a pair for looks and a pair for speed."

Ramos and Falcon traversed the catwalk to the veteran's apartments in the next building. Ramos had a private room overlooking a tree-lined park. He showed Falcon his prosthetics. The first pair looked like muscular legs, tinted to his skin tone. The second pair, ended with curved titanium springs.

"These are my racers," Ramos explained. "I can run as fast as any man with legs, no matter what the surface. I was a long distance runner before I joined up, and I won yearly racing and long distance awards in my platoon. When I got these legs, my life changed."

Seeing Ramos eyeing the pack of cigarettes in his pocket, Falcon asked, "Want a smoke?"

"Thanks man," Ramos said, ushering Falcon to a small patio outside. "The doc made me quit, but it didn't take. When I was doing covert ops in Iraq," Ramos continued, "I was assigned night duty; sweeping buildings. I got this knack for seeing in the dark. The guys in my squad called me 'The Mole'. One night, I was clearing a group of buildings. They were rubble mostly, with a few standing roofs. I swept several tunnels in the floor of these crap holes. I thought I was about to leave empty-handed, when I heard this sound."

Ramos's fingers trembled, as he lit another cigarette. "Out runs this kid, no more than twelve years old. He was strapped with plastic explosives and was holding a trigger device. This kid was pale as a ghost, swaying and weaving. He could hardly stand on his feet. I knew what was coming, so I backed out of the way. Then he says something really crazy, with this pathetic look in his eyes and tears streaming down his face."

Falcon sat erect, listening intently to the soldier's next words.

"Help me," Ramos relayed.

"Help me?" Falcon asked in disbelief. "That's not the usual thing a suicide bomber says."

"You got that right," Ramos answered. "It is the will of Allah, is what they usually yell. So anyway, I do the only thing I can do. I jump. Next thing I know the kid's mincemeat and I'm thrown down a hill. I look down and both my legs are blown apart, flesh, bone, and muscle hanging on by a shred of skin."

Falcon shook his head and asked, "How did you survive?"

"That's the weirdest part I'll never forget," Ramos stated. "This dude in white robes dressed like an Iraqi holy man, walks up to me and kneels by me. He touches my cheek and says, 'You're going to be okay.' Boom, the pain is gone, and I'm still conscious. Next thing I know a chopper shows up. The medic was amazed that my wounds had stopped bleeding. He asked me how I stopped the bleeding so fast."

"I looked at him like he was crazy," Ramos continued. "That's when I passed out like a light. When I woke up in the states, my legs were gone. The doctors were saying it was a miracle that I lived. They were amazed that I knew what to do to save my life. I tried to tell them someone else was there, but they wouldn't believe me."

"Who would stick around knowing the kid was strapped with explosives," Falcon commented.

"Exactly," Ramos replied. "When the army shrink came to question me, I told him what I saw. He said I must have been mistaken. I looked at him like he was loco, but he wouldn't let it go. The official report says I managed to give myself first aid. How I could have done that? "Cauterize my wounds with a hot piece of shrapnel from the explosion? Rather than spend time in a psych ward, I signed the paper. They transferred me here for rehabilitation."

Ramos shook his head and finished with, "When I told Padre what happened, he said it was divine intervention. He claims an archangel had visited me, as a sign from God that my work wasn't done." He stubbed out his cigarette, looked at Falcon in the darkness and commented, "That priest could have convinced Osama Bin Laden to turn himself in. After I talked to Padre a few times, I couldn't wait to hear what he had to say next."

"Did you see anything else strange before this happened, anything out of place?" Falcon pressed.

"Other than the suicide bomber asking for help?" Ramos asked. He sat quietly for a few moments. "Yeah, there was one other thing, I never told anyone."

"Go ahead," Falcon urged.

"Well there must have been an animal scrounging around in one of the tunnels," Ramos recalled. "Before the chopper came, I saw what I thought was a huge black dog behind the blown up shack. It turned to look at me, but all I could see clearly was its eyes, lit up like two gold circles. Whatever it was, it was big, like a wolf. I watched it trot away until the chopper came."

"Thanks, Corporal Ramos," Falcon said as they walked back to Ramos' apartment.

"Al, call me Al." Ramos said.

"When are you getting out of here?" Falcon asked him.

"Doc says I'm good to go, soon as I find a place to stay," He answered, then asked, "Why?"

"My team and I could use your help on the Ripper case," Falcon stated. Seeing Ramos' hesitation he added, "The pay is good, $600.00 a week, plus expenses."

"Hmm—and you say Father Francis wanted me to do this?" Ramos asked. Seeing Falcon's nod, he stated, "I'm down with that. Where do I stay in St. Louis?"

"Well, I just happen to own an apartment building in the city," Falcon replied off-handedly. "The job includes room and board."

"Let me grab my stuff," Ramos replied, wheeling over to his chest of drawers. As he started removing his belongings and stuffing them into a duffel bag he asked, "Where's the apartment?"

"In the Central West End," Falcon answered, grabbing one of the bags.

"Falcon, you're one crazy dude," Ramos commented, with a slight smile. "You're taking me to Ripper territory aren't you?" He shook his head, and added, "Look at me. I must be nuts, I'm already itching to get a piece of that dirt bag!"

As the two men drove into the city, Falcon reflected on what Alberto had told him. Was it possible that before the Ripper had traveled to Africa, he had been on a rampage in Iraq? What if the Keeper drained the Iraqi boy of blood, strapped a suicide bomb on him, and pushed him out into the open? That would explain why the boy was deathly pale and cried for help before the bomb exploded. What a horrendous way to cover up an insatiable appetite. Had there been other similar deaths in Iraq? If so, they had not been enough to satisfy the Keeper's needs. Falcon conjectured that the vampire had migrated south traveling to Katari. Falcon wondered how many other victims marked the Keeper's trail of blood. Their bodies would never be recovered, or documented by African governments too deeply involved in the daily turmoil of survival to investigate a few more casualties of civil war.

Falcon's cell phone began vibrating. It was Dr. Montreau speaking in a tense voice, "Dr. Lugano is in the hospital, he was attacked."

"We just saw him a few hours ago," Falcon returned.

"Michael was trying to find his brother, and it appears that he did," Dr. Montreau explained wearily. "He collapsed in my arms early this morning. Before he passed out he said he killed him."

"Dr. Lugano killed his brother?" Falcon asked incredulously.

"Apparently, the man was a fugitive," Dr. Montreau explained. "He was scheduled to receive treatments under my care. A Freeblood zoo maintenance man brought me the dagger that was used in the stabbing. It was on the ground inside the lion habitat, but the body wasn't there."

"Why did he use a dagger?" Falcon asked.

"As far as I know, a ceremonial dagger is only used to execute a Keeper's family member who jeopardizes the entire clan," Dr. Montreau explained.

"Dr. Lugano is a Keeper?"

"A half-breed Keeper," Dr. Montreau explained. "Michael and his brother had the same Keeper mother, but different fathers."

"Now I understand why Dr. Lugano was so adamant that the Katari Ripper be part of your experiments," Falcon stated. "He wanted to see if the treatments would help his brother too."

"Unfortunately we still don't know his brother's identity," Montreau returned sadly. "Michael truly believed that his brother could change and become a productive member of the vampire and human community. His physical condition is very critical. Several of his ribs were broken and his right lung collapsed. Even with his vampire healing ability, he'll have to stay in intensive care for weeks. One of his broken ribs nearly pierced his heart. He's lucky to be alive. It's impossible to speak with him yet, he's in healing hibernation."

"I hope he pulls through," Falcon commented. "I'll call Colin and Father Francis. They'll want to visit him in the hospital."

"Even if he survives, Michael will be out of commission for months," Dr. Montreau pointed out. "Without a body, we can't even be sure his brother is dead."

"Could the lions have eaten him?" Falcon asked.

"Perhaps, but there would be tissue evidence left," Dr. Montreau explained. "The Freeblood Zoo maintenance technician found nothing, not even traces of blood."

"Someone was very careful about cleaning up," Falcon suggested. "Perhaps Dr. Lugano's brother wasn't alone when they met at the lion habitat." Falcon continued remorsefully, "I feel bad about my harsh assessment of Dr. Lugano's motives. I was too quick to judge before I knew all the facts."

"Don't be too hard on yourself," Dr. Montreau returned. "Michael was over-zealous and too secretive about his brother. The only information we have about the man is from his tattered shirt with the initials H.W.R. on the pocket. Michael's brother was clearly fighting for his survival. For a rogue Keeper, survival always transcends family loyalty."

"Considering what happened to Dr. Lugano, it doesn't bode well for our efforts to reform them," Falcon commented.

"We are in the middle of a difficult struggle to change the survivalist mentality of a race of vampires that has prevailed for thousands of years," Dr. Montreau pointed out.

"Then our main priorities are to find the Ripper, stop the killings, and test him with Alpha-T," Falcon stated.

Chapter 11

The next evening Falcon helped Alberto Ramos move into a street level apartment. Falcon had arranged for special handicap access to be installed in his apartment. He also ordered a side ramp added to the outside stairwell. Falcon went on line and added another cell phone to his account for Alberto's use. His cell phone rang after he finished making the arrangements. It was his cousin, Colin.

"What's up Colin?" He asked.

"Damien is missing," Colin said, with worry in his voice.

"How did that happen?" Falcon asked. "I checked him out of the hospital earlier this evening."

"I gave him a bed in one of the second floor apartments. He's bunking with Beau," Colin returned, "Nicole hooked him up with a job delivering dinner to the clients on my food aid list. He uses my ten-speed to deliver the meals. The bike's here, but he's gone."

"I'll be right over," Falcon replied signing off. He quickly called Alberto, saying,

"Sorry to put you to work already, but I need your help."

"No problemo. Meet you downstairs," he responded.

Falcon waited for Ramos near his Thunderbird, texting Giselle that he would be delayed. Ramos whistled when he saw Falcon's car.

"I like your ride partner," Alberto was much taller than Falcon on his racing legs. He scrunched down and joined him in the passenger seat.

"Thanks," Falcon said. "One of my friends is missing. He was at the scene after Valerie Chouteau was murdered. I think he knows something."

"The guy must have been in the wrong place at the wrong time," Alberto commented.

"We're going to my cousin, Colin's apartment to get the details," Falcon explained. "Damien was last seen at one of his shelter apartments."

"You're cousin runs a shelter?" Albert asked curiously.

"Colin's a minister, he runs the Redeemer Mission and Coffee House, "Java Heaven", Falcon explained.

"Father Francis told me about that place," Alberto returned. "He said if I came to St. Louis, I could find a clean apartment, a friend, and a job."

"Yeah that's Colin's gig," Falcon replied.

Colin was inside finishing evening prayer and worship service when they arrived at the Mission. The two men walked in quietly and sat in the back row. Colin led the music ministry team in a haunting worship song about God watching over the city.

When this last song ended, and the worshipers began to file out, Colin detained them saying, "Remember, be careful out there, and watch out for the children. Don't be afraid to help others. Be vigilant warriors for Christ. Pray with all your hearts my friends. God Bless You."

Falcon walked up to his cousin after the congregation filed out saying, "I like the new song you wrote, Colin, especially the instrumental between the verses."

"Thanks, we've been working on it for a while," Colin replied. "Who's your friend?" he added, nodding to Alberto.

"Alberto Ramos," Falcon said.

"Que pasa?" Colin asked shaking Alberto's hand. "Father Francis mentioned you. I was about to contact you, but I see my cousin found you first."

"I got a weird summons from Father Francis," Falcon explained. "When I went to St. Ignatius' he gave me a memo with Al's name on it in the confessional."

"Did you confess your sins while you were there?" Colin asked.

"Now don't you start," Falcon stated. "You know how I feel about Confession."

"I think your sins are safe with Father Francis," Colin said, smiling. "At any rate, let's go upstairs where we can talk," Colin suggested. Turning to Al he said, "I'm sorry you missed my wife, Nicole, she would have set you up with a fine dinner. However, I do have some tasty leftovers from last night's meal if you're interested."

"Thanks, man," Alberto responded. "It's been a while since I had a home cooked meal, even a warmed-over one."

The three men sat at the kitchen table and ate quietly together. Al looked at the two cousins, and waited patiently. His throat was dry, and he needed a smoke, but he didn't say anything. He had a strange feeling in his gut, the kind he used to get when he went on special ops missions. His belly was telling him he was about to get involved in something crazy and unpredictable.

"Nicole asked Damien to ride to the Food Mart and get more bread and coffee for the soup kitchen," Colin explained. "Damien really felt comfortable around Nicole and would do just about anything for her. She treated him with kindness and respect, like any other person. Damien was more lucid than I have ever seen him, under her influence. Anyway, after an hour Nicole went looking for him, and found his bike in the alley. Two recycle bags of food were tipped over and the groceries were all over the ground like there was a scuffle or he took off in a hurry. That was about two hours ago."

"Can we see his room?" Falcon asked.

"Sure, it's downstairs," Colin led the two men down the stairs to apartment six and unlocked the door. There were two beds in the room; Beau was asleep in one bed, while the other was empty.

Falcon looked around the room. He moved the covers aside on the bed and checked under the mattress. Careful not to wake Beau, he quietly opened the chest of drawers and looked in the tiny closet. Beau had few belongings and the only things missing were his old shirt, pants, and his well-worn trench coat.

"It looks like someone wanted him to blend in with the homeless again," Falcon commented to the two men in the hallway. He pondered the situation a moment then slipped back inside and reluctantly awakened Beau.

When the elderly man stirred sleepily and bolted upright with a look of terror on his face, Falcon reassured him in a calm voice saying, "It's just me Beau. What are you so fired up about? Did someone come here tonight?"

"I ain't saying nothing," Beau answered, eyeing Alberto suspiciously.

"This is my friend, Alberto Ramos. He's a war veteran like you," he explained.

"Pleased to make your acquaintance," Beau said, shaking Alberto's hand.

"Likewise," Alberto replied.

"Damien's gone," Falcon explained looking down at Beau. "Do you know where he went?"

"I told that bugger-eyed creep to stay away from old D," Beau replied. "That tall dude looked right through me with those black peepers. Damien went with him like a zombie or something, staring off into La La land," Beau shuddered saying, "It scared the tar out of me."

"Do you have any idea where they were going?" Falcon asked calmly.

"Can't say," Beau replied scratching his head. "Before that creepy giant showed up, D said he had to go back to the dock and get something. I told him to forget it, but D's stubborn when he has a mind to do something."

"I hear you," Falcon stated. "Beau, lock your doors and windows. No one comes in here but us tonight,"

"Sure," Beau agreed. "I wish I had a little snooker to help me sleep though. I got such a scare, like I just saw the Boogie Man, for real. When I close my eyes, all I can see are those black eyes staring at me, and my skin gets all goose pimply."

Falcon handed Beau a silver flask saying, "Don't tell Colin."

"My lips are sealed pal," Beau said grinning. "I hope you find D. It's mighty lonely around here. I got kind of used to him chattering away to himself all the time."

Falcon said goodbye to Colin asking him make sure the old man was safely locked in his room all night. It had been a week since the last Ripper killing, and something terrible was about due. He and Alberto rode in silence to Forest Park. Falcon parked his car under a street light near the boathouse.

As they traversed the path to the boat dock Alberto commented, "Man, you can see in the dark better than me."

"It's a gift. It runs in the family," Falcon returned.

The night was moonless, and the only lights on the lagoon were the solar lanterns near the water's edge. The boat dock was closed until April and the vessels lay still and silent in the darkness. Falcon walked over to Beau's tiny abode and raised the tarp. No Beau.

His night vision spied something silvery white trapped under a thin layer of ice next to the boat. Falcon motioned for Al to come closer. He pointed to the ice covered water. They could just make out a ghostly, pale face just below the surface.

Alberto balanced on the dock with one leg using the other as a ramrod, breaking the ice with one swift jab. Falcon reached in the slushy water, grabbed the victim's coat and gently lowered him onto the wooden walkway.

"It's Damien," Falcon stated, with a sudden intake of breath.

Falcon and Alberto carried Damien over to the soft snow laden grass. Falcon swiftly removed his soaked, ice-glazed coat, carefully wrapping him in his own fleece lined all-weather coat. He loosened Damien's tattered shirt and placed two fingers in Damien's mouth removing debris. Fingers trembling, Falcon felt a faint pulse in the man's jugular. While Alberto called 911, Falcon began massaging Damien's limbs to bring back circulation.

When the emergency van arrived, Falcon turned Damien over to the trained professionals. The unconscious man was stabilized, put on a gurney, and taken to Barnes Emergency Room, Falcon and Alberto following close behind in the Thunderbird. Alberto looked at his friend's crestfallen face and said, "I found these in Damien's hand."

Falcon parked the car and turned on the dome light. Alberto put the objects in his hand and he stared at them, a cork from a wine bottle and a small brass button. Turning the cork over and over Falcon finally saw what he was looking for, two words stamped in ink, Cordoba Winery.

Albert watched as Falcon studied the button saying confidently, "It's a uniform button. I see them on the brass in the military all the time. My dress blues have buttons similar to this but with the Marine's Corps seal etched in the center."

"Who would Damien follow without question?" Falcon asked aloud. He answered himself with, "A police officer. Damien wouldn't run away from a cop, knowing he had groceries to deliver to the mission. He would have played it straight and cooperated"

"Creeps disguise themselves as cops all the time," Alberto stated.

"In the dark, Damien wouldn't know a real uniform from a makeshift one," Falcon agreed. He took out his camera to take videos of the alley where Damien was abducted. The old bike Damien rode was still lying on its side, its basket carrier broken and twisted from hitting the brick wall. Several muddy footprints near the bicycle could be seen in the circle of the flashlight. Two of the prints were of Damien's familiar old Nike's. The other two were larger with different treads.

Alberto studied the prints saying, "This dude has huge feet. He's definitely over six feet tall. He's was wearing army boots by or possibly steel-toed work boots, by the looks of those tread marks."

"Military boots could be easily obtained at any army surplus shop in the area," Falcon concurred, digesting the clues. There is an Uncle Sam's in north city and south county," Falcon stated, e-mailing the digital photos to Tobias. "Damien was abducted about 9:00 pm.," he continued. "The sunset was 5:15 pm that evening," Falcon conjectured. "The Ripper had plenty of time to kidnap Damien, drive him to

Forest Park, force wine down his throat and hold him under water. To the police it would look like some homeless man had gotten drunk, and had fallen in the icy water."

"That sounds reasonable," Alberto agreed.

"Except for one important detail," Falcon stated. "Damien is a Muslim, and never drinks alcohol."

While Falcon drove to the emergency room, he called his father about the wine cork.

"It's good you called son," his father said, happily. "Your mom is planning Thanksgiving, and wants to know who we can expect for dinner."

"Looks like we'll all be there this year Pop," Falcon answered hurriedly, "I'm bringing a friend, Giselle. Did you hear from Zeke?"

"Giselle," His dad replied interestedly, "What a beautiful name. I love her already. Zeke called last night. He's bringing his girl Barbara too. Isn't love wonderful?"

Falcon, trying to stifle his impatience, asked, "Dad, sorry I can't talk, I'm in a hurry. A friend of mine was attacked this evening, and we're headed to the emergency room."

"What can I do to help?" His dad offered soberly.

"Well you remember the indigent man I told you about, Damien?" Falcon asked.

"Yes, the man with schizophrenia, how can I help?" his father asked, concern in his voice.

Falcon explained what had happened and added, "Damien had a wine cork with the Cordoba label in his pocket. Ring any bells?"

"It certainly does, son," His father replied. "It's not the brand a homeless man could afford. It's very expensive, imported from Madrid. A bottle costs seventy-five dollars here."

"Thanks dad, that explains a lot," Falcon returned. "I'll see you Thursday night. Valerie's wake is Wednesday evening and the Funeral is early Thursday Morning."

"I read about it in the paper," His dad replied sadly. "You're mom sent flowers from the family. Is this Damien thing related to finding Valerie's killer?"

"I never could keep a secret from you dad," Falcon said.

"Son, catch the killer for all of us," his dad added.

"I'll do my best," Falcon assured him. "Give mom my love."

"Maybe that was the clue you were waiting for, boss," Alberto offered emphatically.

Falcon asked, "Say what?"

"You said a serial killer usually slips up," he replied. "Well, this might be the break we've all been looking for: proof that someone tried to silence Damien."

Falcon looked over at Alberto as he maneuvered the car in a parking space close to the ER. "Al, I think it's time you stopped calling me boss. We're partners and, I hope, friends."

"Sure thing, Falcon," Alberto replied, stepping out of the car to join him.

The two men waited in the emergency room for over an hour until a young resident with tired eyes and sympathetic manner walked up to them explaining, "I'm Dr. Levin. I was here when they brought your family member in."

"How's he doing?" Falcon asked worriedly.

"The good news is he's stable," the doctor replied. "The bad news; he has acute hypothermia, and he's in a coma,"

"When will he come out of it?" Falcon asked, steadying his voice.

"In these cases it's hard to tell," The doctor answered with a sigh. "His heart is strong and he's remarkably fit for his age. It's just a matter of time. The next twenty-four hours are crucial. Hopefully, he'll come out of it with no permanent damage."

Falcon walked up to the nurse's station, handing the attendant the papers he had filled out for Damien. He didn't know his last name so he wrote White. As far as the nurse was concerned Damien was his uncle. Falcon left his name as the responsible party, signing the forms to pay for ICU care and later for a private room. He called Eli, and left a message to put a guard on the door the next day.

He walked over to the Hospital Administrator's office and spoke to the physician in charge of the night shift, Dr. Howard, "Mr. White is a witness in an ongoing investigation into the Ripper murders. Tonight my colleagues and I will keep watch. Tomorrow Lieutenant Tobias is sending a full-time guard. No one but medical personnel that we are made aware of are allowed in his room."

Doctor Howard replied, "I'll make sure he has around the clock care and security."

"Thank you," Falcon replied. "By the way, the attending physician tonight, Dr. Levin, please see to it that when he's on duty, he's my uncle's doctor."

"I will personally assign Dr. Levin to your uncle," the doctor agreed.

"Al, I'm going to the drink machine, want a black coffee?" Falcon asked as they walked back to Damien's room.

"I'll get the coffee, you stay with your friend," Alberto insisted. "Call your cousin, Colin. Let him know what's going on."

"Thanks, Al," Falcon replied hazily. "I'm not thinking too great right now."

Falcon called Colin and relayed what had happened to Damien. His cousin said he'd come to the hospital right away. He offered to call Father Francis, who always took an interest in Damien. After he signed off with Colin, Giselle called, in reply to his text apology for being so late.

"I'm so sorry about your friend," Giselle commented in a soft voice. "I'll be right there. I was on the way to your apartment. When you didn't show, I was worried."

Giselle arrived at the hospital fifteen minutes later with Colin and Nicole. She had driven by and picked them up at the mission. Nicole brought six cups of Java Heaven's specialty coffee and began passing them around.

Falcon was relieved as he embraced the two women. "Thanks for the brew, Nicole. Your java will hit the spot. The coffee machine here must be broken. It only dispenses hot, muddy water."

Alberto took a chair and kept watch outside the door, while the rest of the group sat in the small cubicle near Damien's bed. Colin sat close to the comatose man, touching his forehead and whispering prayers for healing. Falcon knew his cousin's devotion; Colin would pray all night. He looked over at Giselle noticing that her head was bowed, her lips moving in prayer as she held Damien's hand.

When his cell phone vibrated, Falcon walked down to the visitor's waiting room and answered the call. It was Eli asking about Damien. He wanted to know if there was any change. He was anxious to get a description of Damien's attacker. Falcon signed off with a sigh. Just as he was about to walk back to the ER, Father Francis called to let him know that a group of priests, nuns, and neighbors were holding a candle light prayer vigil for Damien at the church. He promised to visit Damien the next evening.

Colin stepped into the waiting room and commented, "Why would anyone hurt Damien, he didn't witness Valerie's murder."

"Maybe he unwittingly picked up an important clue that the Ripper left behind," Falcon suggested. "Which means the killer is still looking for it. Is it possible Damien made the call to the police that night?"

"It must have been him," Colin said. "I saw him taking off towards the park, and a few minutes later the police pulled up."

Falcon pulled out his cell phone and scrolled down to memos, saying, "I have a list of Valerie's effects brought in by the police the night she was murdered."

"Tobias gave you that?" Colin asked.

"Without Tobias we would never crack this case," Falcon explained. "He's the one vampire contact I have at City Hall." He cleared his throat and continued, "Look at the list. There's no cell phone here."

"I think you should show this to Nicole," Colin suggested.

Nicole sat down on the sofa and carefully studied the photos of Valerie's possessions. After a few seconds she stated, "Her cell phone is the only thing missing." She looked through her own purse a moment. Pulling out her metallic, blue cell phone, she explained, "It was identical to mine, except hers was purple. Valerie would never go anywhere without her E-phone."

"Damien used Valerie's cell phone to call 911," Falcon deduced. "He called the police, and ran off with it."

"That has to be it." Colin agreed.

"Maybe Damien got scared and dumped the cell phone," Alberto suggested, joining them in the waiting room. "The police were probably all over the place."

"You could be right," Colin agreed. "The local cops are always sweeping the park, moving the homeless folks to shelters, especially when it's bitter cold outside."

Giselle walked into the room with tears in her eyes and said, "Do you know what I just heard on the news?"

"No. What happened?" Falcon asked, putting his arm around her.

"A nurse was murdered a few blocks from here," Giselle said. "She was walking home after her shift ended. She was murdered in the breezeway outside of her apartment building."

"Did the report say what time she was murdered?" Falcon asked.

"Ten o'clock," Giselle said.

"Damien went missing about that same time," Falcon commented, "The Ripper couldn't be in two places at once."

Seeing his disappointment, Giselle offered, "The Ripper could have an accomplice."

"Just like we discussed," Falcon said.

"I read more statistics about serial killers," Giselle continued. "In rare but documented cases they used accomplices."

"If a Keeper is killing these young women, he could be using an Ordinary to help him", Falcon suggested

"Perhaps a misguided person who believes the Ripper can share some great power with him," Colin offered.

"What kind of Ordinary would help a Keeper?" Falcon asked out loud, pondering the situation. A flash of something came to him; an image of the two tickets Colin had given to him the night Valerie was murdered. He said aloud, "The Midnight Supper Club."

Giselle looked over at Falcon stating, "Someone connected with the club is helping the killer?"

"Who else would believe vampires exist, but a club member?" Falcon asked. "The accomplice was led to believe that he could be given immortality in exchange for his help."

The group walked back to Damien's room pondering all these things as the night hours drew to a close. The police guard arrived at early light, as Eli promised, and Falcon gave him instructions.

Everyone was somber and quiet on the trip home. When they stopped at the Redeemer Mission, Nicole was so overcome with emotions that Colin had to help her up the stairs to their apartment. Giselle was silent as Falcon walked her to her apartment. They embraced several times. Falcon touched her chin and tilting it gently to look into her eyes. They were full of tears.

"Poor Nicole," She said. "She's lost her best friend. I wanted to hug her and comfort her, but I don't know her that well."

"Hey, It'll be okay, love," Falcon said reassuring her. "Nicole is grieving, but she has great faith. She knows Valerie is with God. I promise you, we'll find her killer."

"Why did this have to happen in our city?" Giselle asked miserably.

"The Ripper may be here, but remember, we are too," Falcon replied soberly.

"Now you sound like Colin," Giselle said, smiling weakly through her tears.

"Well, maybe I'm beginning to believe there are no coincidences in this world," Falcon replied, touching her cheek. "Now, go tuck yourself in bed, and I'll see you tomorrow evening."

"Thanks," Giselle said touching his lips with hers.

"For what?" Falcon asked.

"For being strong for both of us," Giselle replied.

Chapter 12

While Falcon's day was over, Alberto Ramos' day was just beginning. He was taking his usual morning jog around the trail at Forest Park. Bright sunlight bathed the cold winter day with a welcoming light. Alberto was pleased that he wasn't as winded as he had been the first three times he had run the course. Pausing to take a drink from his water bottle, he noticed an elderly lady walking down the sidewalk, pushing an overflowing grocery cart.

When the white-haired old woman strolled near Alberto, she paused and stared at him curiously. Moving her cart closer she asked, "Would you like to help a homeless woman out young man?"

At first appearances, the old woman seemed bent over and frail. Then he realized she was merely weighed down by the many layers of clothing that kept her warm. Her face was wrinkled, her hair, unkempt, and the smell coming from her was unpleasant, but she peered up at him with sharp, blue eyes.

"I can give you ten bucks," he offered. "That's all I can spare."

The old woman shook her head and said sharply, "I don't want any handouts." She removed several objects from the cart, and displayed them on a piece of stiff cardboard. "For ten bucks, choose what you want, and it's yours," she explained.

As Alberto scanned the objects, his eyes were drawn to a tarnished, purple metallic E-Phone. He held the phone in his hand, commenting, "The battery's dead."

"With a new battery, a phone like that is worth a lot more than $10.00," the old woman pointed out.

"You're right, Abuela," Alberto agreed. He handed her a ten dollar bill, and stuffed the phone in his jacket.

"The name's Effie, and I'm not your granny," the woman called back to him as she moved away.

Alberto turned to wave, but the woman had vanished. He looked up and down the street, but she was nowhere in sight. "That's one speedy, old lady," he said to himself as he headed back to his apartment. He was anxious to show Falcon the phone, but would have to wait until later. Falcon was a night person, and didn't get up until nearly sundown.

Unduly awakened by an insistent pounding on his front door, Falcon sat up in bed and yawned sleepily. He looked at his alarm clock; it was only 4:30 pm. He threw on his robe, and walked sleepily down the stairs.

He opened the door to an excited Alberto apologizing profusely for bothering him. Spying the E-Phone, he told Alberto to have a seat, and called Colin. He ran back upstairs and threw on his clothes. Pulling on his leather jacket he stated, "Come on Al we're going to Colin's."

When they arrived, Falcon was surprised to see his cousin, Ethan sitting at the kitchen table. He nudged Ethan's fist with his and stated, "How long are you staying?"

"Indefinitely," Ethan answered gloomily. "The housing project in L.A. fell through. It usually slows down over the winter, but this year the housing boom went bust, and so did my latest contract."

"Sorry to hear that," Falcon returned with sympathy then added, "It's good fortune for me though. I was just about to call you. I have several projects that need to be finished on my apartment building, and I know this building could use some repairs."

"That's great," Ethan replied, his face brightening.

"I'll write up a proposal for you, and we'll talk later in the week," Falcon stated.

Colin, saw that something was on Falcon's mind and offered, "I filled Ethan in about the Ripper." He placed bottles of root beer, cheese, crackers and pretzels on the kitchen table.

Falcon looked relieved and placed the cell phone on the table. Colin's eyes widened and his hands shook, as he poured the root beer into frosty mugs. He picked up the phone flipped it open asking excitedly, "Where did you find it?"

Alberto spoke up with, "I bought it from an old lady pushing a cart near Forest Park Boulevard."

"What did the old woman look like?" Colin asked. After Alberto gave a detailed description of the homeless woman, Colin said, "It sounds like Effie Banks, she comes to the soup kitchen every week."

"She must have been nearby when Damien dropped the phone in a trash can," Falcon guessed.

While they were talking, Nicole walked into the room smiling, pleased to see the gathering of friends. "What is this, the weekly meeting of the Extraordinary Gentlemen?"

"Something like that babe," Colin said, kissing her on the cheek.

Suddenly the men were looking at her strangely, and she laughed saying, "What? Is my hair a mess? Do I have food in my teeth?" she asked, smoothing her thick black curls and cleaning her teeth with her tongue

Colin handed his wife a soda looking at her admiringly, "No. You look great. Your cheeks are rosy from the cold."

Sipping her soda, she glanced down at the table. Her eyes widened, and her slender fingers were unsteady as she put her drink on the table. "Where did you find Valerie's phone?"

"Al bought it from Effie in the park," Falcon replied.

Nicole's lips trembled as she said, "We used to have such fun sending little text messages when we were apart."

"Too bad it's dead," Falcon commented. "There could have been some useful information on it."

Nicole took the phone and looked at it saying, "It's not dead, but the charge is very low. I'll hook it up to our computer, and we can try it."

"It won't turn on," Alberto mentioned.

"Of course not, it's the new E-Phone-S," Nicole explained. "Only a security code can turn it on."

"Do you know the code?" Colin asked expectantly as Nicole hooked the phone up to their P.C.

"Valerie's college friend who lives in L.A. just had a baby. It's baby Jonah's birth date, 10/01/09."

Once connected to a power source, the phone sprang to life displaying a variety of icons to click on for information. Falcon looked at the selections and asked, "Can I keep this for a while and research Valerie's information?"

"Of course, if it will help the case, but eventually we should give it to her parents," Nicole replied. Handing Falcon a leather bag she added, "Here's an extra charger."

Falcon pocketed the phone as the group went back to the kitchen to finish their drinks. When the discussion steered away from the Ripper case to more family and social interests, Falcon called the Hospital to ask about Damien's latest prognosis.

Dr. Levin explained that Damien's condition had not worsened, but he was still comatose. He informed Falcon that the police guard had been replaced an hour ago.

"If Damien wakes up, call me," Falcon stated. "I don't want anyone grilling him about the attack."

"I agree," Dr. Levin stated. "He may have some temporary amnesia from the trauma he experienced."

Reading a text message from Giselle, Falcon said goodbye to his family, and he and Albert drove to the restaurant. Giselle waved to them from her table. She gave him a kiss on the cheek, and nodded to Alberto. She listened with fascination as Falcon filled her in on the discovery of Valerie's cell phone.

"I'll help you go over the information later if you like," she offered.

"Thanks," Falcon responded, "I can use a tech-savvy woman's perspective on Valerie's information."

When the waitress, an attractive Hispanic woman with thick wavy brown hair and large brown eyes, walked up to their table, Giselle smiled, and announced, "This is Antonia Gonzales, my friend and classmate."

Falcon looked up at Antonia and commented, "So I guess you two ladies spend much of your free time analyzing people."

"Incessantly," Antonia agreed, winking at Giselle.

Falcon cleared his throat stating, "Well, I'm sure Giselle has told you all about me. Tell me. In what category do I belong?"

Antonia looked steadily at Falcon saying, "From what I hear, you're in a category all by yourself."

Alberto chuckled, adding, "Falcon, I keep telling you to loosen up man."

After taking their order Antonia returned with three martinis. Falcon assured Alberto that real men did drink chocolate Martini's. When the drinks arrived, Alberto sipped his and commented, "It's okay but I could really go for a "Bohemia" right now." Gazing at Antonia he said, "No offense ma'am.

Smiling down at him, she replied, "None taken."

When the steak dinners arrived, Antonia sat Alberto's plate in front of him saying, "If you join me at Casa Blanca around ten-fifteen tomorrow night, we could have a Bohemia together."

"I'll see you then, Senorita," Alberto replied, with a pleased grin on his face.

Falcon looked over at Giselle, asking, "How's my little matchmaker tonight?

"Simply marvelous," She answered, clicking his glass in victory. Not wanting to put a damper on the evening by discussing the Ripper case, Giselle asked Alberto about his family.

Alberto put his fork down and replied, "My parents live in San Mateo. My father owns a Mexican Grocery Store, Tiendo del Rio. I haven't seen them in six months. My little sister Theresa is getting married in June, I hope to be there for the wedding."

"Just let me know when you need time off, and it's yours, with pay," Falcon stated.

"By the way, Ethan wants me to be his partner in this new company he's starting in the spring," Alberto said, adding, "I told him I would have to talk to you first."

"That's great news Al," Falcon said. "Go for it. It's a great opportunity. Will it be construction?"

"No," Alberto answered. "Alternative energy; wind turbine and solar panel installation."

"Ah," Falcon commented. "You should grow a mustache. I can see you chasing down windmills, like Don Quixote."

"It beats hunting down insurgents," Albert replied with a grin.

"Father Francis would say you've found a new purpose in life," Giselle offered, "Saving the planet." She took a sip of her drink and asked Alberto, "What do you think of Antonia?"

"She's a fine woman," Alberto answered. "I don't know what she sees in me, but I will never question your matchmaking ability," he added, smiling at her.

As the friends enjoyed their dinner together, they did not see the tall stranger across the room, hidden in the shadows of the dimly lit bar. His eyes surveyed the scene with glittering intensity, studying, not only the pretty young waitress, but her friend with the dark red hair as well. As he watched their movements with interest, he studied one with hunger, and the other with nostalgic desire. He was disappointed that Giselle seemed smitten with her date, Theodore Falcon. He knew his family were respected Freebloods of great wealth. He did not share the Falcon's willingness to coexist peacefully with Ordinaries. His Keeper senses revolted at the concept.

Later that evening, Falcon joined Giselle at her apartment for tea. Falcon studied her as she served the tea and sat down next to him. He finally took her hands and asked, "What's wrong, Giselle? You seem agitated and nervous tonight."

"I didn't want to add to your worries," Giselle replied, looking away.

"Giselle, let's get something straight right now," Falcon insisted. "We're friends, and we shouldn't keep secrets from each other. Now, out with it," he urged.

"I had a visitor the other evening after you dropped me off," Giselle explained. "An old friend of my family showed up out of the blue.

"Who is this old friend, and what did he do to make you feel uncomfortable in your own home?" Falcon probed gently.

"His name is Henri Raven," Giselle stated. "The last time I saw him was at Cannes, ten years ago. He knows my parents, but I never talked to them about that night."

"Did he molest you?" Falcon asked worriedly.

"No," Giselle answered quickly. "I was very young, and flattered that an older man would seek me out. We took a walk in the gardens and he was about to kiss me, when Lancelot, our dog, jumped out of the bushes and stopped him."

"Good for Lancelot," Falcon said. "I like this dog already."

"Nothing would have happened. Henri was younger in those days and not so aggressive like he is now," Giselle reassured him.

"Sounds like he just wanted to see if he could pick up where he left off, with a very beautiful young woman," Falcon surmised. "I can't blame him for trying."

"I asked him to leave," Giselle said. "I'm afraid I had to get harsh with him. Fortunately, I didn't have to follow through. Dr. Lugano showed up and convinced him to leave."

"Dr. Lugano!" Falcon exclaimed. "He was attacked and almost killed last night!"

"Oh no!" Giselle cried out. "Does my father know?"

"Your father is taking care of him," Falcon answered. "Lugano was mauled by a lion at the zoo."

"Do you think Henri had something to do with it?" Giselle asked. "They spoke to each other as if they were friends."

"Dr. Lugano said he killed his brother before he collapsed in the foyer of your father's house."

"Henri Raven is Dr. Lugano's brother?" Giselle asked.

"Half-brother," Falcon explained. "They have the same vampire mother."

"Will Dr. Lugano live?" Giselle asked worriedly.

"He's in hibernation," Falcon said. "It's too early to tell."

Giselle said aloud, "I wonder what Raven's connection with my father could be."

"Perhaps Raven was a patient," Falcon surmised.

"If so, he didn't take his advice," Giselle commented. "He was so different I hardly recognized him."

Chapter 13

"The Ripper just killed another woman about two blocks from my apartment building; Marian Jackson, a nurse walking home after the night shift," was Falcon's comment as he filled in his brother, Ethan about the Ripper case.

"Why do women insist on walking home by themselves with the Ripper lose?" Ethan asked, clearly upset.

"Marian didn't have a car," Falcon explained. "She lived about three buildings away from the hospital. She took a shortcut through a gangway between two apartment buildings. The Ripper must have grabbed her and transported her six blocks away, killed her, and dumped her body early this morning."

"What a monster," Ethan replied. "How can I help?"

"You can help me secure my buildings," Falcon replied. "Right now, I need new deadbolts on all the apartment doors, and wrought iron bars on the first floor and basement windows."

"I know where to get wrought iron materials that are constructed in functional turn-of-the-century style," Ethan stated. "I'll check my contacts on the web."

"You can work on Colin's building first," Falcon commented. "Remind me to give you my business charge. Does fifty an hour, plus the cost of supplies sound fair?"

"That's more than generous," Ethan replied. "It's a deal."

"Al told me about your business partnership for the spring," Falcon commented. "I can just see you, hammer in hand, chasing windmills, after dark."

"Very funny, but I think I'll stick to installing them," Ethan replied. "Al has some interesting ideas for advertising on the internet that don't include the man from La Mancha attacking our products with a sword."

"By the way, Valerie's visitation is tomorrow night," Falcon reminded him.

"I remember," Ethan replied. "I'll be ready when you come by."

Falcon told his cousin about the family get together at the farm on Thanksgiving and signed off. It would be a relief to have Ethan living in his apartment building. His cousin had been a Freeblood police constable for ten years, and Falcon knew he could trust him in a dangerous situation.

Falcon met Colin and Giselle at the hospital while Alberto stayed behind catching up on much needed sleep. Damien had survived the first twenty-four hours, but his condition hadn't improved. Giselle was sitting next the comatose man reading the morning issue of the daily newspaper. She was convinced that Damien could hear what was being said, even if he couldn't respond. After two hours, Falcon reluctantly said goodbye to Giselle. She was fast becoming his best friend. With a courageous heart and an uncomplaining spirit, her compassion for Damien was evident as she carefully applied cool compresses to his sweat-beaded forehead.

He dropped by the Nightwing Arms to pick up Ethan, who was eager to accompany him. He knew the city well, and would be a valuable aide in finding the Ripper. The two cousins walked at a brisk clip down Kingshighway swiftly cutting over to Forest Park. Falcon had an appointment to meet with Eli in front of the Muny Opera, which was closed for the winter. He wanted to show the detective the two clues Damien had clasped in his fist when they rescued him from the frozen lake. The killer apparently hadn't expected his victim to live.

Tobias, who was managing the Ripper investigation with his usual expert capabilities, had kept the details of Damien's attempted murder from the public. He had convinced the reporter from the Post Dispatch that a middle aged homeless drunk's unlucky fall in the lagoon, was only worthy of a back page item in the local crime section. Because of the impending Thanksgiving Holidays, the paper was focusing on "The Hundred Most Neediest Cases, an annual outreach headline, and the Salvation Army's red kettle drive for the city's poor.

While waiting for Tobias, Falcon made a call to Dr. Montreau discussing the details of the latest murder. The learned psychiatrist was confident that the Ripper's voracious appetite for blood would soon abate, requiring him to hibernate before feeding again. Falcon informed the doctor of the probability that the Ripper had an accomplice who was connected to the Midnight Supper Club. He asked that all information pertaining to the case be kept secret.

"I respect Lt. Tobias' need for secrecy," Montreau had responded. "If I can be of any help, don't hesitate to call me. Oh, by the way, Yvonne and I will be attending the memorial for Valerie."

"Thanks, Doctor, I know Valerie's family will be pleased," Falcon returned. "I'm sure I'll call on you for help many times before this case is solved."

As they jogged closer to the Muny Opera House, Falcon spied a tiny red spark in the darkness, the tip of Eli's cigar. Tobias eagerly shook Falcon's hand and nodded to Ethan. Eli had met Ethan two yeas ago and was aware of his reputation for effective police work. Falcon's cousin had made a name for himself five years earlier, arresting an infamous vampire drug dealer in northwestern Missouri. A year later Ethan had retired from the Freeblood force to begin a construction career. He was convinced that his true vocation was to build things, not to kill or arrest criminals who were often released on a technicality.

Falcon informed Tobias that Valerie's phone had been found and that useful information had been discovered in her files and photos. He flipped open the purple metallic E-Phone, touching the photo icon to show Tobias the last picture Valerie had taken the night she died. The digital picture showed the back of the killer's head, and most of his right forearm. Falcon zoomed in on the photo until the tattoo above the Ripper's wrist was visible stating, "I put this information out on the web to see if anyone could tell what the complete tattoo might be. I got a hit from a Dr. Reynolds, a professor of Ancient History at Cambridge. He confirmed my idea that part of the tattoo as an ancient Egyptian symbol, the ankh."

"The symbol of life," Tobias stated. Pointing to the somewhat blurred photo he asked, "What is that inside the loop of the ankh?"

"A swastika," Falcon replied, adjusting the photo to bring the symbol in focus.

"An appropriate symbol for a heinous killer," Tobias commented. "The Ripper wanted to destroy Valerie's phone and all the evidence it contained."

"When the Ripper discovered Damien didn't have the phone, he or his accomplice tried to kill him," Falcon surmised.

"Fortunately, Damien is alive and Effie found the cell phone first," Ethan interjected.

Tobias puffed his cigar, while Ethan and Falcon finished their cigarettes. Rings of smoke curled up into the frosty air, as Tobias explained the kind of clues they had compiled so far. "I'm inclined to agree with you that the Ripper has an accomplice; probably a pliable Ordinary to assist him during the daylight hours while he sleeps. To date the Ripper has killed five young women, all Ordinaries," Tobias stated, then specified, "The first woman was, Susie Martin, the second was Gloria Stevens, the third was, Maggie O'Connell, the fourth, Valerie Chouteau and the most recent, Marian Jackson. All were attractive, well-educated, single women, under the age of thirty."

"The Ripper was drawn to each of these women," Falcon guessed.

"Right," Tobias agreed. "He was looking for a special type, as serial killers often do. We know the profile of his victims. Now we need to find out how he finds them."

"Giselle thought the Ripper might use a dating service, or a social web site to find them," Falcon offered.

"Professional Match.com," Ethan suggested. "That's where men look for attractive women with education, a career, and class."

"And you know this because?" Falcon asked, waiting for his response.

"I used the web site myself," Ethan explained. "It was a good way to meet women that I had a lot in common with."

"If Dr. Montreau is correct, and the Ripper is hibernating, we have about two weeks to find him. If we locate his accomplice, we may get closer," Falcon stated.

"His accomplice probably contacted the girls," Tobias stated.

"What kind of man would help the Ripper kill those women?" Ethan asked angrily.

"Someone desperate enough to believe the Ripper can share his powers," Falcon suggested.

"That makes sense," Ethan agreed. "The accomplice is not only obsessed with vampires, he wants to be one."

"Unfortunately, our only evidence is the photo on Valerie's cell phone, which is very inconclusive," Tobias admitted. "There was no PC in Valerie's room at her home on Lindell," he added. "Don't you think it's odd, that an educated professional like Valerie would share an outdated PC with her parents?"

"That is strange," Falcon commented. "We'll just have to dig deeper," he added quietly.

"Well, if you find anymore clues keep me posted," Tobias said, discarding his half-smoked cigar and walking briskly away.

"What was that all about?" Ethan asked, shoving his cold hands into his jean pockets.

"Tobias doesn't need to know everything," Falcon stated.

"Are you saying we can't trust Tobias?" Ethan asked.

"I don't trust the plain clothes officer in the black sedan who circled the block at least three times while we were standing here."

"Do you think he's following Tobias?" Ethan asked.

"Not necessarily. It's possible Tobias put him there as a back up," Falcon conceded. "I just hope we aren't dealing with a departmental spy checking up on Eli."

Falcon sprinted away into the park, with Ethan close at his heels. From the relative ease of their evasion, it was evident that the man tailing them was not a vampire. Falcon felt himself slipping deeper and deeper into a constant state of paranoia because of the Ripper case. Every shadow seemed to hold an unseen enemy, and every night that the Ripper remained at large seemed painfully long.

When the two cousins finally halted, Ethan studied his feet, trying to control his inner rage toward the Ripper. Even though he had admitted to seeing Valerie's profile on Professional Match while he was browsing the website, he had met her long before that.

Two years earlier, Colin had called him about a possible construction job in St. Louis. Pierre Chouteau was rehabbing an old office building in the Benton Park neighborhood, and needed a subcontractor. Ethan, whose construction job had ended a month earlier, eagerly sent Mr. Chouteau his resume. The businessman called him, and they made an appointment to meet.

When the two men met at the work site, Mr. Chouteau expressed his acceptance of the interesting plans Ethan had for updating the buildings, and the landscaping of the property. Not only did he want the fifty offices redone and equipped with the latest technology, he planned an on-site daycare facility and walking park for the employees. The Chouteau Group, a software and marketing research company, served customers throughout the Untied States and many European countries.

Mr. Chouteau had handed him the keys and he had spent several days studying the old building. He was pleased that the structure of the building was sound. Once inside, however, he was crestfallen to see that mildew and water damage to the offices was extensive. Even though the framework and joists were still in tact, the walls would have to come down and be replaced. The old carpet was stained and the tiles beneath it were cracked and chipped. Every room would need a factory fan to dry it out, after which a durable, sub-flooring would have to be installed before new tiles were laid.

Considering its age, Ethan deemed the exterior of the building to be in above average shape. The bricks could be tuck-pointed and sandblasted to their original red color. The roof would have to be replaced right away, to insure no further water damage would be incurred.

The basic systems would have to be updated to meet city codes. Utility contractors would have to update the wiring, add central air, and replace the outdated boilers with gas furnaces. After three days, Ethan typed up his suggestions in his proposal for renovating the facility and dropped them off at the Chouteau Group.

Three days later, Pierre Chouteau was beaming with delight when the butler ushered Ethan into the den of his luxurious home for their meeting to discuss his proposals.

"Fantastic ideas, Mr. Falcon," he had commented, shaking Ethan's hand. "You've given me such a fair bid, but I checked around and your hourly cost is much too low, so I edited your figures to reflect the industry wages."

"Thanks, sir and please call me Ethan," He had replied. "I read the article in Time Magazine about the computers you're foundation is sending to developing countries, so that children can get a modern education. I think it's a great thing to do for kids."

"Ah yes, I can only take credit for part of the funding on that project," Mr. Chouteau had informed him casually. "The Learning for Life program is my daughter Valerie's brain child. I'm very proud of her concern for children. A good per cent of the money invested comes from her trust fund."

At that moment, Valerie had walked into the room bringing light that had little to do with the fixtures in the room. Ethan tried not to stare at the lovely young woman. Her thick ebony waves were pulled back into a ponytail. She was sipping a tall glass of iced tea through a colorful straw.

She wore one of her father's old button downed shirts over grass-stained, rolled-up Bermuda shorts. There were dirt smudges on her knees and her pecan hued legs. What pulled at his heartstrings the most were her luminous brown eyes, peering at him from under thick, eyelashes. Her eyebrows were raised slightly in interest and her lightly glossed lips turned up into a smile as her father introduced him saying, "Valerie, this is Ethan Falcon, the new contractor for the Benton Park project."

"Pleased to meet you," Valerie had returned. She had taken his arm and walked him to her office saying, "I've been dying to show someone my ideas for interior design for the building. I need your expert opinion as to whether or not they will compliment the architecture." For the next two hours he and Valerie had poured over drawings of her creative vision for the building.

Later that evening Janet Chouteau had declared, "Valerie, not only did you whisk Ethan away before I could meet him, but you've kept him far past his dinner time."

"Oh, Ethan, I'm so sorry," Valerie had apologized. "I lost track of the time."

"Valerie, ask Ethan to join us on the patio for a little barbeque your dad has cooked up," Janet had suggested. She took Ethan's arm gazing up at him kindly. In spite of being in her sixties, her face was smooth and her ash blonde hair perfectly coifed. Her figure was slender, and she moved with the graceful carriage of a dancer.

Ethan had observed that Pierre Chouteau and he liked their steaks cooked in the same manner, rare and succulent. To compliment the beef, Janet had prepared asparagus, roasted rosemary potatoes and a fresh salad of field greens. Tall glasses of ice-cold lemonade were passed around to cool their palates. During dinner he and Valerie had discussed the cost of her simple, yet elegant office designs, and how they could be modified to work in the newly renovated space. Dessert had been his favorite, French Silk Chocolate Pie covered with fresh raspberries and topped with whipped cream.

After an enjoyable evening, Valerie had walked him to the door and promised to stop by the work site after a week or so, and bring him lunch. Janet Chouteau had taken Ethan's arm and strolled across the lawn to his parked car, saying, "When Pierre and I visited the Homeless Children's Orphanage in Northern Africa and saw Valerie, we decided to adopt her and bring her back to the states. I was forty and Pierre was pushing fifty. Pierre and I granted an endowment to the orphanage and improved living conditions for all the children. We recruited physicians for a two-year stint in the Marion Infirmary. I was asked to chair the adoption board for the United States. The three of us became a family in an era when eyebrows were still raised about adopting a child of a different race."

"You must have endured a lot of criticism," Ethan had commented.

"We lost a few friends in the process," Janet had agreed. "Valerie is the joy of my life and an intelligent caring woman in her own right."

Valerie, true to her word, had visited the work sight nearly once a week to bring lunch for Ethan and his crew. She was a welcome sight for them and enjoyed watching the rehab progress. After ten months the job was finished, and Ethan had returned to California.

Until her death, Valerie had never failed to text him or e-mail him every month or so to keep in touch. When she had called and invited him to a Charity Dance for the Learning for Life Foundation, he had booked a round trip ticket, bought a tuxedo and patiently waited for the weekend to arrive. The event would have taken place on December 5th. Sadly, Valerie was killed the twenty first of November.

He had fallen in love with Valerie, but because he was much older, and a vampire, he hesitated to reveal the depth of his feelings. When Ethan finally raised his head, Falcon was studying him with concern.

"It really makes me angry that five young women were killed, just as their lives were beginning," Falcon stated. "I'm especially outraged about Valerie. From what I've learned, she was an angel to everyone she knew."

Ethan looked over at his cousin in misery, commenting, "It makes you wonder how a God, who supposedly loves us, could allow such a thing to happen."

Falcon walked beside Ethan in a quandary. He was unsure of how to answer his question. He took a deep breath and said from the heart, "God didn't kill Valerie, a monstrous man chose to take her life, and then, tried to cover it up. We'll find her killer, and he'll get what he deserves."

Ethan sighed, and said, "I didn't know you had such strong beliefs."

"People can change," Falcon commented, adding, "even if they're pushing three centuries of age."

Falcon dropped Ethan back at Colin's building listing the security work for his cousin to complete. Falcon knew that keeping busy with hard work would help Ethan to focus on living each day.

"How do I keep going?" Ethan asked as he got out of the Hummer.

"I'll tell you how Great Grandpa Falcon handled it when Great Grandma Lucy died," Falcon offered, "There were three things he did every day to get through; work, eat, and sleep."

Falcon reminded Ethan to meet him later at the hospital where the family would gather to visit Damien. He called Giselle to tell her he was on his way. He couldn't help feeling miserable for his cousin. Carrying a torch for Valerie was not an easy thing to let go of.

Giselle saw the pain in his face and asked, "Are you okay? This whole thing is a strain on you isn't it?"

"Ethan was in love with Valerie and never told her," Falcon replied, accepting her embrace.

"I'm heartbroken for him," Giselle returned. "It's a burden he'll have to carry a long time."

"He never had the chance to find out if she felt the same," Falcon stated, sadly. He took the cup of hot tea she offered, and asked. "Did you find anything else when you checked Valerie's phone?"

I went through Valerie's music yesterday and checked her memos," Giselle answered. Flipping open the phone she scrolled down to a memo saying, "Valerie's favorite songs were oldies from the 60's and 70's. Nicole told me that Valerie found one song really relevant with the problems in the economy lately: Too Much of Nothing, by Peter, Paul, and Mary."

"I seem to remember that," Falcon commented. "Read me the lyrics."

"I'll do better than that, I'll sing them," she responded, singing in a bluesy style. When Giselle got to the refrain Falcon listened carefully to the words:

"Say hello to Valerie, Say hello Marian,

Send them all my salary, on the waters of oblivion"

"Interesting how the words seem to apply today as well as they did in the sixties," Falcon observed. Something in the haunting melody troubled him, but he couldn't quite understand why. It was simply an old folk song, yet he knew it had a deeper meaning than a commentary about social upheaval. "Giselle sing the last few lines again," he asked.

When Giselle repeated the last two lines, she stared at Falcon saying, "Valerie, Marian, the names of the last two Ripper victims!" She commented excitedly.

"He picks his victims names from songs then searches the web for the perfect woman to fit the profile," Falcon suggested, rapidly scrolling down through his notes on his cell phone, scanning the names of the other victims. "The first girl was Susie Morrison-Susie Q by Buddy Holly," Falcon suggested. "Margaret; Maggie Mae, by Rod Stewart, and Rhonda; Help me Rhonda, by the Beach Boys."

"The Ripper is one seriously disturbed man," Giselle commented, holding onto Falcon's arm.

Falcon and Giselle went through memos and messages from the last few months of Valerie's life. Ethan was a frequent caller and a more frequent subject of Valerie's memos, which were written in journal form. After the couple read the last ten messages, sent and received, Falcon switched the phone off saying, "The messages go on and on. I'm getting really uncomfortable reading the web messages of a dead woman."

"Ethan and Valerie really had a good friendship," Giselle commented. "Nicole never mentioned they were sweet on each other."

"According to Nicole, Ethan was sweet on Valerie, but she only thought of him as a friend," Falcon replied. "He asked Nicole's advice on how to approach her."

"What did Nicole tell him?" Giselle asked curiously.

Falcon replied with, "She gave him good advice; continue being friends, see where it goes, and don't pressure for more."

"Ethan seems like a good man," Giselle commented. "Valerie and he came from different worlds though," she added, with melancholy in her voice.

"In more ways than one," Falcon agreed. "Still, they deserved a chance to have a relationship. The Ripper took that chance away, and ruined a lot of other lives in the process."

"You can't blame Ethan for falling in love with an Ordinary. There aren't a lot of female Freebloods in this part of the country," Giselle observed. "Did he date anyone while he was working in L.A.?"

"If he did, he kept it a secret," Falcon observed. "Ethan never told me about Valerie, but I knew there was someone he was in love with. I've never seen him happier than in those months."

Chapter 14

"I called Nicole and asked her about Valerie's P.C," Giselle said as she and Falcon discussed new clues to the Ripper case. "Valerie did have her own computer, but when the police went to her parent's home, it wasn't there."

"Call Nicole as soon as possible and have her talk to the Chouteau's," Falcon suggested. "Maybe you two can pay a visit and ask Janet about Valerie's computer."

"Good idea. I'll call her right now," Giselle stated, dialing the number.

While Giselle was talking to Nicole, Falcon's cell phone began vibrating. It was Colin. Moving into the other room, he talked a few minutes then signed off. Returning to Giselle he explained, "Colin called about a prayer meeting at the hospital for Damien."

"Is Damien okay?" Giselle asked with a worried look on her upturned face.

"He's slipping deeper into a coma," Falcon answered soberly. "We better get over there right away."

"What can anyone do?" Giselle wondered aloud.

"If I know Colin, he'll want us to pray for a miracle," Falcon replied softly.

"By the way, Nicole and I are going over to talk to Janet Chouteau early tomorrow evening before we drive to St James," Giselle informed him.

"That's good news. Let's hope there's something on Valerie's computer that will help us," Falcon said.

When they arrived at the Barnes Hospital ICU, Ethan met them in the hall. He was still wearing his painter's clothes and spots of paint dotted his curly blonde hair. Colin and Nicole were already there, talking softly to Damien. Colin held the Bible in his hand and the other was raised in prayer.

Colin motioned for the others to join hands and gather around Damien's bedside. Damien's face looked like a pale skull. His head was sunken deep into the pillow. The pallor of his skin was mottled gray, and the dark circles under his eyes were more pronounced. His mouth was slightly open and a ventilator tube now assisted his breathing.

"Damien went on full life support this morning," Colin said. Seeing their stunned expressions he added, "We must keep watch and pray. The enemy is close. We're his best hope, and we need to pray for his delivery from this attack."

Falcon was surprised to see Beau enter the ICU shuffling miserably over to his friend's bedside. He had a manila folder in his hands and an envelope. He walked over to Colin and handed him the papers saying, "I thought you might like to see D's papers. He asked me to hold on to them when I moved in."

Colin thanked Beau and opened the folder, sharing the information with the others, "Damien Ahmed, was in the Gulf war, he served in the army for five years and was honorably discharged. He came to St. Louis shortly after his military stint to work for McDonnell Douglas. These papers say he was a fuel engineer. He owned a home in North County, but sold it when he was laid off after a nervous breakdown. He was diagnosed as borderline schizophrenic with post traumatic stress syndrome. These other papers are discharge papers from the State Hospital. The hospital lost its funding for extended care, and Damien ended up living on the street."

Colin lowered his eyes and looked intently at Damien. Placing his hands on the comatose man's forehead, he prayed aloud, "Lord, if you are willing, your servant Damien needs your help. We gather here in your name to ask that our friend to be healed, that every nerve and brain cell be restored, and that Damien live to fulfill your special purpose for him."

When no change was evident, Colin lowered his head and repeated his words kneeling on the floor, head bowed in supplication. Damien's friends joined hands and prayed for his recovery. While their eyes were closed in concentration, their voices were crying out to God.

After a few minutes, Falcon opened his eyes to look at Damien. There was a noticeable change in his appearance. The gray pallor of his skin had disappeared, and was replaced by a more normal hue.

"Look!" Giselle exclaimed in a whisper. Damien's eyelids fluttered and opened.

Dr. Levin came in and looked at Damien pleased with the change in his appearance. Because he appeared to breathe on his own he removed the ventilator tube.

"It's amazing," Dr. Levin stated. "He made it through the crisis sooner than I'd hoped." He checked his vital signs and was pleased that he could remove Damien from all life support.

Within the next hour Damien was sitting up and asking for something to eat and drink. He was confused about where he was, and had little memory of what had happened to him.

Dr. Levine pulled Colin aside admitting, "I never understood the power of prayer until tonight."

"We can do nothing without God's help," Colin told him.

"I can see that now," The doctor agreed. "I just need your help with one more thing."

"What?" Colin asked.

"When can you and your friends come again and pray for the other patients on this ward?" Dr. Levin inquired.

"I'll call you tomorrow and we'll set up a schedule," Colin answered.

Falcon joined the two men in the hall stating, "Doctor, please don't let this new development go any further than this room."

"Do you think Damien is still in danger?" Dr. Levin asked, concern showing on his weary face.

"I'm going to remove Damien to a private facility, for his safety," Falcon informed him. "Damien saw his attacker who may be the killer of five young women. When his memory comes back, he should be in a safe place with ample security to protect him from retaliation."

"Damien saw the Central West End Ripper?" Dr. Levin asked. He quickly added, "I'll have Damien ready to go before the shift changes. There is usually a lull after the second shift goes off duty. It's a good time to discharge a patient quickly. Meet me on the basement level, near the morgue, after midnight."

"I'll be in a black hearse with silver eagles on the doors," Falcon said.

Falcon called Dr. Montreau to apprise him of Damien's condition. The doctor was relieved that Damien had recovered, and agreed to meet Damien at Happy Grove Rehabilitation Center. After placing a call to Father Francis, Falcon called St. Louis American Mortuary and reserved a hearse from Bob Stands, who was also the President of the

Knights of Columbus chapter that met each month at St. Ignatius Church.

Damien was released from the ICU and put in a private room at the end of the hall near the elevator. He rested comfortably while his friends watched over him and discussed the amazing events of the evening. Damien soon fell asleep, listening to the comforting sounds of their discourse.

Falcon, still confused about what had happened, had to admit Damien's recovery was nothing short of a miracle. Colin's eyes were intensely focused on Damien as he and Nicole discussed the importance of what had occurred. Falcon urged Colin to keep Damien's recovery a secret to protect him.

"Don't worry," Colin agreed. "We and the doctor are the only ones who know what happened. Besides, it wouldn't be right to gloat over something that was God's doing, not ours."

Chapter 15

St. Ignatius church was filled to capacity for Valerie Chouteau's funeral mass. The beautiful African American socialite was well loved by everyone in the community. Her parents and extended family sat in the first five rows of pews, and her friends and acquaintances, numbering in the hundreds, behind them. The church was inundated with the aromatic fragrance of hundreds of flowers placed near the sanctuary.

Nicole and Colin held on to each other, bereft and exhausted. The life of their friend, Valerie had been cut short by a killer who still roamed the streets of their city. Falcon and Giselle sat next to them with Ethan and Zeke, who had arrived the previous evening. Ethan's eyes were red and swollen and his hands shook as Valerie's casket was brought to the front of the church near the sanctuary. Zeke watched his brother vigilantly, in case he needed help. In spite of his efforts, it was no secret to his family members that Ethan had loved Valerie.

Falcon gazed at the stranger who sat next to Valerie's parents. He surmised that he was Valerie's friend, Trey. According to Nicole, Valerie had won the handsome entrepreneur, Trey Hawkins, at the charity auction for MS foundation, and they had continued to see each other after the contest. His username, "tenderheart4," was at the top of Valerie's friends list on her E-Phone and the subject of numerous e-mails on her PC.

Trey stood up, visibly shaken at seeing the Valerie's casket only a few feet away. Valerie's parents had requested a closed casket for the requiem mass because the body had already been viewed earlier that day. Tears streamed downed Trey's face as he reached out to touch the final resting place of his beloved friend.

Father Francis led the mass wearing ceremonial robes of vivid white. He shunned black vestments at funerals, because he viewed death as the doorway to a new life in heaven. His young face was paler than ever, and his usually bright eyes, were dull, from lack of sleep. The priest had befriended Valerie five years ago, and considered her a true Christian. They had laughed together many times, as they cleaned and polished the gleaming wooden pews of the church. She had been a light to the city, exhausting herself in good works, locating the homeless, and driving them to Colin's soup kitchen, visiting the cancer victims at Children's Hospital, and faithfully donating large sums from her trust to help the poor. She lived her faith, and thanked God for the blessings of her parents every day.

As Father Francis gazed over at Janet Chouteau, his heart went out to the grieving mother. No loving parent wanted to outlive their child. Pierre Chouteau gripped his wife's hand, unable to stop his own from trembling, silent tears trailing down his quivering cheeks. Next to him stood Trey Hawkins, Valerie's close friend, and the love she had been praying for. The grieving man was having a difficult time controlling his emotions. He sobbed out loud several times, and needed help getting up from his seat.

While father Francis continued celebrating the mass, Falcon watched Trey with increasing curiosity. The man had only known Valerie about six months. Falcon understood how quickly one could become involved with a beautiful, intelligent, and loving woman, yet he sensed something more coming from the distraught man.

Giselle had never met Valerie, but after hearing such wonderful things about her at the memorial the previous evening, and listening to the words Father Francis poured out for her at the pulpit, she felt overcome with sadness that the world had lost such a treasure. Her tears were shed for what might have been; a close friendship between the two of them, that was lost now with her death.

She became aware of Falcon looking at someone in the front pew. Giselle turned her gaze curiously to the person he was studying so intently, Trey Hawkins. She squeezed Falcon's hand and felt him grip hers in return. Perhaps he was imagining how it might feel to loose the love of your life in such a cruel manner.

"Valerie's memory will live on, not only in our hearts, but in our city." Father Francis announced. "Janet and Pierre Chouteau have generously donated the money to renovate a large home in the Central West End to be used for family stays in cooperation with Children's Hospital. It will be called the Valerie Chouteau House." The priest paused a moment, composed himself, and continued. "I have it on good authority, that there are dedicated members present today who are working tirelessly to find the lost soul that killed Valerie and the other four women. With the help of God, we will stop this killer from doing his evil deeds in the darkness."

The choir sang Valerie's favorite Christmas hymn, "O come O come Immanuel" as the congregation filed out into the cold November air. White fluffy snow had fallen steadily all morning, and the temperature had plummeted to single digits. The cloudy, gray day was adequate protection from solar damage for the vampire entourage that attended the funeral. Falcon, Giselle, Colin, Ethan, and Nicole got into the black limo that awaited them outside. Valerie would be buried at the family grave site in Calvary Cemetery, the oldest Catholic cemetery in St. Louis.

A large green tent awaited them at the cemetery. Bitter winds drove family and friends under the canvas flaps. Father Francis prayed over Valerie, and all who stood beside her coffin. He commended her spirit to God as the casket was lowered into the ground. As family and friends filed by dropping bright pink roses onto the casket, Pierre Chouteau quickly caught his wife's as she collapsed near the grave. When he looked around for help, Ethan rushed over in a blur. He gently lifted Janet and carried her to the family limousine.

Falcon told the others to go ahead while he remained. He wanted to ask Father Francis a few questions. The priest was still praying over the casket as it was covered with earth. He ended his words softly, pulling his coat collar up against the wind. Falcon looked into the grief-stricken eyes of the priest and asked, "How much do you know about Trey Hawkins?"

"I know that Valerie won a date with him in the Most Eligible Bachelor auction last summer for the MS foundation. Trey owns a trading company in the Central West End, the Midwest Mercantile Co. Ltd.," The priest answered.

"How did he really feel about Valerie?" Falcon asked.

"From what I have seen, I believe he cared deeply for her," Father Francis replied. "Do you believe Trey was involved in her death?" The priest asked, in an astonished whisper.

Seeing the priest's worried expression Falcon stated, "That's what I'm trying to figure out. When Giselle and I discovered that Damien and Marian were both attacked at approximately the same time, we came to the conclusion that the Ripper had an accomplice."

"You mean an Ordinary is somehow leading the Ripper to his victims?" The priest asked with interest.

"The other way around, Father," Falcon explained. "The Ripper stalks the girls on the internet, or in the neighborhood news. His accomplice meets them and sets them up for him."

"I understand where you are going with this, but Trey was in love with Valerie," The priest replied shaking his head. "Two weeks ago, he came to me about posting marriage bans in the church paper, and expressed his desire to become a Catholic. Trey was going to propose to Valerie on St. Nicolas Day. He planned a romantic dinner at Tony's, where they had their first date. He showed me the engagement ring he was going to give her, a magnificent Marquise diamond; a keepsake from his mother, if I remember correctly. Theodore my friend, I can't believe Trey is the one you're looking for. You've got the right idea about an accomplice, but Trey can't be your man," the priest insisted.

Falcon returned to the limo, and sat in silence as the chauffeur drove their group to the Chouteau residence in St. Louis Hills. Because the circle drive was crowded with other cars, the girls were dropped off at the front door. After the driver parked the limo, Falcon and Ethan walked back to the house. Falcon gazed over at his cousin and asked, "How're you holding up?"

"Not good," was Ethan's tearful reply. "I have this feeling in my gut that Hawkins was involved in Valerie's murder."

"I don't know if it's any comfort," Falcon offered, "but I'm inclined to agree that Trey had something to do with Valerie's death. If we're right Hawkins has completely fooled Father

Francis. He doesn't believe Trey was involved in Valerie's death."

The two men entered the Chouteau home wading through the exquisitely furnished rooms packed with friends and acquaintances until they found the others. Ethan sought out Colin and Nicole, while Falcon walked toward Giselle who waved to him from the right side of the spacious dining room. Falcon reached for glass of dark red wine she offered him, trying not to drain it in one gulp.

"It's been a difficult day," She said, watching him as he struggled to remain composed. "The death of someone so good is always a blow."

"Especially when it comes before it should," Falcon commented, finishing his wine.

"How is Ethan taking Valerie's death?" Giselle asked, touching his arm.

"He's miserable," Falcon said, sighing. "When someone is brutally killed, it's understandable to question why God would allow such a thing to happen. It shakes your faith."

"Perhaps it's as simple as a man choosing to do an evil act for his own personal gain," Giselle suggested. "Besides, Valerie's death got us on the case. That's a good thing, right?"

"I'm going to find that blood sucker and when I do, he'll wish he had never been born," Falcon stated between clenched teeth.

"Remember my father's plan for him," Giselle said, alarmed at his sudden rage.

"I didn't say I was going to kill him," Falcon replied, relaxing his fists.

Chapter 16

On the evening of the Thanksgiving trip, Giselle arose sleepily when her alarm clock bellowed two hours earlier than her usual waking time. She dressed quickly, packed her suitcase, and stowed it in the trunk of her Chevy Cobalt before she picked up Nicole. They had arranged a meeting with Janet Chouteau at her home, before they were to meet Colin and Falcon. When she arrived at Java Heaven, she helped Nicole put her suitcase in the trunk. Nicole turned and kissed Colin goodbye, and got in the passenger's seat.

A cold snap had hit the area, with a threat of snow in the forecast, and the wind was biting cold on their bare cheeks. As she drove away Giselle touched Nicole's arm and asked, "How are you doing?"

"It's hard. I miss Valerie, but I know she's in heaven," Nicole said with a sigh. "How are you and Falcon getting along?"

"Falcon and I are becoming very good friends," Giselle answered with a smile.

"He's really crazy about you!" Nicole stated emphatically. "He's usually so quiet. I don't think I've ever seen him this open or communicative."

Giselle looked over at her asking, "Are you going to be okay with this visit?"

"Janet and Pierre have been really good to me," Nicole offered. "They're the parents I never had. My mother died when I was born, and my dad couldn't handle me. When I was four, he dropped me off at an orphanage. After going back and forth to foster homes, unsuccessfully, I might add, the state gave up, and I stayed at St. Barnabas Home for Children until I was eighteen."

"I didn't know." Giselle said sympathetically. "What a sad childhood you've had."

"Valerie was like a sister to me," Nicole stated. "When she and I became friends, it added a lot of happiness to my life. Because of our friendship, her parents grew to love me like a second daughter. I should have visited Janet days ago, but the last time I called her, the servants refused to wake her. When I finally got through last night, they insisted I see her as soon as possible."

The Chouteau's lived in a private gated street in Saint Louis Hills, but the guard at the gate knew Nicole and let them through. It was nearly twilight when they reached the Chouteau Residence, a large three-story French Second Empire home with tall towers and mini turrets. It looked like a small version of a European castle.

"You should see the grounds in the spring," Nicole commented. "The fountain is alive with sparkling sprays, and the flowerbeds are breathtaking. The Chouteau's use landscape designs similar to the Botanical Gardens. They even have a mini Japanese Garden in the back with a rounded cherry wood bridge spanning over a fresh water pond filled with Water Lilies and Japanese Goldfish."

Nicole added tearfully, "Valerie really enjoyed gardening. The English Garden on the side of the grounds was her creation. She spent hours researching and designing how it should be laid out. I spent many a Saturday afternoon helping her care for that lovely spot. She always said that working in the soil helped her to keep her perspective."

"I'm so sorry you lost your best friend," Giselle said nearly in tears herself. "I hope we'll become good friends. I know I can't take Valerie's place, but I feel that we have become closer because of this tragedy."

Nicole turned toward Giselle and said, "Your friendship is helping me get through a difficult time. Thanks for being there for me."

After drying their eyes, the two women walked up to the Chouteau's front door. They were hastily ushered into the entryway by the maid, Betsy, who uttered tearfully,

"Miss Nicole, it's so good to see you, madam is anxious to see both of you."

Nicole and Giselle walked up the winding staircase arm in arm. Along the dimly lit hallway, the picture frames were draped with large black crepe swags with deep crimson roses. A light at the end of the hall led them to the master bedroom.

Janet Chouteau was sitting up in bed wrapped in a dark blue satin robe, her hair hastily pulled back by a satin headband. Her face, without makeup except for light pink lip rouge, looked pale, drawn, and twenty years older.

Nicole rushed to her side and fell into her waiting arms. Giselle sat in the bedside chair as they cried together, her own eyes brimming with tears. Nicole got a damp cloth from the bathroom and gently wiped Janet's face.

"I can't believe she's gone," Janet said, speaking in a husky cracking voice.

"Janet, we're all working hard to find the person responsible for Valerie's death." Nicole reassured her. "I hope you don't mind. I brought Giselle, she's Theodore Falcon's friend. She's been involved in Valerie's case from the start."

"It was so good of you to come," Janet said, looking over at the pretty young woman with dark red hair who hastily wiped away her tears with a tissue.

"Janet, I need to ask you a few questions about Valerie," Nicole stated. "Are you okay with that now?"

Janet sat up straight and looked at Nicole levelly, saying, "I'll do anything to help you find Valerie's murderer and stop that madman from killing someone else's daughter."

"What happened to Valerie's computer?" Nicole began. "It wasn't on the property list of items relating to her case."

"Valerie took that to her apartment several weeks ago," Janet replied. "I didn't think it necessary to tell the police, since she never got a chance to live there."

"Valerie had an apartment?" Nicole asked in surprise.

"She moved some of her things there the week before she was murdered," Janet replied. "While we were all having dinner about a month ago she told Pierre and I that she had rented an apartment in the Central West End, in the newly renovated Melrose Apartments. It was a lovely apartment. She had a great view of the city from the top floor. It had two spacious bedrooms, a kitchen, living room, and an attractive latticed balcony. I was only there one time to meet the drapery hanger, George. He was coming over to measure the windows. Valerie had to chair the Race for the Cure, and couldn't make it."

"She never told me," Nicole said in a quiet voice.

"Valerie was going to tell you last Sunday," Janet said. "She wanted to surprise you. She always wanted a place of her own, closer to the church community and her friends," Janet explained hesitantly.

Giselle looked at the woman and commented gently, "You don't sound so sure about those reasons for Valerie's move. Was there something she didn't want to share with you, like a man in her life?"

"Were my feelings that transparent?" Janet asked, abject misery in her voice.

"Giselle is not only a psychologist, she's a very empathetic person," Nicole explained.

"I was happy she was seeing Trey," Janet offered. "Valerie was very mysterious about him. That's how I knew the relationship was getting serious. We would have talked and laughed about a casual suitor, they were usually not her type and short-lived."

Janet took a sip of water and continued, "Trey had Valerie totally charmed. She moved around the house in a dreamy state like a teenager, and didn't really tell me where she was going most of the time. I wasn't surprised when Father Francis told me Trey was going to ask her to marry him, but I didn't expect it so soon."

"Can we see her apartment?" Nicole asked tentatively. "There could be information on her computer that may help us find the killer."

Janet fished in the drawer of her bedside table and handed Nicole a key chain. "Please go ahead. I'll call the landlord after you leave," Janet replied sadly. "She paid ahead for the year, and the landlord said to take my time about removing her things. He wanted to give me her money back, but I said he could give me the balance later, after I moved her things out. I just haven't had the heart to go through her apartment yet."

"I'll help you with that," Nicole said taking her hand. Giselle leaned forward and placed her hand on the woman's arm, nodding in agreement to help too.

"Thanks, I may take you up on that offer. You two girls go ahead," Janet said settling back down on the pillows. "Be careful. The killer might be trying to find her P.C. to cover his tracks," she added tearfully.

"Very perceptive Janet," Nicole observed, kissing the drowsy woman's cheek.

"Don't be strangers you two," Janet said as the women waved goodbye.

As they walked down the stairs the two women heard Janet on the phone talking to the landlord. Nicole and Giselle looked at the slip of paper Janet had given them, the address of Valerie's apartment was, number 555.

Mr. Hudson, the landlord, met them at the security entrance and led them up the stairs. Most of the apartments were still empty, but he assured the two women that the building would be full by the first of the year. The smell of fresh paint assailed their nostrils as they walked to the elevator. The walls were painted a bright cream color and the wood molding was deep brown. Valerie's floor was painted light blue with dark gray molding. A tall window at the end of the hall had a view of swaying, gnarled trees, creating eerie shadows in the dimly lit hall. Seeing their unease, the landlord commented that the new light fixtures, brightly lit sconces, mounted between each doorway, would be installed the following week.

When Nicole unlocked the door and turned on the light switch, she and Giselle were transported to another world. Giselle and Nicole walked slowly into the enchanting Victorian apartment admiring the brightly papered walls covered with tiny purple and blue violets on a white background. They noted the intricately carved crown molding of natural oak. White stamped tintype tiles covered the ceiling. An antique turn-of-the-century, globed chandelier softly illuminated the spacious living room. Directly across from where they stood, two large arched windows with purple and blue striped swags overlooked the site of the future courtyard and urban garden.

The highly polished hardwood floors of burnished oak gleamed brightly as they padded quietly around the room. Area rugs in deep purple were scattered about to give warmth and texture to the floor. A long Victorian Couch of cream-colored brocade, decorated with tasseled throw pillows in different shades of purple, lilac and white, sat elegantly in the middle of the room. On the left side of the room, two navy blue wingback chairs flanked either side of the gray tiled ornate fireplace.

"It's beautiful," Nicole stated, as they walked into the kitchen.

The kitchen was decorated in china blue and white, from the white and blue damask curtains to the blue cornflowers stenciled on the white cabinets. White glazed tiles gleamed like glass on the kitchen floor. The many-paned kitchen windows overlooked a leaf-strewn brick walk way that would be bordered by flower beds in the spring.

Giselle walked down the short hall to the first room and commented, "There's no PC in here, Nicole, although this must be Valerie's office."

Nicole scanned the pleasant room with mint green walls and white molding. It was incomplete, had little furniture, save a dark mahogany cabinet. Framed art prints lay against the walls waiting to be hung. Several sets of ivory mini-blinds were still in their plastic packages, and two dark brown wooden filing cabinets were still in boxes. When Nicole tentatively opened the brass handled doors of the cabinet, they found a hidden desk with Valerie's computer sitting on it. Giselle pulled up the rolling chair for Nicole and scooted over an elegant needlepoint chair for herself.

"Do you know Valerie's password?" Giselle asked curiously.

"I helped her set it up last year when she bought it. We worked together on the web sites. Nicole deftly logged on to Valerie's settings and clicked on the internet icon. She clicked on the most recent web site Valerie had accessed; Professional Match.Com, just as Ethan had said. Nicole opened Valerie's e-mail and clicked on history. The dating website had begun only six months ago. It was easy to spot Ethan's messages on her e-mail, his user name was sanguineguy1. Valerie's user name appeared as renaissancegal.

"Well here goes," Nicole stated nervously, opening a few of the e-mails. The most frequent hits were tenderheart4, blackbird, and ironmandaddy. Ironmandaddy is a fifty-year old rocker with his own band called Forced Retro.

"Valerie loved music and this rocker guy knows a lot about the history of oldies. Look at this one, they had a mutual exchange about how "music has gone to hell in a hand basket," to quote I-daddy," Nicole observed.

"What about blackbird?" Giselle asked

Nicole clicked on the messages sent by blackbird saying, "He identifies himself as a new Zoo Friend. He mentions a large contribution to the zoo, over $100,000. He wants Valerie to take him on a tour of Big Cat Country when he's in town."

"Try tenderheart4," Giselle asked. "That's an interesting username."

"Why does that name seem so familiar?" Nicole mused aloud. "Look, here's the first reply, "You won me fair and square, now wine me and dine me."

"Look at her blog," Giselle stated. "All's fair in love and war, but this is for charity."

"I know what they're talking about now," Nicole said excitedly. "Valerie told me about this crazy auction for MS. Women at the dinner would bid on a selection of eligible bachelors in the St. Louis area. Remember, it was on the news. Taylor Riggens, the winner on American Idol a few years back, was the guest performer. He sang two songs from his album. That's how she met Trey. He was one of the contestants. Valerie made the top bid and won a date with him."

"Lets go to stltoday.com and find the event, it might list who the other bachelors were," Giselle stated

Nicole typed in the St. Louis web site and easily found events for September. Clicking on the MS Bachelor Auction, she scrolled down the article. Nicole read the names of the men for sale aloud, "Connor Gentry, owner, Cabanna Club, Sean O' Riley, Child Advocate Lawyer, Dr. Leran Johnston, Maryland Ave. Family Dentistry, Trey Hawkins, owner Midwest Mercantile Co. Ltd."

"Hold it right there," Giselle stated. "Remember when we checked Valerie's text messages for the last few days before she died?"

"Yes, did you see something?" Nicole asked turning toward her friend.

"There were at least ten funny little texts to "TH,"" Giselle said.

"Giselle, you're right," Nicole exclaimed. "T.H., Trey Hawkins."

"Valerie's friend," Giselle confirmed. "I remember reading about the auction in the paper. Valerie took him to Tony's for dinner. I'm not surprised they started dating. No wonder Trey was so sad at the funeral. He must have really loved her."

"Valerie was so happy when they started going out. She was getting really serious about him after only a few months," Nicole added. "She said that Trey even started going to church with her. We should talk to Trey and find out what kind of person he really is."

"Do you think that Trey was involved in Valerie's death?" Giselle asked.

"I don't know," Nicole answered. "Maybe he unwittingly introduced her to the Ripper," Nicole suggested.

Clicking on stlcareers.us, Nicole scrolled down to St. Louis businesses, quickly finding Trey Hawkins' company. Nicole clicked on history and read aloud, "It says here Trey has been in business for almost six years. He took the family business after his father died suddenly in 2004. He is in the import-export wine business. Here's the address: 425 Market Street."

Nicole dialed Colin and filled him in on the details of their visit to Valerie's apartment. He agreed they should see Hawkins before they went out of town.

"I'll call Falcon. Meet us at his apartment," Colin stated. He phoned Falcon and let him know what the two women had found.

"This can't be a coincidence. There must be a connection between the Ripper and Hawkins." Falcon commented.

"I hate to say it," Colin replied. "Trey could be the Ripper's accomplice, but why would he betray the woman he clearly loved?"

"We're missing something in the equation, Colin," Falcon commented. "Trey wouldn't willingly give up Valerie to the Ripper. Maybe he was tricked.

"Whatever Trey wanted from the Keeper, he didn't realize Valerie would be killed because of it," Colin conjectured.

"That would explain his out of control behavior at the funeral," Falcon agreed. "He wasn't just sad about losing her. He was overcome by guilt because he was partially responsible for her death."

Chapter 17

In a corner office of the Midwest Mercantile Company Ltd., a green desk lamp illuminated the solitary figure of Trey Hawkins. He sat upright, in an imported leather swivel chair behind an enormous, glass-topped, oak desk. A formerly handsome man, tall and slim, in his late twenties, Trey's pallor was now shockingly grey. The dark shadows under his pale blue eyes were the most prominent feature of his face. With shaking fingers, he gripped a large manila envelope, hesitating, even dreading, the moment he would open it and study the contents within.

Mustering much needed courage, Trey quickly opened the envelope and slipped out the two large x-ray films inside. His stomach lurched as he viewed the proof he had denied for so long; the cancer in his bones had spread to his lungs, liver and kidneys. Once touted as the most eligible bachelor in the Midwest, he would soon be reduced to an emaciated stranger.

Three months earlier, the doctor he had seen suggested that that twinge in his side he had been feeling for over a year, warranted a closer look. The effects of the cancer they had found and treatment to decrease its spread, were slowly transforming his athletic body into that of a sickly, frail man. Throughout the extensive treatment; chemotherapy, radiation and alternative therapies, Trey had firmly believed that he would not only beat the cancer, but was convinced he would go into full remission. He remembered the day he told Valerie about his cancer. With tears in her eyes she told him she loved him and they would fight the disease together. That's when he decided to ask her to marry him.

Tears rolled down his cheeks as he replaced the two x-ray films in the envelope. He grabbed the iced tea tumbler sitting on his desk and filled it from the half-full wine bottle next to it. He almost laughed aloud, remembering the oncologist had advised him to give up alcohol. Trey no longer felt the need to stop drinking-the one thing that eased his emotional pain.

On his last visit, Dr. Reynolds, usually ebullient with hope, sat stonily silent behind his desk. Trey's upbeat smile had died on his lips as he sat across from the sober looking Oncologist and asked forcefully, "Whatever the prognosis, we can fight this thing, can't we?"

The doctor has looked over at his young patient with abject misery. "We fought the good fight Trey. Nothing more can be done."

Tray couldn't believe it. He had swallowed the rising outrage and hysteria that threatened to explode inside his gut. He had taken the envelope the doctor offered him and asked, "How long?"

"It's impossible to say," Dr. Reynolds had answered.

"Come on doctor. How long have you done this job, twenty years?" Tray had commented sarcastically. "I have to know. How long!" he had insisted.

"Six months at the most," Dr. Reynolds had answered. "There is an experimental treatment that you could apply for. It may change the prognosis, and give you more time without pain. It won't be easy Trey, it could be a long drawn out process. There are no guarantees."

"Okay! Okay! I get the picture," Trey had exclaimed. "You can chalk it up as another shining moment in the annals of modern science. I can't wait that long to get better.

I've got plans," he had added. He had stormed out without speaking, vowing never to return to the hospital again. Now he wished he had chosen to take the treatment the doctor recommended. The whole future would have changed and most importantly, Valerie would still be alive.

Sitting at his desk, drinking steadily to get inebriated, Trey studied a small photograph he had removed from his wallet. It wasn't the best photo of him and Valerie, but the day it was taken had been the happiest day of his life. They had gone to the Washington University's Carnival 13 and taken the picture in the narrow confines of a curtained photo booth. They had smiled at each other as the camera captured the moment in black and white. His eyes glistened as he studied the faces of the two young people in the photo; the couple from a more hopeful time. The ecstatic smiles on their faces were real, not phony, their love for each other, innocent and true.

Hawkins set the picture down, picked up his phone, and dialed the number on the business card he held in his hand. Imbibing in too much alcohol caused his fingers to fumble stupidly, and he had to key in the number three times before he got it right. The moment he heard the deep resonant voice on the other end say, "Blackbird here," Tray blurted out, "I need to talk to you right now!"

To his dismay, the voice had been a recording and it continued with, "I can't come to the phone right now, but leave your name and number, and I'll get back to you as soon as possible." A short excerpt of Night on Bald Mountain in the background ended with a loud beep. Hawkins shouted frantically, "Pick up! Pick up! I don't have much time!"

A few seconds later a snarling, gravelly voice came on the line, saying "I told you I would call you when I got up. What is so pressing that you had to awaken me from my sleep!"

"I'm dying, Henri," Tray confided, his voice shaking. "You've got to help me before it's too late!"

"Well, a promise is a promise," Blackbird stated sarcastically. "I'll be there in a jiffy my impatient friend."

When the line went dead, Trey began sobbing with relief. He rose from the desk grabbed his cane, and shuffled into the washroom to freshen up. Reaching up toward his dark black wavy curls, he yanked and pulled until the wig came off, throwing it into the drawer under the sink. He looked at his hairless head in the mirror, massaging his itchy scalp with trembling fingers. He peeled off the neatly trimmed mustache above his trembling lip. He could hardly stand to gaze at his ghostly white death's head reflection in the mirror. Although he had lost weight, the muscles on his lean frame hadn't yet become slack. Somehow he had to suspend the inevitable before his body became an empty shell.

Tray removed his clothing and stepped into the shower. Once drenched in the warm flow of steamy hot water, he tried to relax. As the shower brought increasing sobriety, he felt a pain in his heart stab him like a knife. The realization of what he had done drove him to his knees.

Grabbing onto the shower curtain to steady himself, he cried out," Valerie, NO! NO! Dear God! I don't want to remember!" His desperate prayer went unanswered, and the truth flowed over him like the murderous waves of a Tsunami. How could he do it? He asked himself. He had found women for Raven in exchange for the promise of the cessation of his cancer and a long life with Valerie. He had no clue Raven was the Ripper and had brutally murdered the two other women, not until Marian was found dead.

How could he have been so blind? He should have guessed Raven was up to something that night after the Lion King play when he met Valerie. Raven couldn't stop looking at her. Sobs wracked his body over and over, the guilt he felt nearly unbearable now.

While he was communicating with Marian, Raven had abducted Valerie, taken her life's blood, and mutilated her body. Trey now realized that he knew Raven was interested in Valerie. He grilled him about her every time they met. His own need to live had blinded him to the truth. Because of his selfishness, he had been blind to Raven's evil motives which had resulted in Valerie's murder. Deep in his heart, he hoped that someday God would forgive him for unwittingly helping the monster who killed her.

After Valerie's death, Raven had again appeared in his office, towering over him, staring down at him with two hungry eyes demanding, "Hawkins, I need more!" He had plopped down an old issue of the St. Louis Post Dispatch and pointed to the photo on the front page. He had circled the face of the young woman, Marian, who had won the St. Louis Marathon charity race two years earlier. "Remember her? You promised to introduce me to her."

"I can't," Trey had refused. "Valerie is dead, because I couldn't protect her. How can you ask me to help you anymore?"

"BECAUSE, LITTLE WORM, I'M STILL HUNGRY!!" The maniacal vampire had insisted, putting his two vice like hands around Trey's neck, squeezing the life out of him with very little effort.

"Okay! Okay! Please!" He had gasped.

Coming to his senses in the shower, Trey tried to calm himself before Raven arrived.

In spite of himself, Trey's mind backtracked to the evening he had first met Raven. He had received free tickets for the Midnight Supper Club's monthly reception, eagerly reading the bio about the guest speaker, Henri Raven. Trey was intrigued by the world traveler's riveting descriptions of his encounters with real vampires. He had entered the club a few minutes early, and was met by Rascal Gold who escorted him to his seat. Trey had looked up at Rascal and commented, "I'm impressed by this month's guest speaker."

"The tip of the iceberg," Gold had replied, flashing a smile that showed too many pearly white teeth, and unusually pointy, canine incisors. "I'm trying to line up a real vampire for November."

Tray had stared at the emcee in disbelief as he was ushered to his VIP table, second row center stage. As newly appointed treasurer of the Midnight Supper Club he enjoyed all the privileges of a VIP guest. The Vice President of the club, Rhandi Gupta, and his young wife, Preeya, were already seated at the table. Trey had nodded a quick hello.

Rhandi had nudged Trey excitedly saying, "Isn't this special, Mr. Hawkins? My wife and I have been looking forward to seeing the remarkable Mr. Raven. On our last trip to Nepal, our family village was rampant with rumors of vampires living in the hills. Perhaps Mr. Raven will have such a story to tell."

"From what I have read about the man, whatever he says will be riveting," Trey had answered in agreement.

Suddenly the houselights dimmed and the emcee, Rascal Gold, had stepped up to the microphone announcing:

"From the deepest recesses, within the darkest shadows, where the whims of pleasure seekers are fulfilled throughout the world, I present you the prince of adventure and encounters with the unusual, Henri Raven III."

Raven, nearly seven feet tall, had walked regally across the stage and took the microphone. He had bowed to the audience, motioning with two hands for them to be seated. While sitting on the high stool, he had taken a deep breath, and had relayed his experiences, beginning with the question, "What would you do if you came face to face with a vampire?"

After the audience murmured in anticipation, he had continued with, "That is exactly what happened to me one summer a decade ago when I was invited to the Cannes Film Festival. I had spent the evening holding the arm of a lovely young starlet. We were invited to the after party celebration in a wealthy French Vintner's hillside villa. The guests were transported in Limos to the estate where only VIP's partied all through the night. The champagne was plentiful, and the banquet table overflowing with French delicacies. My date, Michelle, a model turned actress, was tall and graceful, with a breathtaking face and willowy figure. We danced all night long and as you might have guessed, I became captivated by her."

Raven, had taken a deep breath, as if luxuriating in his fantasy about the lovely girl he described and had narrated, "Her hair was burnished auburn and hung in thick shining waves below her tiny waist. She wore an emerald green satin gown that enhanced her dark green eyes. As you can imagine, I couldn't take my eyes off of her. To my good fortune, she felt the same about me."

Raven had paused to sip his drink and continued, "About three in the morning, I became restless and left my bed to take a walk on the edge of a tree-lined bluff. I strolled several miles by moonlight, enjoying the soft, cool breezes coming off the sea, basking in the peaceful solitude of my nightly ritual done in an exquisite setting."

Raven had arisen from his stool and had strolled across the stage. Locked in the spotlight, he had turned toward the audience and announced excitedly, "Suddenly, I realized I was not alone. Ahead of me a dark, robed figure holding a lantern, glided toward me, an enormous Mastiff trotting at his side. I have traveled to the ends of the earth, and never shied away from an encounter with man nor beast, but I can tell you that when the monk came nearer, and I could see his eyes, I was overcome with a primal fear that I could not shake."

His account had struck fear in the hearts of the crowd. They had shifted nervously in their seats as he continued, "If the eyes are the windows of the soul, the robed man's eyes projected something I dreaded to see. I lit a cigarette to still my shaking hands. As the smoke curled and was taken on the wind, I tried to appear nonchalant. When the cleric walked within inches of me, I bravely said, "Good evening Friar." He walked past me slowly, heeling in his enormous snarling pet, and replied in a hoarse gravelly voice, 'Only immortals dare to walk the cliffs at night.' He stopped a moment, his lips twisting into a thin smile asking 'I trust you received your heart's desire tonight?' I smiled back at the monk and replied most arrogantly, 'Tonight I feel as if I could live forever.' As he moved past me, the friar sighed, and said in a dull monotone, 'Immortality is grossly overrated, my son.' When I turned to stare at his retreating figure, he was gone. In that instant, the cleric and his terrifying pet had melted into the shadows."

Trey had listened in rapt attention as Raven ended his presentation. He had been mesmerized not only at Raven's daring encounter, but with the possibility of becoming an immortal.

How could he have known that there would be a monumental price to pay for that privilege? Lowering his head, he wished he had never met Valerie. She would still be alive now, living the life she dreamed of, with another, worthier man.

The MS Ball, the social event of that summer, had been held outdoors in the Botanical Gardens, on a perfect summers evening, temperatures were in the high seventies. There was a light balmy breeze blowing the potted palms and with a cloudless starlit night as their canopy. The round patio tables with peach colored cloths and Bird of Paradise flower center pieces were overflowing with guests paying $500.00 a plate to enjoy an evening under the stars.

Party goers had filed in, dressed in their summer finery; the men, in white or pale gray suits, the women, in soft flowing sundresses and sandals, with lacey shawls to cover their bare shoulders. Trey, had worn a Ralph Lauren summer suit with an unstructured blazer and raw silk slacks, and had mingled confidently with other professionals who were invited to participate in the Most Eligible Bachelor Auction for Multiple Sclerosis. Along with himself, a vice president of Southwest Bank, the owner of the Cabana Club, a noted child advocate lawyer and a firefighter captain would be auctioned. Trey didn't expect to win the event, but the competition was great advertisement for his company. Besides, it was a chance to mingle with other professionals.

Dining had been an elegant affair with a sumptuous buffet of gourmet foods provided by local restaurant chefs who happily displayed their culinary talents. Trey had walked over to sample the selection of seafood, greeting Mr. Gutpta, who stood next to him in line. He had nodded to Gupta's pretty demure wife, who was stunning in a rose-colored silk sari trimmed with embroidered birds of golden threads. Her shining blue-black waist-length hair was adorned with tiny flowers and pearls. She returned his nod with a shy smile and downcast eyes.

Jack Matthews, Trey's overseas rep, who strolled up and shook his hand, had good news for him: their Missouri Wines exports had found a market in Sweden. He had added lightly, "The Sanguine label is finally within our grasp. I've arranged to talk with the Falcon brothers next week. With any luck, their wine will be a delightful addition to our exports. By the way, we snagged the Cordoba wine order out of Spain again."

"The Cordoba account is good news," Trey had said. "When you contact the Falcons remember to ask for a small shipment. Don't try to overbuy, it's a family owned business, and they're reluctant to expand."

"That in itself is strange," Jack had returned, sipping his champagne. "With the faltering economy, I understand being cautious, but wine sales are up."

"The bottom line is, they don't need the money," Trey had reminded him. "They make wine because they enjoy creating their family label. If they choose to export it to other nations, that's icing on the cake for us."

At that moment a petite blonde walked up and stood on tiptoes to give Jack a kiss. Penny Meyers, a local actress, had been featured in national wine advertisements. Jack had met her through their ad man, Kent Williams. Trey had to admit to himself, they were good together, which had made it all more depressing that he didn't have a serious relationship.

At nine, the emcee and Chair for the MS foundation, Jennifer Fields, had announced that the auction would begin. She had reminded the audience that coffee and dessert would be served directly afterwards. The single women in the audience had move toward the front tables to have a better view of the bachelors they would bid for. Jennifer Fields had stated the rules of the auction.

"As each bachelor comes forward, I'll read his dossier, and you can see with your own eyes how attractive he is. The highest bidder will win a date with the bachelor of their choice. Each couple will join each other for dinner: ladies choice. The winner of the highest auctioned amount will receive a Cash prize of $1000.00. Remember, all proceeds will go to the MS foundation, so let your generosity shine. Now girls lets start the bidding with bachelor number one."

Paul Stanton, the tall African American owner of The Cabanna Club, was the first to be called. The women were very excited and verbal about his degree of attractiveness. After hearing his impressive accomplishments, Stanton did well; he brought $2000.00. The lady, who won the bid, walked over to claim her prize. The first winning bachelor and his date were driven by horse drawn carriage to the Jewel Box for their society photo.

Trey was the fifth bachelor to be called. He strolled across the stage confidently, his suit immaculate, his shirt slightly opened at the neck. He wasn't prepared for the reaction of the women. His aunt Monica had commented that he resembled a young Gregory Peck, but when he looked in the mirror he couldn't see it. However, the ladies obviously liked what they saw, because they began clapping and screaming as he moved across the stage. Ms. Fields had to quiet the women down so they could hear Trey's dossier. The bidding that followed was fiercely competitive. He scanned the crowd discretely to see which ladies were raising the bet to win a date with him. A rather attractive middle aged woman in a purple dress seemed to be ahead, until a willowy, young African American woman with the most beautiful eyes he had ever seen, suddenly jumped ahead in the bidding and won.

"The winner of the bid, at $5,000, is Valerie Chouteau," Jennifer had announced.

Trey had been in a fog when he walked off the platform and held out his arm for her. Valerie had smiled up at him, and from that moment, their relationship had rapidly grown from a casual, to serious involvement.

Chapter 18

Two months later, he and Valerie had gone to the opening of the Lion King at the Fox Theater. Trey remembered what a joy it was watching Valerie's different reactions to the musical. He enjoyed her reactions to the play as much as he enjoyed the rhythmic music and moving dramatic scenes. They had left the theatre in a very ebullient state, holding hands as they walked to the car.

While they were dining at the Drunken Fish in the Central West End, Trey's spotted Henri Raven having a drink at the bar. Raven had met his gaze, nodded, and walked over to their table.

He had gazed openly at Valerie as he explained, "I was meeting a friend, but sadly, she called and canceled. I had tickets for the Fox, but couldn't find another companion at such a late hour."

"Wasn't the Lion King wonderful?" Valerie had asked.

"Exceptional," Raven had concurred, sitting in the empty chair to her right. "It reminded me of the time I went on Safari in Kenya." He had taken a sip of his brandy and stated, "But I won't keep you. I don't want to interfere with your dinner."

"Please stay," Valerie had protested. "I would love to hear your story about Africa."

The next hour they had listened intently as Raven narrated an intriguing mystery that occurred while he was on safari. He quickly assured them that the expedition was not the hunting kind, but a tour of the nature preserves in Kenya to experience how animals lived in the wild.

"During the third week," he had relayed, "our team discovered that poachers had invaded the preserve. They brutally killed two bull elephants, slashing off their tusks and leaving their carcasses to rot in the heat. It's not uncommon for poachers to attack elephants at night. You can imagine how outraged the team was."

"I suggested that we prepare a trap," he continued. "We tranquilized and tagged a large bull elephant that we isolated from the herd, and waited patiently in the bush, hoping to catch the poachers in the act. When I checked the perimeter about two A.M., I discovered that all the guards and my guide, Schneider, had fallen asleep. I couldn't blame them. We'd had a long day in the very oppressive heat. I climbed up a nearby tree and waited. Suddenly, I saw two of the guards creep away from the group. It was apparent that they had drugged the others, and I suppose, planned to kill me, and take the elephant's tusks. However, they never made it to the grazing behemoth. While they were scrambling around in the dark, they had fallen into the pit. They lay stunned and injured twenty feet below. In the morning we threw them a rope and pulled them out. They came away willingly, tired and listless, mumbling incoherently about an evil spirit that had visited them in the night, and fed upon their blood. We tied them up, put them into the back of the truck, and took them to the authorities."

Tray was increasingly uncomfortable with the effect Henri was having on Valerie. She seemed mesmerized with the man and her face showed disappointment when he said,

"I should leave. I've taken up too much of your evening."

"Thanks for joining us," Valerie had returned. "Your adventure was fascinating." She smiled as she watched him walk away.

"Valerie, don't take too much stock in what Mr. Raven says," Tray had warned her. "He's a professional story teller."

"Trey, you sound jealous?" She had responded, her eye dancing.

Trey had leaned forward, took her hand into his, and whispered, "I guess I'm a little jealous of anyone who takes you away from me, even for a moment. You see, I've found the woman I want to spend the rest of my life with." Valerie had squeezed his hand and smiled at him. Leaning over, he had kissed her softly. That was the last kiss they had ever shared. The night she had died, instead of going with her to the Midnight Supper Club, Raven had required his help to meet with a young woman named Marian.

Shaking off his painful nostalgia, Trey finished his shower, quickly dried off, and pulled on his robe. Walking past his desk, he picked up the picture again, wishing he could turn back the clock and right the terrible wrong he had done.

Raven had told Trey a homeless man named Damien had killed Valerie, while she was on her way to the club. Raven knew where to find Valerie's killer. He was a powerful man with contacts among the criminal element, and those who walked the streets of the city at night. In a grief stricken rage, and hungry for revenge, Trey had blindly followed Raven's leads.

Wearing a policeman's uniform, Trey had gone after Damien, forced wine down his throat, knocked him on the head, and dumped him in the icy cold waters in the Lagoon near the boathouse in Forest Park. He murdered him and made it look like an accident.

In return for his silence about Damien's murder, Trey had arranged a meeting with any young women the vampire had desired. When Marian was found murdered, he realize it was Raven that had killed Valerie. He had committed murder, and had become the accomplice of a deranged serial killer. Everything he thought he knew about Raven was a lie. Fortunately, the arrogant vampire had fallen for his trap. He had successfully lured Raven to his office so he could kill him.

Hearing the flapping of wings, Trey realized he was not alone. A large crow had flown into the room and landed atop his bookshelf, staring down at him with cold, beady eyes. Trey looked up at the bird and said aloud, "How did you get in here? A window must be open somewhere."

As the large blue-black bird continued to sit statue-like, staring down at him, a rushing noise like a freight train startled Trey, and he instinctively backed away. Henri Raven, tall and imposing, dressed in black like the grim reaper, had entered the room. He glared down at Trey, his bushy brows knitted together, and his mouth twisted into a sneer. His eyes, two bottomless dark pits, followed Trey's every movement.

Raven took a newspaper from his overcoat and threw it on the desk in front of him. Trey rapidly shifted his position, slowly moving behind the security of his solid oak desk.

"See the lovely Asian girl on the cover?" he asked. "She works at the Golden Lantern. I want her."

Trey glanced at the paper. It was a copy of Sauce, an entertainment magazine that reviewed local restaurants. The young woman, Judy Kim, was holding two specialty dinners the restaurant offered. Sauce had given her the Restaurant Manager of the Year award for her excellent customer service. Miss Kim looked proudly into the camera lens, her two lustrous, brown eyes sparkling with happiness.

Glancing from the photo, to the looming figure in front of him, Trey clenched his teeth with determination stating firmly, "No! I won't be a party to anymore killing."

"YOU DARE DENY ME?" Raven's booming voice raged. Seeing Trey's stubborn look, he leaned down and placed his larges hands on the desk. He stared steadily into Trey's eyes, saying in a carefully controlled voice, "You're dying of cancer my friend. I thought you wanted me to save your life."

Shaking his head violently, Trey stated, "I don't want anything from you! You're a liar and a killer. You never intended to give me immortality, because you don't have it to give, you're not God, you're a monster! You killed Valerie and I'm going to kill you!"

Raven moved swiftly around the desk grabbing Trey by the collar of his robe. Trey twisted out of the garment and ran to grab the broadsword that was mounted on the wall above his mini-bar. Although weakened from his illness, he managed to raise it over his head and bring it down towards Raven's chest, screaming,

"I murdered a man for no reason! I got women for you, and you killed them! You murdered the only person I ever loved!"

Raven stepped back too late, grunting as the sword sliced through his leather coat. In one swift action he swatted the sword out of Trey's hand as if it were a plastic toy. Caught off balance, Trey fell to the ground stunned.

Raven stared down at him saying, "You didn't kill anyone you stupid fool! Damien is alive! I let you think you killed him, his friends kept him hidden so he would be safe from me. As for the women it was a small price to pay for the promise of a long life with Valerie. Don't kid yourself. I didn't *make* you do anything. You chose to take the easy way out. Valerie made a bad decision too. If she hadn't refused me for the sniveling cowardly likes of you, she would be alive now. She chose you—a weak, loser, dying of cancer, over me—the greatest vampire of all!"

Raven growled, lifting Trey high off the floor, until his feet dangled in the air. The vampire carried him into the washroom and threw him into the shower stall. His head hit the stone tiles with a wet crunching sound.

As Trey weaved back and forth in a semi-conscious state, he heard Raven whistle loudly. Seeing the crow diving for his face, he frantically raised his arms to protect his eyes. The bird hovered over him squawking loudly.

As Trey lost consciousness, Raven brought his arm down, slashing the helpless man's torso with the razor sharp tiger's claws he held in his hand. Blood poured from the gaping wounds, running down the tub in crimson rivulets that quickly emptied into the drain.

"Nevermore," Raven commanded. "Enough!" The bird flew up and perched on his shoulder, its wings fluttering to keep balance. Raven turned the hot water on full blast and watched as billows of hot steam surrounded Trey, turning his skin bright red.

Raven's chin was quivering with rage as he turned to leave. Frustrated at being thwarted by his sycophant, Raven punched his fist into the bathroom mirror, cracking it. His nervous pet soared to the ceiling, flying frantically back and fourth, reacting to the vampire's violent emotions. Slamming the bathroom door, Raven flew into a full-blown tantrum, knocking over chairs, bookshelves, and the potted palm. With a loud grunt, he upended the solid-oak desk as if it were a cardboard box. All the papers on the desk flew up into the air, floating back down like falling leaves.

Hearing a car pull up outside, Raven streaked down the hall and out the side door whispering under his breath, "You won't be joining her in the next world, my friend. I've seen to it that you'll burn in hell."

Raven sped to the warehouse where thousands of bottles of wine lay in their cases, cool and untouched. Removing an object from his pocket, he placed it under a wine cask and set the timer. Dashing to his hidden motorcycle, the vampire moved slowly, until he was down the street, out of hearing distance. Once on the main thoroughfare, he gunned the motor, sped three blocks and turned onto Grand Avenue.

The wound inflicted by Trey's feeble attempt to kill him was already healing.

Chapter 19

Falcon and Giselle met Colin and Nicole at Java Heaven as planned, eager to investigate the Midwest Mercantile Company owned by Trey Hawkins. Nicole leaned against Colin in the Hummer, exhausted from lack of sleep. She had insisted on joining the others because she wanted to do something to find Valerie's killer.

It was nearly midnight when Alberto received a call from Falcon to meet him in front of the apartment building. He had unable to sleep when he returned from his dinner with Antonia and her four-year old, Maria, and was relieved to get the call. After he got in the car and greeted everyone, Falcon's cell phone rang, interrupting their discourse.

"It's Tobias," Falcon stated as he flipped open his cell phone and answered with, "Eli, what's going on?"

"I have some new information about the Ripper," The detective replied soberly. "Meet me at the entrance to the zoo A.S.A.P."

"I'm on my way," Falcon assured him.

"How was your date with Antonia," Giselle asked, twisting around and smiling at Alberto.

"It was awesome! I finally met her daughter, Maria," Alberto replied happily. "That little girl is an angel and she's really smart," He explained. "We made quesadillas together. I think she likes me," He explained, his dark eyes twinkling happily.

"What's not to like?" Nicole asked, smiling at him.

"You're just what that little girl needs," Colin agreed.

"Not to mention the effect it probably had on Antonia," Falcon commented.

"Do you think it's too soon to tell her how I feel?" Alberto asked with a hopeful look in his eyes.

"Don't waste time, if you love her, go for it," Falcon stated, gazing over at Giselle.

Falcon parked the Hummer at the main entrance to the zoo and they waited for Tobias. He left the heater on, got out of the car to look around. Alberto and Colin followed suit, pulling up their collars against the cold. The temperature had dropped, the winds had picked up, and a light snow began to fall. The men moved from one foot to the other, tamping their feet on the ground to keep warm.

Giselle and Nicole gazed out the windows, scanning the lighted parking area across the street. Peering into the wooded area behind the lot, Giselle scanned the bushes and suddenly cried, "There's something out there!"

"Where?" Nicole asked nervously. "I don't see anything."

"There, in the back of the parking lot, in the holly bushes," Giselle stated. "Two eyes staring at us."

"Yes, I see them now," Nicole said in a hushed whisper. "It's an animal, a really large one. I hope it didn't escape from the zoo."

"I don't think so, we would have heard about it on the news," Giselle consoled her, "More likely it's a raccoon or a stray dog."

Falcon walked back to the car when he heard Giselle talking excitedly. She told him about the glowing eyes. He snuffed out his cigarette, and signaled Colin and Alberto to follow. The men walked slowly across the street. Falcon motioned for Alberto to stay near the chained lot entrance, while he and Colin checked the wooded area. Climbing agilely over the six-foot security fence, the two cousins raced to the end of the lot. Alberto watched the two men in amazement. Not only did they easily surmount the fence, but they reached the edge of the woods within seconds.

Hearing a warning snarl from the bushes, Falcon stooped low and spread a few branches apart. Colin crouched close by, ready to intervene. Falcon was suddenly looking into the pain-ridden eyes of an injured Great Dane. Somehow, the animal had made it to the woods after being brutally attacked. When the canine gave him a warning growl, he stared directly into the dog's silver gray eyes with his own unwavering black ones and said softly,

"You're going to be all right. Now hold still, and let me have a look at you."

Falcon and Colin lifted the pony-sized animal from his hiding place and laid him down on the snow-covered grass. "Look at his left hind quarter," Colin stated. "He has two gashes."

The both studied the wound noticing that blood was matted and dried on the upper end of the two gashes, but still dripped from the lower end. Colin held the dog's head while Falcon held the edges of the wounds together. He took a small tin from his pocket and spread a healing salve on the edges of the wounds, watching them seal together. The tin contained a mixture of glycerin oil and preserved vampire cells. When they hit the dog's skin they were activated and became a catalyst for rapid healing. No longer in pain, the dog's breathing relaxed and the grateful animal licked both their faces, completely unafraid, as the two humans petted him.

Standing on his four feet, the canine was nearly three feet high at the haunches. He was solid black with dapples of white fur on his brow line. The white fur above his eyes moved expressively as he glanced from Falcon to Colin. When the eager dog tried to walk, he whimpered and favored his right front paw. Colin touched the injured paw tentatively.

"Here's the problem," he stated. He extracted a two-inch hawthorn sticker that had pierced one of the dog's pads. Once the thorn was removed, the dog bounded happily back and forth between the two men.

Falcon looked at the animal and commanded, "Come." The Great Dane cocked his huge head, barked softly, and followed them across the lot.

When Alberto saw the huge canine he asked, "Is that a dog or a horse?"

"He's the largest Great Dane I've ever seen," Falcon commented. "He doesn't have a collar or tags, and by the look of his skinny frame and matted fur, he's been on the run a long time."

The two cousins climbed back over the fence. They paused a moment, trying to figure out how to get the dog over the barricade. The next thing they knew, the dog was galloping toward the chain link fence. With one graceful movement, he bounded up and over. He paused and looked over at Falcon, his tongue hanging out, his tail wagging.

"Rufus," Falcon said petting the animal's enormous head. "Your new name is Rufus. Eat your heart out, Hound of the Baskerville's," he added, referring to the fictional canine nemesis in the Sherlock Holmes mystery.

When the men returned to the SUV, Giselle was waiting to let the dog in the way back. She had found an old army blanket, folded it and placed it on the floor for the dog to curl up on. Rufus, who was overjoyed to see the two ladies, stuck his huge head over the seat and stared at them with luminous eyes, waiting to be petted. Fortunately, the roof of the Hummer was high enough for Rufus to sit up. Nicole and Giselle cooed and talked baby talk to the animal as they stroked his fur.

"Rufus," Giselle said, "You need a bath."

"And a good grooming," Nicole added, combing his fur with her fingers.

"Tobias should be here by now," Falcon commented worriedly.

It was nearly one and the detective hadn't arrived. Falcon turned on the wipers as blowing snow began to accumulate on the Hummer's windshield. Flipping opened his phone, he dialed Tobias, but to his dismay, the detective's phone kept ringing until it transferred to voice-mail.

Outside, the sirens of fire engines, medical units and police cars blared loudly into the night. On impulse, Falcon turned on the police band, and listened as the dispatcher reported a vehicular accident on Forest Park Boulevard. A truck had jackknifed on the icy streets and smashed into a dark blue sedan. Falcon put the engine into drive and raced to the accident sight. Giselle looked over at him worriedly. Colin and Nicole prayed quietly and Alberto, a look of concern on his face, stared out the window.

The street was blocked off when Falcon arrived on the scene. The eighteen-wheeler had jack-knifed, skidded and ultimately fallen over on its side. Underneath the trailer, jagged pieces of crushed metal from the other vehicle were illuminated by a fallen streetlight.

Falcon parked the car and ran over to the accident. Using vampire speed he rushed around the trailer in a blur, past the firemen and police. He squatted down, nearly crying out when he saw the crushed body of his friend Tobias. He was trapped in his vehicle; impaled by the broken gearshift; a fatal injury no vampire could survive.

It would take special equipment to lift the heavy truck off the crushed car and recover the agent's lifeless body. Fearful an autopsy would reveal Tobias' vampire nature, Falcon took his lighter and ignited the fuel that had seeped into the car. He jumped back as his friend's mangled body was consumed in flames and incinerated within minutes.

Falcon streaked back to his vehicle and drove slowly away. A crowd had gathered and the police and firemen were too busy to notice them. Falcon, outraged at the unnecessary death of his friend stated passionately, "Someone just made sure our meeting with Tobias never took place. Obviously, Eli was going to give us some important information about the Ripper."

Before Falcon angrily turned off the police scanner, he heard one of the officers commenting that the driver of the big rig, who had made an illegal right turn from a side street, couldn't be found.

"Falcon," Giselle asked. "Was Tobias killed instantly?"

"Yes. His heart was pierced by the gear shaft," Falcon returned huskily. "We better get over to the trading company and see if we can talk to Hawkins. I think he's the person we're looking for. The last time I talked to Tobias he said he was checking his activities for the last six months. This Keeper is cunning and evil. If someone like Tobias can be fooled, we could be in deep trouble."

As they pulled into the parking lot of the Midwest Mercantile Trading Co. Ltd., Falcon stated, "Stay here. I'll walk around back and see if there's a way in."

Moving with determined strides, Falcon ducked around the corner of the building. The light was on in Trey's office. He scaled the side of the building and hopped on the roof. Discovering an unlocked skylight, Falcon carefully dropped down to the floor of the office. The room below looked as if it had been ransacked. Even the solid oak desk had been turned over. He ran back to the main hall and opened the front door. Giselle, Nicole and Albert moved cautiously into the building, with Colin leading them through the darkened hall. When Falcon's entourage entered the room, they were shocked to see the room in disarray and the huge oak desk on its side.

"That desk has to weigh over two hundred pounds!" Alberto exclaimed. "My commanding officer owned one. When he bought it last year, it took four of us to lift that baby and carry it into his office."

Falcon stepped around the overturned desk and picked up an object on the floor. Scanning the room he noticed a long area of lighter paint over the mini bar where the object had been mounted. He walked into the center of the room carrying the heavy bronze broadsword.

Alberto studied the blade of the sword and exclaimed, "That is one cool replica of a medieval sword! Look, there's dried blood on the edges."

Colin walked over and studied the stain, which glittered wetly in the overhead light. "There was a battle here," he stated.

Falcon looked around the room stating, "From the looks of this room, Trey must have pulled the sword off the wall and attacked Raven with it."

"It kind of fits with your idea that Trey was unaware that Valerie was one of Raven's intended victims," Alberto pointed out.

Giselle scanned the room spotting something behind the overturned potted plant. It was a group of photos from a photo mat. She picked it up, looking at the pictures of Trey and Valerie. She handed it to Nicole who looked at it wistfully, commenting, "Trey really cared for her. I'm glad she experienced love before she died."

Falcon found the manila envelope and he and Colin looked at the x-rays. Nicole walked over and observed, "If those x-rays are Trey's, his body is riddled with cancer. I have a friend who's a radiologist. She showed me her practice x-rays and how to read them."

"What if Raven promised Trey that he would make him immortal?" Falcon asked.

"Raven would want something in exchange," Alberto added.

"The girls," Colin stated. "Ethan told me that Valerie had a casual friend she was e-mailing a lot, some kind of adventurer. His user name was blackbird."

"Henri Raven," Giselle stated in a half-whisper.

"The man who showed up at your apartment, the night Dr. Lugano was attacked," Falcon stated.

"That's why Lugano was looking for him," Giselle said. "Henri Raven is his brother! He must have helped him escape from Katari."

"Dr. Lugano wanted Raven to take Alpha-T," Falcon conjectured.

"He wanted to cure his brother," Colin pointed out.

"Raven must have refused to see my father when he first came here," Giselle guessed.

"He had other plans," Colin added. "He couldn't resist his insatiable need for human blood."

"Raven chose the girls," Falcon suggested. "Trey set them up for him. Trey had no idea he was the Ripper and was going to kill them. Trey must have been the one who tried to kill Damien while Raven was murdering Marian.

"Why would he want to kill Damien?" Colin asked. "The papers stated that there were no witnesses to the murder, just like Tobias asked them."

"Unless Raven put him up to it," Nicole conjectured.

Alberto offered, "Maybe that was the lie."

"I see where you're going with this," Falcon commented. "Raven must have told Trey that it was Damien who killed Valerie. What an ingenious way to cover up Valerie's death and maintain Trey's loyalty."

"Until Marian was killed," Nicole pointed out. "Trey had to realize that Raven was the Ripper when that happened."

"Trey couldn't save Valerie," Giselle stated sadly.

While the others were searching the main office, Nicole, walked quietly into to the washroom to splash water on her face. The circumstances surrounding Valerie's death were becoming more and more horrifying, and she grew dizzy with emotion. When she opened the lavatory door, the sound of the shower startled her. Hot steam had filled the room, making it impossible to see. Backing out of the bathroom, she called out frantically,

"Colin!"

Colin rushed over to Nicole and pulled her out of the steam-filled room. Giselle grabbed a bar towel and dried the shaking woman off.

Falcon motioned for everyone to stand back. Wrapping his hand with a dry towel, he reached around the shower curtain and turned off the tap. When he pulled the shower curtain aside to open the window, he turned away saying, "Oh no!"

Hearing Falcon's shocked voice, Alberto raced over to see if he could help. What he saw made his stomach lurch. Trey had been thrown into the shower and lay like a broken rag doll. His blackened, dead eyes stared out of a bright red face. His skin had burned and peeled from the hot steam. The blood that had dripped into the tub from three large gashes carved into his side was mixed with water, creating a rust-colored stream whirling around the drain. Curiously, blackbird feathers stuck on the ceiling and walls, floated downward once they began to dry.

Colin peered into the shower and cried, "God help him!" With trembling hands and shaky legs, he commended his soul to the Creator, adding, "It looks like Trey finally did the right thing and refused to help Raven. It cost him his life, but perhaps this last, selfless act saved his soul."

"Trey didn't know that Damien is alive," Giselle stated. "He wasn't directly responsible for anyone's death."

Falcon motioned for Giselle to stay with Nicole. Falcon blinked several times trying to get the picture of Trey's face out of his thoughts. He closed the bathroom door and said in a pensive voice, "Keepers are usually loners, but often have pets to keep them company. It looks like Raven brought a large crow with him to rattle Trey." Shaking off the gruesome sight, Falcon turned to Alberto requesting, "Al call 911 and report the murder."

Turning to the others Falcon requested, "Search the office. Collect all the evidence you can before the police get here." Falcon hoped this distraction would get their minds off Trey's brutally murdered body in the other room.

Outside in the car, Rufus was barking, howling and scratching on the door to get out. His superior sense of smell had detected the suspicious odor of smoke coming from somewhere in the building. Frantic to warn the others, the dog pushed his snoot on the door handle and let himself out of the Hummer. Jumping down from the vehicle, Rufus loped to the front door. Unable to detect the scent of any of his friends there, he galloped around the side of the building until he saw a light in the office window. Hearing the humans talking excitedly, Rufus stood on two hind legs to reach the window ledge. Balancing with two paws, he gripped onto the sill, peering through the windowpane, he began barking loudly as he saw Falcon and the others picking items off the floor.

"Look," Nicole said, gesturing toward the window. "It's Rufus."

Falcon, who was stuffing files and news clippings into Trey's briefcase, turned to look at the excited dog. The animal was barking frantically, staring at him wildly, Rufus was sensing some danger that they had been too distracted to notice.

"Something's not right," Falcon thought out loud. "Everybody out!" he ordered loudly.

The group moved swiftly towards the exit. Rufus met them at the Hummer whining and howling, pacing nervously until they were in the car. Falcon turned on the engine, backed out of the parking space and pressed the accelerator to the floor. The Hummer's motor screeched and its tires burned rubber as they sped out of the lot and raced away.

An instance later, ear-splitting explosions shook the two buildings and the ground around them. The passengers in the Hummer twisted around, gaping at the searing, flames and billowing, black clouds of smoke that engulfed the office building. Soon, the flames spread to the warehouse, igniting the boxes of stored wine, initiating more thundering blasts. The sky was filled with smoke, fire, and flying debris that could be seen for miles.

Alberto reported the fire then called Antonia to let her know he was okay. She knew he was on the case and would be frantic until she heard from him, especially when a five-alarm fire was probably being reported on a Breaking

News segment. He didn't envy the firemen assigned to such a difficult and dangerous job of extinguishing a fire, which was being fueled minute by minute with alcohol.

"Raven must have set a timed explosion to destroy any evidence of the murder," Falcon commented.

Seeing his wife's face suddenly turn gray, Colin gripped Nicole's hand and put his arm around her trembling shoulders. "Falcon, take us home will you. I want Nicole to rest before we leave for St. James."

"I'm on my way," Falcon agreed, cutting over to Kingshighway Blvd. "I think we've been traumatized enough for one night. We can sift through the evidence later." As he dropped them off at their apartment building he added, "I'll pick you up in three hours. Tell Ethan to be ready."

"If there is a memorial service for Tobias, Nicole and I want to be there." Colin offered as he and Nicole stepped out of the car.

"The second funeral in a month," Giselle commented miserably, as they pulled away from Colin's building. "How many more friends are we going to lose trying to stop that beast?"

"No more," Falcon replied firmly. "We'll make sure of that"

"I got your back," Albert agreed. "We have to find that loco hombre before he hurts anyone else."

Falcon nodded, thinking of what he promised Dr. Montreau. Was it right to turn the killer over to be part of the doctor's rehabilitation experiment? He had made an agreement, but when he came face to face with Raven, he wasn't sure he could keep his end of the bargain. With every fiber in his being, Falcon wanted to kill him.

"I wonder what we can do now." Giselle pondered as they drove to her apartment.

"We haven't been beaten yet." Falcon commented trying to reassure her. So far Raven had been one step ahead of us. Sooner or later, Raven's arrogant belief in his own superiority will cause him to make a critical mistake, and we'll get the upper hand. He almost met his match with Trey. I have great respect for the man. I'm sorry he was killed. He did love Valerie and fought for her in the end."

After dropping Giselle off at her apartment, Falcon took Rufus for a long walk. The happy canine didn't mind wearing his leash, and trotted alongside his master, tongue lolling out, happy to be out in the cold November night. Wanting to expel residual nervous energy, Falcon broke out into a jog. He was pleased to discover that Rufus could easily keep up with his pace. The loyal dog had probably saved all their lives. Without Rufus' warning, Falcon and the others might have tarried, and been killed. Falcon was beginning to understand how one could get used to having a pet around, especially an unusually smart one.

While Falcon jogged home with Rufus trotting amiably at his side, he thought about Al. He had become a valuable ally and friend. He seemed to understand that Trey's obsession with vampires led him to believe they existed. Everyone had skirted around the truth because of Al's presence. Falcon wondered how he was going to tell him about his own peculiar nature. Sooner or later he, or one of the others, would slip and reveal themselves. He worried that once Alberto knew the truth their friendship would come to a screeching halt. A vampire took a calculated risk befriending an Ordinary, even though Ordinaries and Vampires were locked in the same struggle for survival. Whether they were aware of each other or not, they were allies, not enemies.

He packed his suitcase for the trip to the country for Thanksgiving. In an hour, he would pick up Giselle, Ethan,

Colin, and Nicole. Al wasn't going with them. He was spending the holiday with Antonia, and her daughter Maria. For the time being, Falcon was saved from having to tell him too much too soon.

As he loaded the Hummer with his belongings and placed a sleeping pad in the back for Rufus, along with his favorite dog food, Falcon's cell phone rang. Flipping it open he answered, "Falcon, here," Recognizing the voice on the other end he said. "Father Francis, what can I do for you?"

"The memorial service for Mr. Tobias is being held at Abraham Temple, Monday evening at eight, my friend Rabbi Steinberg is giving the service. He would like you to say a few words about your friend."

"It will be an honor to speak about Eli," Falcon answered solemnly. "He was a brave man, and a good friend. We'll all be there."

"I heard an interesting report on the news about the Midwest Mercantile Warehouse fire," Father Francis continued. "That was quite a coincidence, considering you were going to question Trey about Valerie's death."

"Trey was already dead when we got there," Falcon explained. "All the evidence we collected points to the probability that Hawkins unwittingly helped the Ripper. We discovered his name is Henri Raven."

"Henri Raven, Dr. Lugano's brother," Father Francis said. "No wonder Michael was so anxious to find him. His own brother, the Ripper, how terrible for him. As for Trey, he put his trust in the wrong person. How did he die?"

"He died trying to stop the Ripper with a medieval broadsword." Falcon informed him.

"Then he died a valiant death," Father Francis stated. "With God's forgiveness he will meet Valerie again."

"Do you think Raven will be hibernating for a while?" Falcon asked.

"He's created a big disturbance in the city at this point," Father Francis began. "If he's as cunning as I think he is, he'll at least lay low for a while. The city should be safe for a few days."

"By the way, there won't be any evidence connecting Trey to Valerie's death," Falcon informed him.

"That alone will spare Valerie's family more pain," Father Francis replied. "When you get back to the city, stop by. I need to talk to you about something that has been bothering me. My caretaker may not be who he appears to be. He has been acting strangely."

"I'll see you when I get back in town," Falcon agreed. "I have a contact in the FBI that may be able to help research Victor's background for you."

"Thanks Theodore," Father Francis said in relieved tone. "Have a restful holiday."

Falcon locked his apartment building's outer doors and turned on the security alarms. He and Rufus scanned the hallways of the building to make sure that no intruders were lurking in the shadows. They scoured the grounds around the building, checking the locks on the security fences and the four-car garage.

"Come on boy," Falcon commanded. Satisfied that the area was safe he added, "Let's go pick up the others."

Once Rufus was safely ensconced in the way back, Falcon looked at him in the rear view mirror saying, "Thanks pal. Thanks for saving our lives."

The Great Dane looked back at his master with luminous eyes, gave a little contented sigh, and stared out the window at the passing scenery.

Chapter 20

When Father Francis got off the phone with Falcon, he lowered his head deep in thought. Trey's death was troubling to him. The man had been in love with Valerie. Francis was convinced Trey had been tricked by Raven. He knew Falcon would explain the details of what happened after the holiday weekend. In the meantime, he prayed for the fire and police personnel who had to deal with murder and arson on this dreadful night in the city.

There was a knock at his study door and Victor, the church caretaker, popped his head in to say, "I saw your light on and brought you some tea."

Father Francis looked over at him with a slight smile, replying, "Bring it in by all means, and thank you."

Victor moved slowly holding the teacup and saucer in one hand and his cane in the other. Although only forty, the man was plagued with bouts of painful arthritis and moved with difficulty. Victor had told the priest that he had taken a bad fall as a child, breaking both legs. Because of his family's poverty, he could not receive extensive medical care. As a result of poor healing, Victor was unable to straighten his legs to his full height. Now in middle age his condition was exacerbated by arthritis. He appeared to be in some pain, yet he never complained. Victor set the tea cup down in front of the priest, nodded, and turned to leave.

"Victor, what are your plans for the holiday?" Father Francis asked.

Victor turned his heavily bearded face toward the priest and replied, "Well, I'll take my dinner at the Soup Kitchen on Fourteenth Street. They have a fine Thanksgiving Feast every year. I don't have any relatives, and my only friend, besides you is dead."

Valerie Chouteau had been one of Victor's only friends. She had been the first person to reach out to Victor when he came to work for St. Ignatius Church and School. Valerie, who always had a kind word for Victor, was the only one who could make him smile.

Father Francis had been eager to hire Victor based on Reverend Colin's reference alone. Victor proved to be a hard worker and much stronger than he looked. Whenever there was a fish fry, a wedding banquet, or a bingo night, he single-handedly set up all the chairs and tables, even though the priest had offered the help of the eighth-grade school boys on such occasions.

Father Francis had been thoroughly satisfied with his new, albeit unusual, caretaker until about four weeks ago. It wasn't his daily behavior that was disturbing, because Victor always remained his cheerless, dour, yet respectful self. After Father Francis finished carving pumpkins for the Harvest Festival he had stepped outdoors to get a breath of fresh air. Although it was nearly two in the morning, he spied Victor walking down the sidewalk, moving rather quickly, without his cane. At first the priest attributed this behavior to the caretaker having an especially pain-free day. When Victor displayed similar behavior for several weeks, the priest became troubled, suspecting the caretaker was feigning his infirmities.

After his visit to his family, he would talk to Falcon. He was intuitive about people's motivations. He would be able to help him find out if there was any connection between

Victor and the killings. If anyone could succeed in ending the Ripper's killing spree, Theodore Falcon could, with the grace of God behind him, of course.

A few hours earlier and several miles from the burning warehouse, Raven looked down at his hands, a look of disgust twisting his features. Trey's tainted cancer-ridden blood was still glistening on his fingers. Nevermore, his pet crow, sat on his shoulder eyeing him quizzically. The bird hastily flew up as Raven sped over to the fountain in front of a nearby apartment complex. Although he frantically washed his hands over and over again in the icy cold water, the feelings of revulsion that were churning inside his stomach did not ebb. His nausea was not caused by the horrendous brutality of his attack against Trey, but the realization that his pliable confidant had betrayed him. The weak Ordinary had suddenly acquired some courage and refused to do his bidding. Trey had sacrificed his life, as a result of that decision.

Stopping off at the Rectory to talk to Father Francis, disguised as Victor, help Raven establish an alibi for his whereabouts when the murder and arson occurred. After exchanging pleasantries with the priest, the vampire was eager to work off his mounting frustration. Changing from his caretaker costume, Raven streaked down the street to his garage.

Climbing on his Harley-Davidson Hog, Raven sped away, his black coat flying, his long, bushy hair blowing behind him, the look of a madman on his pale angry face. The rage inside of him was building and he had to alleviate the pressure before he burst. An ugly smile spread on his deaths head continence. His large eyes were deep black holes as he flew west down highway 44 like a demon racing out of hell. The vampire swerved around any driver ahead of him on the road, leaving behind a trail of smoke, dust, and a cacophony of noise, from his bike's overtaxed muffler.

Sixty miles from the city he pulled into the lot of the Half-Moon Roadhouse, which was still open. Its dirt and gravel lot was filled with well-maintained motorcycles. When Raven opened the creaking door of the tavern, it closed behind him with a loud bang, getting everyone's attention. The bikers ceased their raucous chattering to look at the frowning stranger that burst into their bar. The exceedingly tall man, dressed in calf length black leather coat, black, silk shirt, and black jeans, removed his leather skullcap, walked up to the bartender, and demanded a double whiskey. Holding the glass in his large fist, Raven swallowed the burning liquid in one gulp. He then scanned the room like a hungry lion on the savannah.

A huge bald-headed man wearing an open leather vest, revealing a pair of cobras tattooed on his chest, swung his two muscular, sleeve-tattooed arms and sauntered up to Raven with a grimace exhorting, "This is no place for the likes of you." He walked around Raven sizing him up, laughing loudly stating, "We got a private party here, dude, and you're a little too dandified for our list. So, take your trench-coated butt out of here before I make you sorry you were ever born."

Raven placed his empty shot glass on the bar, drew himself up to his full seven foot height, and stared down at the hulk in front of him, as if her were a pesky fly to swat. With one swift movement of his arm he pounded the biker on top of the head. The stunned man toppled over like a fallen tree trunk and lay unconscious.

The other bikers, who had been observing the confrontation, moved closer to get a better look at the man who had beaten their leader. A long-haired biker with a ring in his nose and tattoo of a skull on his bare chest, pushed his way through the crow toward Raven, suddenly reaching out his hand saying,

"Welcome to the Hell on Wheels Club."

Raven shook the man's offered hand and proclaimed, "I'm now your leader by process of elimination." He looked pointedly down at the unconscious man who lay at his feet. After the milling crowd's noisy laughter ebbed, Raven continued with, "If you follow me you'll be known as The Death's Head Crew!"

No one in the room voiced an objection because as he made his bold statement, Raven leapt up in a blur and landed on the bar. Looking down from the gleaming counter, he roared, "Let's Ride!"

Fifty bikers left the bar en masse and mounted their black and silver cycles. Behind them, the Half-Moon Roadhouse suddenly burst into flame as the proprietor and his employees rushed out.

Raven led the unholy caravan of fellow bikers down the road and onto the ramp of I-44 West. He had it on his mind to ride to wine country and visit the Two Brother's vineyard. What he planned to do once he got there he hadn't decided yet. Before Raven had mounted his bike, he had locked eyes with a feisty biker woman, with bright blonde hair sporting tattoos of hearts, skulls, and roses on her shapely arms. She wore black jeans, a skimpy black T-shirt, and a black leather vest with a white skull embroidered on the back. The woman who called herself, Ava, smiled back at him and climbed up behind him placing her arms around his torso.

The bikers shot off down the highway creating a thundering noise, racing as fast as their machines could carry them. Whomever they followed before was forgotten in light of Raven's display of power. They were now his to do with as he pleased.

Chapter 21

It was nearly 3 a.m. when Falcon, Giselle, along with family and friends, reached the Two Brothers Vineyard. Rufus, who had been happily snoring in the way back, popped up when they finally arrived at the Falcon family home, curious about where they were. After the group got out of the Hummer, and Falcon opened the rear door, the gangly canine leaped from the vehicle and darted around the front yard marking every tree and bush.

Everyone grabbed their overnight bags and walked to the front door of the large anti-bellum home. The enormous white frame house had been restored to its original post Civil War ambiance. Walking up the stars of the portico, two forest green doors with oval windows etched with delicate grape vines opened to reveal Falcon's parents, Jonathan and Clara. Behind the couple, hardwood oak floors gleamed in the soft turn of the century lamp light.

"Theodore, come in. It's so good to see you," His mother cried, embracing him and kissing him on the cheek. She turned toward Giselle and said, "Welcome my dear. I assume that you're responsible for the contented look on my son's face?"

"I think so, Mrs. Falcon," Giselle answered, immediately taken with the energetic, petite woman with a short, sandy-colored bob, and large brown eyes.

"Clara, please call me Clara," she admonished the girl gently. "We are going to be such good friends. Let me show you the rest of the house." Turning to Nicole she touched her niece's face saying, "Come along my girl. I'm so sorry about that sweet friend of yours, I really loved her."

"That's where I've seen you before," Giselle stated. "You're Lenoir. I saw a photo of you in Valerie's room. You were helping her hang one of your paintings. I love your big cat paintings. I have several of them in my apartment."

"You've guessed my secret. Lenoir is my middle name. Teddy tells me you are quite an artist yourself," Clara answered. "He described your pastel Tigress for me. She sounds enchanting."

While Giselle was given a guided tour of the Falcon's home, with Nicole following to see the latest décor, the men took the bags upstairs and claimed their rooms. The rooms were elegantly designed to display a World's Fair Era home. Falcon chose the room he grew up in, second floor last door on the left, overlooking the back flower gardens and grounds. Colin and Nicole would use the room across the hall with a clear view of the vineyards.

Fur trees lined the boundaries of the family property, adding a forest green color to the drab brown and gray winter scenery. The stakes and wires of the vineyard were bare of leaves, the grape vines having been cropped for the winter season. Beyond the vineyard were the Quonset huts of the winery. A covered ramp led to the Two Brothers warehouse where the barrels and boxes of wine were stored. Beyond that, on top of a rolling Ozark hill, was his Uncle Frank's large rustic log home, surrounded by tall, stately, pine trees.

When Giselle joined Falcon and gazed languidly out of the large arched windows in room at the winter wonderland outside, the stress, that had been wearing her down, slipped from her shoulders like a heavy weight. Snow had fallen earlier that day and a thin white carpet lay on the countryside, reflecting light from the enormous harvest moon that glowed above the hills.

The room itself took you away to another era, without the noise of trucks, cars, the constant hum of electric appliances, and technology, to a more serene way of life. The elegant four-poster mahogany bed was covered with a handmade white quilt decorated with tiny embroidered red hearts and flowers, with a crocheted lace bed ruffle. Two large red satin covered bolsters and two pink heart shaped bed pillows, invited the guest to cuddle down under the cover for a good days rest. Two colorful Tiffany lamps sat on the tall marble topped bed tables, which gave a lustrous glow to the satiny cream wall paper decorated with tiny red bell-flowers. Thick double lined red Velvet drapes covered the arched windows. The top arch of the glass widows held a flower garden in stained glass.

Giselle hugged Mrs. Falcon in appreciation of the lovely room. "It's perfect. I feel as if I have traveled back to a more sedate time, away from the maddening crowd of the city."

"That was our intention when we bought this old house in the 1940's." Clara Falcon explained. "It had been so neglected, we got it for a fair price and have spent twenty years updating and changing it to reflect the true artistic and architectural style of the era."

Falcon walked into the room with fresh firewood and set the wood in a pile in the fireplace. He carefully opened the flu and set a fire. Using old newspapers, he started the fire, watching as the logs heated up and burst into warmth-giving flames.

Rufus, who had finished his frantic foraging in the old house, yawned widely, made two circles in the front of the fire place, and settled down on a thick maroon area rug.

The contented canine faded off to sleep, listening to the comforting voices of his new family.

"Well," Clara Falcon replied, "I'm off to the kitchen. There's a turkey that needs basting."

"Let me know if I can help you," Giselle suggested.

"Can you whip up a sweet potato casserole?"

"My mom just gave me her traditional sweet potato recipe," Giselle answered smiling.

"Wonderful. I'll put the yams on to boil. Come back in an hour and you can whip up your creation," Clara stated beaming. "Teddy, get in that Hummer of yours and take Giselle on a tour of the vineyards while the moon is still out."

Falcon and Giselle spent the next hour traversing the vineyards, driving up and down country roads, gazing at the shape of the Ozark Mountain ridges through the tall leafless trees. Snow had begun to fall again as the two reached for each other's hands.

"This whole ordeal would be a lot harder without you around," Falcon stated brushing her hand with his lips.

"Maybe this awful situation is why we've become close, so quickly," Giselle replied, her eyes shining.

"When this thing is over, and the Ripper is in a deep dark prison, we have to talk," Falcon said, pulling her into his arms.

When they returned to the family manor, Falcon was pleased to see Zeke's Safari Van parked in the driveway. His brother had promised to bring his fiancé, Barbara to meet the family. Colin's parents would arrive the next evening to share the holiday feast.

While Giselle and Falcon were touring the grounds, Ethan had unearthed his old motorcycle from the shed to take it for a ride. The dark clouds overhead were bursting with snow as Ethan turned on to highway 68. The brisk wind whipped about his face. It was cold, well below freezing, but he wore a knit face covering under his helmet and two layers of clothing under his leather jacket. Fur-lined gloves kept his fingers from going numb. He was speeding down the roadway listening to his favorite song, "Born to Be Wild," on his I-Pod

When Ethan merged on highway forty-four he saw a curious sight. A caravan of fifty bikers sped by him, their mufflers sputtering loudly. Feeling young and impulsive, Ethan turned onto the ramp and raced to catch up with the pack. As he got closer, he noticed their leader, a tall man with long bushy hair and lustrous black eyes. Ethan was convinced he was a vampire, yet his crew seemed to be Ordinaries.

The cold wind whipped against Ethan's face as he increased his speed. It seemed as if he would never catch up with the bikers. He finally saw the tail end of the pack around the next bend. Not wanting to be seen, he pulled back and followed at a slower pace. They rode at breakneck speed, as if their lives depended on arriving at their destination as soon as possible.

They pulled off the highway at Robertsville and entered St. Francis State Park. The park was closed for the winter, but that didn't seem to deter them. When the approached the blocked off entrance they sped up popped wheelies and flew over the obstruction. Some of the bikers leaned low to right themselves. Their pedals scraped the pavement and sparks flew.

Keeping his distance, Ethan maneuvered his more streamlined motorcycle around the barricade and followed the noisy pack deep into the park. Looking at the moonlit Ozark Mountain ridges, he spied a ranger's lookout tower jutting out in stark relief above the white hills. As the pack retreated down the next hill Ethan followed, wondering what the biker's wanted in the park on such a cold night.

A few seconds later, as he hit the top of the rise, he saw the bikers again. They had stopped in a clearing, and were busily gathering firewood. Hiding himself in a grove of fir trees, Ethan studied the crew as they laid a fire. Huge logs were placed around the fire for long seats. Setting up camp and starting a bonfire out of season was illegal. Aside from that, they were facing a winter storm that would dump ice and snow on them in a few hours.

Ethan watched as the pack's leader began waving his arms and shouting at them. He towered over the seated bikers giving order like a general addressing his troops. His gestures and deep baritone voice seemed vaguely familiar to Ethan as he studied the man. A sudden revelation nearly bowled him over. The leader of the pack fit the description of Henri Raven, the man Giselle had described in her text messages filling him in about the brutal murder of Trey Hawkins. Moreover, according to Falcon, Raven was the Ripper who killed Valerie and the other young women.

Walking his cycle through the trees, he moved in closer to the group. Most of the bikers were drinking beer, and talking loudly. A voluptuous woman with waist length hair was drawing Raven away from the group. Taking his hand, she smiled up at him, leading him to a secluded spot.

Ethan leaned his motorcycle against a tree and traversed the forest until he could clearly see the couple under a pine tree with low hanging branches. The woman had pulled the tall man down onto the pine needles and they were embracing. Suddenly a moonlit kiss turned into a struggle, the woman's legs began floundering and kicking. Within seconds, she stopped moving. Raven was hunched over the woman's side, probably imbibing in her warm, fresh blood.

Infuriated, Ethan crashed through the bushes and hit the vampire over the head with a heavy log he had found nearby. A choking sound erupted from the startled man's throat. He turned his head with a grimace to see who had assaulted him. Raven gave Ethan a look of outrage before his eyes rolled back in his head, and he lay still on the snow-covered grass.

Ethan squatted down to check the girl finding her pulse perilously weak. Raven had already drained several pints of her blood. Running back to his bike he dialed Dr. Montreau, asking him to send his emergency van.

He took a cable from his tool kit, attaching one hooked end to the prone vampire's belt. Climbing on his bike he started the motor moving slowly, dragging Raven closer to the road. The members of the pack seemed uninterested in looking for their boss while he was with a woman, which gave Ethan time to take him away. Ethan dragged the unconscious vampire across land, away from the gang's bonfire.

He called the state police informing them about the illegal rendezvous in order to disperse the bikers. The authorities would find the camp long after the emergency vehicle got the unconscious girl to the hospital. He had explained to Dr. Montreau that she lost a lot of blood and would need several transfusions. He then dialed his cousin, Falcon, and told him he had captured Raven at St. Francis state park.

Falcon entered the park from the opposite direction, leaving his headlights off. As he rambled in, he was relieved to see the gang of bikers scatter after hearing police sirens in the distance. Together Falcon and Ethan lifted Raven into the car, throwing him face first onto the back seat. Rufus growled when he saw the vampire and guarded him watchfully as they drove away. The two cousins decided to drive back to the farm, drop off the bike, and then take the killer to Renfield Sanitarium.

Raven didn't move as they secured him with a heavy cable. Ethan found a bottle of chloroform in the Keeper's pocket, wetted a rag, and applied it to the vampire's nostrils. He would be kept unconsciousness for the whole trip.

Falcon examined the tattoo on Raven's limp forearm. It matched the photo Gary had blown up from Valerie's cell photos; a golden ankh with a swastika in its top loop. Falcon couldn't fathom why anyone would want such a tattoo, but it was a fitting symbol for a psychotic Keeper who thrived on hatred. It proved without a doubt that Henri Raven was the Central West End Ripper.

Minutes later the van from Faith Hospital arrived and removed the injured woman. The ambulance sped back to the hospital, lights flashing and siren blaring. The two men watched as the van pulled away, relieved the biker woman would be taken care of discretely. Once she was healed, she would be released, remembering little about the reason for her confinement.

Falcon flipped opens his vibrating cell phone, and answered his brother, "Hey Zeke. Sorry I missed you. I'm dealing with a situation."

"Is everything okay?" Zeke asked worriedly.

"Ethan and I caught the Ripper," Falcon replied. "He's all tied up for the moment. We're taking him to Renfield."

"The Central West End Ripper is all the way out here?" Zeke asked. "I guess things got too hot for him in the city. What are you going to do with him?"

"I wanted to kill him, but Dr. Montreau needs him for his experiments," Falcon commented.

"Would that experiment have anything to do with what we talked about my last visit?" Zeke asked hopefully.

"I can tell you this it's definitely related to our discussion," Falcon said.

"I don't think I have your restraint bro," Zeke replied. "Are you sure he won't wake up?"

"No danger of that," Falcon answered. "I gave him a dose of his own chloroform. It was enough to knock out an elephant. Rufus is standing over him right now watching his every move."

"Who's Rufus?" Zeke asked, curiously.

"A Great Dane I found at Forest Park," Falcon replied.

"You need my help?" Zeke asked.

"Not necessary," Falcon answered, "I have the orb you lent me. If all else fails, I'll zap him until he glows. Stay by mom and dad. Let them know what's going on. We'll see you later."

An hour later, Raven was safely locked behind a reinforced steel door in a secured room behind four, rubber-lined twelve-inch thick, reinforced concrete walls. A bomb could have dropped nearby, and Raven would have been unscathed. Dr. Knepper, the night physician, would monitor Raven's medication to make sure he remained unconscious, until Dr. Montreau arrived later that night.

While driving back to the farm, Falcon turned to Ethan saying, "I'm glad you stayed calm. One false move and I was ready to go medieval on him."

"The only thing stopping me is Dr. Montreau's experiment," Ethan commented soberly. "Something good has to come out of Valerie's death. After the experiment is finished, Raven better find a deep, dark catacomb, and hide there the rest of his life"

"Becoming a lab rat for Dr. Montreau's maze of treatments is what he deserves," Falcon replied. "Once the tests are over,

I'm sure the Freeblood Court will decide his fate. Fortunately we didn't have to use Plan B to stop the Ripper."

"What was Plan B?" Ethan asked.

"Plan B was Giselle's idea," Falcon returned. "She was going to use herself as bait."

"I'm glad it didn't come to that," Ethan stated, "Enough young women have died because of that homicidal maniac. Besides, if he had hurt Giselle you would have ripped his head off with your bare hands."

"Let's just say there wouldn't have been anything left to experiment on," Falcon agreed.

When the men returned from Renfield, The Falcon family and friends spent the rest of the Thanksgiving holiday enjoying each other without dwelling on the Ripper and his victims.

Barbara, Zeke's fiancée, a statuesque, hazel-eyed beauty with a lovely smile, had a refreshing knack for making everyone laugh. Giselle and Nicole listened in rapt attention as she described her life as a Las Vegas showgirl. After her discourse, she explained that the showgirl part of her life was over. She had already enrolled in nursing school for the spring term.

As his family chatted happily over Thanksgiving dinner, Falcon acknowledged to himself that he had a lot to be thankful for; the family was in good health, they were getting along peacefully, a beautiful young woman now shared his life, and the monster that had terrorized the city had finally been caught, and the secret community of Freebloods was safe. In spite of this, a persistent feeling of dread kept gnawing at his peace of mind. The relative ease of the Ripper's capture was troubling.

Chapter 22

While Falcon's family and friends dined on a delicious Thanksgiving feast, Raven was sitting on the hard cement floor leaning against the padded wall of his cell. He was swathed in a straight jacket and his pale face showed little emotion. His dark eyes could barely be seen under their half-mast lids. Heavy sedation had been administered every three hours.

When Raven was conscious again, Dr. Montreau utilized his first interview with his newest patient to explain the procedures that would follow. He sat in a chair facing the seemingly docile Keeper explaining, "You will be given a special elixir every two hours while we observe any side-effects as they occur. The chemistry of the liquid will replace your need for blood from any source. You will no longer have an addiction to warm blood of any kind."

Raven stared up at Dr. Montreau, stating emphatically, between clenched teeth, "You incompetent fool. I don't drink human blood because I have to. I do it because I want to! It's my right!"

"I'm well aware of what you think your rights are," Dr. Montreau stated. "In time, you will no longer be able to stomach real blood. With repetition and training you will learn behaviors that are accepted by civilized beings, and be of no danger to others."

"Ordinaries are not beings," Raven commented coldly, "they're food." Looking down at his shackled wrists and feet he added calmly, "I will get out of here, my friend."

"I'm not your friend," Montreau countered, "I'm your psychiatrist. I know you tried to kill your brother using your influence on the lions. If you weren't part of this experiment, I would dispatch you myself. Michael is my friend. He has so much more to offer the world, even though you tried to rob him of his existence. You better hope that he lives, and as long as you cooperate with me, you'll live. After the test results are confirmed, you will be remanded to the Midwestern Vampire Court and judged by your peers. They will not be as humane towards you as we have been."

"Peers?" Raven asked, with wide and piercing eyes, "I have no peers. No one on this world is my equal."

"Nevertheless, I wouldn't count on the court being merciful, considering all the people you wantonly killed without mercy," Dr. Montreau returned. Preparing to leave, he added, "By the way you might as well drink your elixir and eat your food. You won't get another meal until tomorrow evening." As Dr. Montreau locked the steel door behind him, he could still hear Raven's ranting.

"I'll get out of here!" the vampire raged. "I'll have my revenge! I'll bleed you and your cohorts dry!"

As the doctor retreated down the long hall, a small, wizened figure darted from the shadows. The creeping man stood up on his tiptoes and peered in the tiny five by five window of Raven's cell. Knocking on the window to get the vampire's attention he mouthed the words, "Don't worry master. Old Beau will get you out of here," Beau moved hurriedly to the stairwell and crept back to his room.

He had been admitted to the hospital for alcohol addiction three days earlier. Smiling to himself, Beau removed a bottle hidden under a lose slat in the floor of his closet. He drained the rest of the cheap wine, and whispered aloud, slurring his words, "The master will remember me when I bust him out of here, he won't break his promise."

Tossing the empty bottle behind the extra blanket on the closet shelf, Beau went over his plan for Raven's escape in his mind. When the doctor made his rounds the next evening, he would be ready. He chuckled to himself when he thought of how easy it was to get out of his room. He had wadded up a piece of soap and stuck it in the door jam. As a result, the dead bolt failed and the door opened easily. After the orderly left with his dinner tray, he hid in the pantry until two am.

"Just because I'm a drunk, doesn't mean I'm stupid," Beau complained aloud to know one in particular. "Folks always think I'm a retard. No retard could have survived on the streets as long as I have."

Shuffling back to his room, he closed the door and lay on the bed waiting for sleep to come. The next day would be long and boring; they would wake him at the crack of dawn, make him swallow some pills, eat breakfast, go to the group meeting, hand him two more pills while the orderly watched with beady eyes. He would be forced to listen to other drunks share their horror stories about booze. Beau laughed to himself thinking of the good sob story he would relate to play along. After lunch he would sneak in the pantry and find the bottle he had lifted from an orderly's locker.

"Stupid uniform thought he could keep his stuff secure using a simple lock and key," Beau commented aloud.

Using a paper clip he had scammed from the nurse's station, Beau had easily opened the lock, and stolen the wine. One drinker could always tell another. Jimmie, the lumbering, overweight orderly, had red eyes early in the morning, and took a swig any chance he could get. Beau could smell it on his breath. Did he think one breath mint could hide that scent from a die-hard boozer like himself?

The next evening when he was taken to Dr. Montreau's office, and as usual, the doctor asked the hulking orderly to wait outside. Beau thought the doctor was okay for a medical type. In fact, Dr. Montreau was one of the few people who spoke to him man to man. He almost felt guilty for playing him for a fool. Shuffling into the room, Beau sidled around the large metal desk and shook the doc's hand. Like a gentleman, the doc stood up and gripped his offered hand. When Beau feigned dizziness, a true side effect of the heavy medication he was taking, Dr. Montreau held onto him until he was steady. While the doctor was worrying about his patient falling, Beau deftly lifted the keys from his pocket.

"I think its time to reduce your meds," Doc said pleasantly as Beau took his seat in front of his desk. "You've been eating well and complying with the program."

"Thanks doc, the meds make me awful dizzy and sick to my stomach," Beau replied breathing hard. "When do I get out of here?" he asked. "I want to play checkers with my friend Damien, and I miss my bed at the mission."

"You're happy at the mission?" Dr. Montreau asked gently.

"Yeah, Ms. Nicole is teaching me how to make bread," Beau replied inanely.

"If you're doing as well on 20 milligrams as you've done on 40, you'll be ready to leave soon," Dr. Montreau assured him.

"Sure thing Doc," Beau said getting up to leave. He turned around and looked at the doctor levelly saying, "I appreciate all you've done for me. I know my life is going to change real soon."

Beau appeared to be sleeping soundly, even snoring, as Derrick the night orderly walked by and peered into his room. Once the orderly had made it to the other end of the hall, he went back to the nurse's station to talk with Renee Johnson, the night nurse he was sweet on. Beau popped up, climbed out of bed and went to the door. Pushing the door gently, the dead bolt disengaged, and Beau escaped into the dim hallway. Checking the area carefully, Beau minimized his body by scooting along the wall hiding in the shadows, like Raven had shown him. When he reached the stairwell, he opened the security door with one of Dr. Montreau's keys and ducked inside, holding the door until it shut quietly.

The rest was easy. He walked down the stairs and quickly looked through the steel-meshed security window of the lock down ward. Seeing no one about, Beau opened the door and scooted inside. Raven's room was the last one on the right. Tiny cameras moved back and forth, but Beau had that covered too. He had scammed a scrub suit and white coat from the employee's locker room and walked confidently like he belonged there. His head was lowered, scanning the medical papers on the clipboard he had taken.

Beau rapped gently on the window and peered into Raven's room. The vampire was sitting in the corner, hidden in the shadows. Only his pale, rugged face with its piercing eyes could be seen. Beau swallowed nervously because the sight made him think of a floating skull he had seen in a horror movie when he was a kid. When the door swung inward Beau jumped back, Raven was already there, towering in front of him. How did he get there so fast? Beau thought. His teeth chattered uncontrollably despite his attempts to remain calm.

In another part of the city, Doctor Montreau was getting out of his car in front of his Lindell home. He reached into his pocket to unlock the front door, and realized he didn't have his clinic keys. Did he leave them locked in his desk again? He was sure he locked the office door behind him. As he rapidly went over the day's agenda in his mind, he recalled Beau's dizzy spell and how he had supported his swaying body until it passed. Did the street-smart patient lift his keys? Did Raven know Beau? Frantic at this sudden insight, Montreau called the hospital and asked them to check Raven's room and initiate the alarm system. Placing the flashing red emergency light on the top of his car, the doctor sped back to the sanitarium.

Raven looked down at Beau with a slight smile on his ghostly face. The vampire hadn't fed on real blood in days and felt weakened by the bitter tasting elixir Dr. Montreau had authorized for him. Did the man really think that such a gross concoction could pass for the sweet taste of pulsating warm blood? What kind of weak vampire was Dr. Montreau anyway? Turning swiftly, he headed for the stairwell.

Suddenly, the shrill sound of an alarm nearly deafened his sensitive ears. In one swift motion, he was bounding up the stairs, slamming his body against the door to the roof, knocking it off its hinges, and squeezing past the broken door.

Beau scrambled frantically after him, whispering, "Why are we going up on the roof? How are we going to get out that way?"

Once on the roof Raven ran from one end to the other scanning the grounds below. Unaware of the vampire's unusual escape route, orderlies were scouring the halls, rooms, stairwells, and grounds for the two escaped patients. Raven grabbed Beau, and both dashed quickly to hide behind one of the many chimneys on the rooftop. Unable to find the missing patients, the two orderlies got into the emergency van and roared down the street.

Raven stood up and walked to the edge of the building that faced a wooded glen: part of the natural scenery that was supposed to calm the patients as they looked out the windows or went on their daily outdoor walks.

Before Beau could react, Raven leaped off the edge of the four-story building, landed on two feet with knees bent, and instantly sprang up to a standing position. Raven gazed up at Beau who stared down at him in consternation. A helpless expression lingered on his aged face as he stood near the edge of the roof.

"Jump my friend," Raven ordered. "Jump! You can trust me!" Raven coaxed, staring up at Beau's hesitant form.

With blind faith, Beau jumped, plummeting downwards, his baggy hospital clothes flapping in the wind. Within seconds, his body slammed onto the pavement, landing within inches of Raven's feet. A pool of blood formed under the back of his head. Beau's eyes were glazing over as Raven squatted down and whispered into his ear.

"I kept my promise old man, I have changed your life," The vampire stated bluntly. Ripping Dr. Montreau's keys from the dead man's fingers, Raven located an ambulance in the parking lot, started the engine, and raced away.

Raven drove to the city impound, and abandoned the vehicle on the street. Climbing the chain link fence he searched the parking area for his motorcycle. Removing the secret key hidden under the fender of the front tire he started the engine idling quietly down the drive. Once past the entrance he revved the engine, the cycle tires squealing, as he roared off the exit ramp. He popped a wheelie and crashed through the exit barricade. Still undiscovered, the vampire casually drove two blocks and parked in his private garage two blocks from St. Ignatius' church.

Before he arrived at the side entrance of the church Raven put his black hood over his dark hair, and slumped down. Dragging his right leg, he assumed his caretaker persona. After he passed through the doorway, he sighed, stretched, and stood up. Pulling a gray wig from under the pillow on his bed, Raven carefully placed it on his head, shoving his thick black hair underneath. Adding a tinted melanin cream to the exposed skin on his face and neck Raven was able to transform his ghostly pallor to a swarthy brown. Taking the salt and pepper colored mustache and beard from a hidden panel in the chest of drawers, he carefully glued them in place. He wore his disguise throughout the night in case Father Francis required his help.

The digital clock on his bed table read 5 am. The sun was burning over the horizon as he sat down on his small, but comfortable bed. His stomach growled incessantly, but there was no time to feed, instead he grabbed the newspaper to read. Raven's eyes soon became riveted to an article in the Metro section. Underneath the photo of a familiar young woman, surrounded by a group of pre-teens, was the caption:

"Nicole Falcon, co-owner of the Redeemer Mission, and the popular, Java Heaven, a non—for profit coffee house, volunteers to take the winning team of the Giving Project Contest to the Winter Holiday Zoo Party, Tuesday December 1st. The special holiday project is sponsored by the St. Louis Archdiocese. The Zoo has earmarked proceeds from the special event for the homeless in the metropolitan area."

The raven-haired woman in the picture had the face of an angel. There was something vaguely familiar about her, and Raven didn't know why. He had only seen her a few times when he had accompanied Valerie to the Redeemer mission. Licking his lips, the vampire sighed and tried to fall asleep, his belly was nearly empty and his metabolism was slowing down. "Relax," he told himself, "in two more days you'll feast like a hungry lion." Since his weak Ordinary was dead, he would just have to locate a suitable meal all by himself.

Getting up slowly from a semi-conscious state, Raven's hibernation instinct told him to return to his cave at the zoo. Retreating to his secret den, would give him a chance to heal more quickly.

He smiled at how correct his brother had been when he observed that he preferred the company of big cats, over those of his own kind. The reason for this idiosyncrasy was simple: he knew what to expect from the large felines. They displayed no guile and held no secrets. When he entered their domain, they accepted him as the alpha male, and behaved accordingly.

Chapter 23

After a quick visit to Faith Hospital to check on Dr. Lugano's condition, Falcon decided to pay a visit to the lion habitat at the St. Louis Zoo. It was nearly dawn, yet he was hopeful he would catch Raven returning to the den for hibernation, as Dr. Montreau had suggested.

Falcon scaled the sixteen-foot stone barrier near Big Cat Country, jumped down the other side, and took the walkway the lion's habitat. Leaping across the safety moat, he landed silently on the grassy hillside near the den. Pausing a moment, he took a deep breath and entered the mouth of the man-made cave.

As Falcon moved silently in the darkness, the male lion rose to his feet and ambled quietly toward him with a warning growl. Falcon was prepared for such a response and calmly took the raw T-bone steak in his coat pocket from its plastic bag, laid it down on the soft dirt floor, and backed away.

The lion looked at the meat suspiciously at first, gingerly sniffed it. Finding the succulent meat acceptable, he ate it with relish. When he ate his fill, the females of his pride trotted over and consumed their share. Happily satiated, the male lion padded over to Falcon sniffing him curiously. Deciding the vampire was not a threat, he allowed Falcon to stroke his thick, curly mane.

Proceeding further into the den, Falcon scanned the area carefully while stirring the hay and dirt around with his boot. He gingerly touched a spot of freshly dug soil.

Crawling on all fours, Falcon dug into the moist soil with a hand spade. As the ground gave way, he found himself sliding into a hole. He controlled his speed by fully extending his arms and pressing the sides of the tunnel with his fists. Landing upright on two feet, Falcon scanned the area. He paused when he spied Raven's empty sleeping mat and supply of bottled water. His nostrils twitched as he smelled the vampire's nearly rancid stash of raw meat; too old for Falcon's taste, but acceptable to a hungry Keeper deprived of human blood. Raven was quite amenable to living like a wild animal. Although he disagreed with the Keeper's methods, Falcon could understand his instinct to survive at all costs. After all, they shared a common ancestry.

Using his vampire agility, Falcon repelled upward. Grabbing the edges of the hole, he pulled himself out. As he walked by the resting pride, the lions yawned sleepily and watched him leave, their tails twitching and their eyes drooping. Once outside, Falcon took deep breaths of the cold, pre-dawn air, relieved to be free of the musty odors of the den.

As he prepared to leap across the chasm of the safety moat, he hesitated, sensing someone behind him. He whirled around just in time to see Raven rushing towards him. The two men crashed into each other, dropping near the edge. Rolling over and over, they tumbled feet first into the moat, still clutching each other's throats. Falcon pressed down on the vampire's neck constricting the arteries until his eyes began to bulge. Frantic and nearly out of oxygen, Raven brought his knees up and rammed them into Falcon's jaw, sending him flying against the cement wall. Backing away swiftly, the Keeper stood up and brushed the dirt off his clothes.

"This is not your business, Freeblood," Raven stated, watching Falcon rise unsteadily.

"You attacked and brutally killed five women in my city. That makes it my business!" Falcon exclaimed.

"Your excessive outrage at the death of a few Ordinaries makes me think there is more here than a territorial dispute," Raven said. "Perhaps your rage is inflamed by jealousy over the lovely Giselle. After all, I knew her before you."

"Don't try subterfuge with me," Falcon stated, glaring back at him. "You used the lions to try and kill your own brother! No one is safe with you around. Your carcass is mine!"

"Nevermore!" Raven commanded. Mimicking the raucous cry of a crow, he looked to the sky.

Suddenly the gray dawn was filled with the sound of hundreds of flapping wings. A teeming flock of blackbirds swooped down toward Falcon, their pointed beaks racing toward him like stilettos. Remembering the torn face of Trey Hawkins, Falcon covered his head with his hood and flattened himself to the ground, sliding and crawling until he could climb out of the ditch. He sped to a nearby concession stand, ramming his shoulder against the door. He scrambled inside slamming the door and holding it shut. Outside, the deafening sound of hundreds of birds thudding against the flimsy walls of the building, reverberated throughout the park.

Finally, when he thought he would go insane, the nerve-wracking crowing and incessant thunder of beating wings, died away. Falcon left his sanctuary and raced back to confront Raven, but he was gone. The avian attack had given him time to escape. Frustrated that the Keeper had once again eluded him, he swiftly scaled the walls of the zoo entrance, running back to his apartment at top speed.

Chapter 24

It was early December, and although the Raven was still at large, Nicole looked over at her husband Colin stating, "I promised to take the winners of the Giving Contest to the Winter Party at the Zoo, do you think we should cancel?"

"I just talked to Falcon," Colin said. "Raven was hiding out in the lion's habitat but he's convinced he won't return. One of the Freeblood Zookeepers, Nathan Wolf, agreed to guard Big Cat Country to make sure. There will be plenty of security and hundreds of people, I don't think Raven will attack in a crowd like that, but I would feel safer if you took someone along. I wish I could go, but I have the men's prayer group."

"Valerie was supposed to come with me," Nicole reminded him. "The kids loved her. They'll be sad about that. Whom could I ask at this late date?" she added, morosely.

"Ask Giselle," Colin suggested. "You two seem to hit it off well."

"Why didn't I think of that?" Nicole wondered aloud. "I'll call her." As Nicole dialed Giselle's number, she remembered Falcon telling her about Giselle's gutsy attack on the stalker in Forest Park.

"Giselle, this is Nicole," she said, after her friends voice registered a cheerful hello, "Are you busy tonight?" she continued.

"Not at all," Giselle answered. "What's up girlfriend?"

"How would you like to join me and six great kids for the Winter Party at the Zoo tonight?"

"Sounds like fun," she replied. "What time should I be ready?"

"I'll pick you up at six," Nicole replied, quickly adding, "Thanks for being such a good friend."

"I'm glad you thought of me," Giselle returned. "See you later."

A little before six pm, Nicole pulled in front of Giselle's apartment with six excited pre-teens. After she introduced the group to Giselle, they drove to Forest Park. The Zoo sparkled with colorful twinkle lights and decorations. As they walked into the main entrance, two of Santa's elves handed out programs for the evening's activities. Police and security guards were a welcomed presence throughout the park.

After the group signed their names in the giant wish book, they headed for the banquet in the Lakeside Restaurant. Guests were already waiting in the buffet line to pick their favorite foods from the splendid array of culinary delights, including two giant turkeys with all the trimmings. By the time Nicole's group went through the line, their plates were overflowing with good foods. Zoo volunteers in safari wear took their order for soft drinks.

Kevin, a young boy of twelve, wearing a multicolored knit cap, looked over at Nicole with big brown eyes, and announced through a bite of toasted ravioli swimming in marinara sauce, "I want to see Big Cat Country."

Sierra jumped in saying, "Me too, then, I want to see the elephants, and the gorillas."

"I have a great idea." Nicole stated. "Let's see the Living World first, then head for the new sting-ray exhibit. After that, we can follow the guide and see all the animals you want."

"Sounds like a good plan," Giselle agreed. "Where are the rays?"

"Between the Lakeside Café and the Living World," Nicole informed her. "It's a special opening for the holidays that will be expanded this summer."

The Stingray's at Caribbean Cove was the newest interactive exhibit for visitors to enjoy at the Zoo. Giselle read the description about the exhibit while the children were eating dessert: "There are 28 cow nose rays and seven southern stingrays, swimming in the 17,000 gallon, warm, saltwater pool. Before petting the rays, visitors have to wash their hands to clean off foreign substances that might contaminate them," Giselle said, pausing to enjoy a bite of raspberry ice. She continued with, "The Aquatic Zoo Keepers will show us the proper way to pet the rays when we get to the exhibit"

Ellie, a tiny eleven year old with short African braids and dark brown eyes looked over at Nicole and asked, "Will they sting us?"

"Not if you pet them properly," Nicole replied. Gazing across the table she asked, "Does the pamphlet say anything about that Giselle?"

"The rays have their stingers clipped," Giselle explained, "kind of like when we clip our nails, so they won't hurt anyone. The pamphlet goes on to say that rays can't bite because their teeth are way up inside their mouths. It also says that they love to swim really fast, stirring up the water. Watch out you might get splashed!" she added mirthfully.

"Is a stingray a fish?" Tommy, a tow headed boy with glasses asked.

"They're related to sharks and skates," Nicole stated, scanning the brochure. "They aren't scary and dangerous like some sharks though. Did you know that many types of rays are endangered species?" she continued. "Does anyone know what that means?"

Gregory, a tall pensive boy, put his spoon down saying, "I think it means they might die and never come back, if people don't stop killing them"

"That's right," Giselle agreed. "I think it's sad that Sting Rays get killed when they're accidentally trapped in nets used to catch other kinds of fish."

"When you're done with dessert, please clean up your area," Nicole announced to the group. "While Giselle and I are finishing our coffee, you can go out on the deck and look at the lake, but make sure you stay where we can see you, and don't wonder off. Gregory, I'm putting you in charge," she added. She smiled as the group obediently walked off with Gregory in the lead.

While the children were looking at the sparkling lake illuminated with colorful torches, Nicole and Giselle sat side-by-side, sipping their coffee and keeping an eye on the children through the large picture windows.

"You're great with kids, Nicole," Giselle commented.

"You are too," Nicole said smiling back at her. "Valerie planned on coming with us tonight," she commented sadly. "The kids miss her, but I think they're happy you came to help. They're having a great time."

"Thanks for letting me be Valerie's stand in," Giselle commented, touching Nicole's arm.

"You're not just a stand in," Nicole assured her. "You're becoming my new best friend. I hope you don't mind."

"Really" Giselle asked, beaming at her. "I never had a best friend, and I don't have any sisters. Someday I hope we'll be both."

"Is Falcon going to propose to you soon?" Nicole asked.

"I hope by this time next year, but if not, I fully intend to ask him," Giselle replied with a ghost of a smile.

"You might have to," Nicole stated. "He's definitely in love with you, but he's scared. He could use a healthy nudge in that direction."

The group's first stop was the Living World, one of the favorite interactive exhibits at the Zoo all year round. There were a variety of animal displays designed to intrigue and educate students of all ages. The two women interacted with the group when they asked questions. At the arachnid section, the spiders were met with shudders and gasps, but the children were awed by the amazing designs of their intricate webs.

Nicole and Giselle led the group to the Sting Ray exhibit where the children spent an hour petting the rays and watching their antics in the pool. When they got splashed with warm salt water, they laughed and went back for more. The attendants gave them towels to dry off with before going back out into the cold weather.

After leaving the exhibit, Nicole decided to split the group in half. Each adult would take three children and explore the outdoor animal exhibits they were interested in. Nicole chose Brandon, Ellie, and Shannon, while Giselle would lead, Gregory, Tommie and Sierra. They agreed to rendezvous in an hour at the Lakeside Restaurant, for hot chocolate and the sing-along holiday finale.

Nicole took the road to the left and walked up the hill toward Big Cat Country. The trail was well-lighted and wound around huge boulders. Brandon pointed to the cage in front of him, and everyone marveled as the female panther stared down at the group from a tree branch above their heads. The animal appeared to be lying sleepily between the branches of thick trunk, her tail twitching lazily, but her large yellow and black eyes were riveted on the children's every movement. Nicole stared at Panther without blinking, until the female turned away and stopped tracking them.

A shadowy form, moving atop the boulders in the Tiger habitat, caught Nicole's attention. She walked ahead of the children, wondering why a trainer was walking in the exhibit thinking, "Surely the zookeeper's feed the animals before the children come to the park."

Suddenly the figure leapt down to a lower rock formation, crouching silently as Nicole and the children walked by. She could feel eyes studying her as she stared into the darkness. Getting the children's attention, she urged them to turn back the other way towards the crowd of people. Motioning to Giselle she cried, "Take them to the concession stand!"

In spite of their disappointed protests, Giselle led the children toward the lighted concession stand saying, "Are you coming too?"

"I'll be right there." Nicole replied trying not to show concern in her voice. "I have to check something out first. Make sure the children are safe."

After Giselle nodded, Nicole turned toward the shadows demanding, "I know you're there. Show yourself and stop playing games."

The dark figure jumped down and was upon her within seconds. Nicole twisted and strained, trying desperately to escape the being that enveloped her and lifted her from her feet. A large gloved hand clamped an acrid tasting rag over her mouth. She tried to hold her breath, but a few minutes later, she was forced to breath in the noxious chemicals.

Within seconds, everything went dark, and she felt herself go limp in her abductor's arms.

When Nicole awakened, she was locked in the small damp room of a basement. A single, naked bulb pierced the darkness with a small orbit of light. The room consisted of four windowless cement walls and a locked door. Its only furnishings were a narrow bed and a small wooden table. Her hands and feet were bound with rope and the gag, tasting of blood and chloroform, was still on her mouth. Tears sprung to her eyes as she bowed her head. She prayed that the children were safe, and somehow, she would make it back home. She thought to herself miserably, "When I get out of here alive, the first thing I'm going to do is tell Colin how much I love him."

Nicole rose to a sitting position and swung her legs over the side of the bed. The wrist restraints were not as tight as she first thought. She began rubbing her hands together to create heat friction, hoping that if her hands became sweaty, she might be able to squeeze out of her bonds. She breathed heavily through her nose, trying not to think about how smelly the gag was, and how much she felt like vomiting.

A ray of hope lifted her spirits as she spied a splintered piece of wood on the door, above the tarnished brass knob. Rolling off the bed and standing up, Nicole hopped the three feet to the door, lifting her wrists until the rope snagged the sharp splinter of wood. Sawing back and forth, she managed to break several layers of twine. Working so tenaciously, sent rivulets of sweat pouring down her face. She bent her head forward letting the perspiration drip her wrists. The rope soon became slippery, and she was able to twist and tug, freeing one hand and then the other. She took out the gag and dropped it on the floor with relief. Hopping carefully back to the cot, she sat down, and freed her ankles from their bonds.

She heard a noise outside the door and viciously hit the lone bulb above her with her shoe, jumping away as it popped and shattered. Flattening herself to the wall behind the door, she waited, holding her boot heel forward.

The door opened slowly, creaking at the hinges. Nicole got a glimpse of her kidnapper through the crack in the door. Swallowing hard she raised her boot heel higher and higher. Her attacker was so tall that he had to bend his head to get through the door. "It's the Ripper" was the thought that came to Nicole's terrified mind. Fear was replaced with anger and Nicole gritted her teeth. When the attacker cleared the doorway, she jumped up and stuck him in the face so hard with her boot heel that she rebounded and fell to the floor. Instead of a crying out in pain, the Ripper let out an amused laughter that bounced off the walls of the room.

"I admire your courage," The Ripper stated, "but you're no more of a match for me than you're friend Valerie was."

"You killed her?" Nicole cried, backing away. "Why? She never hurt anyone!"

To the Ripper's surprise, Nicole jumped up on the bed bouncing as high as she could. She catapulted off the bed and came down on the surprised vampire's head with the heel of her boot. This time the tall shadowy figure groaned loudly, and stared at her with the enraged eyes of a wounded animal. A purple bruise began to form right between his glaring eyes. Within moments, he controlled himself and chided, "Nicole, Nicole, you're only a weak woman. You're all alone. There are no Freebloods here to save you now."

"God is here," Nicole retorted with surprising calm. "Whatever happens to me tonight, He'll know, and you'll answer to Him. When He shows up, you'll be the one trembling in fear."

"He's taking his time about it then," Raven said blandly. "I don't know you're God. I answer only to Ra," he stated, showing her the Egyptian tattoo on his wrist.

"A lot of good praying to an idol will do you, Ripper," Nicole stated vehemently. "No false god told you to kill Valerie. You did it because it was the easy way out. You didn't have to kill any of those poor women. You chose to murder them because you're a coward!"

"I'm a coward?" Raven asked slyly. "Pray tell, how I, the most superior vampire there ever was, am a coward?"

"Only a cowardly man would prey on innocent women," Nicole rebutted. "You took the path of least resistance every time, like the pettiest, most gutless criminal would do!"

"Enough!" Raven bellowed. "You begin to bore me. All inferiors bore me eventually. They are amusing for a little while, until they cease to please me, except for Valerie. She was quite enchanting. Too bad she had to fall for such a weak man."

"What are you going to do?" Nicole asked. "Are you going to kill me like all the others?"

"Sorry," Raven said, sighing. "You weren't the one I chose, but I can't go without nourishment forever." With this remark, he leapt across the room, flinging himself at the horrified woman. To the vampire's dismay, he grabbed nothing but air. The impetus of his leap slammed his body against the cement wall. With a grunt he held his aching head and whirled around.

"How can you move so fast?" He yelled, reaching out for her. He was frustrated by her strength. He suspected she might be a half-breed. After all she was married to a Freeblood. Raven would normally deny himself vampire blood, but if he didn't feed soon he could lapse into a starvation coma.

Nicole dropped down and speedily crawled away from his grasping hands. "It's a gift, it runs in my family," she boldly replied from the other side of the room.

"Sooner or later you'll get tired," Raven responded. "Why put yourself through all this. I promise your death will be quick and painless."

"But your won't," Nicole stated grimly. "Come near me again and I'll gouge your eyes out with my nails until I reach that perverted brain of yours."

"In the end, you'll die," Raven stated coldly, ignoring her retort.

Raven's stomach was churning violently with hunger. He felt himself weakening, a scary emotion for a Keeper, who was at his weakest when deprived of food for a long time. Unable to reach her with speed, Raven rushed to the wall, pushed off with his feet and flipped over backward, catching Nicole off guard. He fell on the startled woman, wrapping his arms around her and carrying her to the cot. Searching for a tender spot on her right side, he bent down to feed. As Raven sunk his teeth into her warm flesh he felt a raised birthmark in the shape of a rose, just below her rib cage. Suddenly, he grimaced, removed his incisors, sprang away from the cot, and streaked out of the room.

Nicole lifted herself to a sitting position and groped for the sheet, tearing off a strip of cloth. She wadded it up and pressed it into the tiny oozing wounds. Ripping away another long strip, she tied it around her rib cage to hold the makeshift bandage in place. Scrambling from the room, the weeping woman ran out of the building and into the alley.

The area looked vaguely familiar. Turning to the right she saw the spire of St. Ignatius Church and realized she was in the basement of a local CPA. The building would be vacant until January when the owner would set up his satellite office for tax preparation.

Racing to her apartment building, Nicole pounded on the front door. The stairway light went on and Colin's worried face peered through the window. He cried out with relief and hurriedly unlocked the door. Once inside, Nicole fell into his arms sobbing.

Colin held her tightly, whispering, "Thank God you're okay. I got a call from Giselle about an hour ago. She was an emotional wreck. We tore the zoo apart looking for you. She and Falcon are on their way right now."

Falcon's Thunderbird pulled up a few minutes later. When Giselle saw her friend she ran over sobbing, saying, "Thank God, I thought we lost you!" The two women embraced, weeping in each other's arms.

Colin and Falcon looked at each other with misting eyes. Falcon wiped the tears from his eyes while Colin unabashedly let his fall. Colin helped his trembling wife up the stairs while Giselle and Falcon walked behind them.

"Are the children okay?" Nicole asked, drying her eyes.

"Yes," Giselle answered, "I told them you took ill and had to find a restroom. I don't think they were convinced though. I left them with Father Francis, and he called their parents."

Colin held his wife's trembling hands saying, "Nicole, what happened?"

"Raven was at the Zoo," Nicole explained. "He was hiding in the Tiger Habitat."

"Raven has a freakish kinship with Big Cats," Falcon commented.

"One minute we were walking on the path," Nicole relayed, "the next moment, I saw his shadow above me. I told

Giselle to take the kids to safety. After that, it's all a blur. I remember he jumped down from a boulder and grabbed me. He put something over my mouth, and I blacked out."

"The demon chloroformed you!" Colin exclaimed angrily.

"He took me to the basement of the CPA office near St. Ignatius." The shaking woman continued. "When I came to, I was lying on a small bed, in a basement room with no windows, just a door and four cement walls. There was a gag in my mouth and my wrists and ankles were tied with twine."

"He took you to one of his safe houses," Falcon conjectured. "He probably has them all over the city."

"I managed to get myself untied," Nicole returned, explaining how she had loosened the ropes, using the splintered wood to unravel her bonds. She looked down at the painful welts encircling her wrists and ankles.

Colin brought four ice packs and covered his wife's wrists and ankles with them to bring down the swelling. He handed her a glass of water, and gave her two aspirin. He touched her tear stained face gently and said, "Dr. Montreau is on his way to look at your wounds. Go on babe, tell us the rest."

"After I got myself untied," she continued, "I heard someone walking outside, so I hid behind the door, holding one of my boots. Raven must be seven feet tall! He had to bend down to get through the doorway. When he did, I jumped up and hit him right between the eyes, which didn't seem to affect him at all. He tried to grab me again, but I slipped away. In the end though, I couldn't stop him, he pinned me down on the cot and bit me on my rib cage. I was making my peace with God, when he suddenly stopped, made a funny sound, and took off. I waited a few minutes, in case it was a trick. When he didn't come back, I got out of there."

"Thank God he let you go," Colin said, a look of relief on his worried face.

"Think about it. Why would a hungry vampire suddenly stop feeding?" Falcon asked curiously. "What makes you different from the other women Raven abducted?"

"He must know I'm half vampire," Nicole stated. "There's nothing else different about me unless he has a phobia about birthmarks." Nicole stated.

"What kind of birthmark?" Giselle asked.

Colin looked at her and stated, "Nicole has a curious birthmark under her ribcage, a strawberry mark that looks like a rose."

"That wouldn't stop anyone," Falcon stated. "The biker girl, Raven nearly killed, was covered with tattoos." He explained. The girl Raven attacked at the state park was still recovering at Good Faith Hospital, a private hospital and safe haven for vampires, run by Dr. Stanley. Falcon thought out loud, "Vampires never feed on their own kind, even Keepers, unless it's was a matter of life and death. Raven must be close to starvation."

"Nicole," Giselle commented looking at her friend. "You said you were raised in an orphanage after your father abandoned you, right?"

"Yes that's right," Nicole agreed. "My mother died in childbirth and my father left me on a church doorstep in Canton, Ohio when I was four."

"Why weren't you placed in foster homes?" Giselle inquired.

"My foster parent's couldn't stand me," she replied.

"My social worker, Ms. Taylor, talked to me about it when I was eighteen and released from state care," Nicole explained. "She said I was unique, which to me meant that I was a freak. I was allergic to the sun, slept all day, and would get up and play all night. I refused to anything but rare meat. I was criticized for bringing home stray animals. The last family I had, the Mueller's were really nice, but they got upset because I brought home a wolf pup and wanted to raise it. I hid him in the woods and kept him a secret for over a year. One day he escaped and found me at the farm. The Mueller's freaked out. A wildlife rescue officer came and took Wolfie away. I cried for months over that. I ran away several times and they brought me to St. Louis. I was placed in St. Barnabas Home for Children and released when I was eighteen."

"That's when she met Father Francis," Colin stated.

"He spoke at my graduation," Nicole informed them. "What he said changed my life. He said that we were God's children, and given unique gifts. He told us that through education we could find out what those gifts were. I met with him after the ceremony and talked to him several hours. That's when he said he had observed me with the children and saw the depth of my love for them. He offered me a job at St. Ignatius Grade School as an evening counselor for the after school program. On evenings when I wasn't working with the children, I went to college."

"That's where I met Nicole," Colin said. "Father Francis asked my music team to play for his youth group."

"Father Francis was the first person to tell me I was part vampire," Nicole said. "It scared me at first, but later, when I thought about it, it made a lot of sense. I realized I wasn't a freak, I was different. I was elated when he told me there was a small nation of Freebloods like myself in the world and that he was one of them. I decided that if a good man like Father Francis was a vampire, I would be okay."

"When we started dating, Nicole began to see that my family was a little different too," Colin interjected.

"I knew Colin was different right away," Nicole revealed. "There was a special light in his eyes and he worked tirelessly. When I met his parents and all of you, it never frightened me, because you were always kind and accepting of me. Being different myself, I understood how hard it was to be accepted in this world."

"One night we finally talked about being Freeblood vampires," Colin said. "We knew that only God could have brought us together. That's when I finally told Nicole that I loved her. I still do, and will, for the rest of my long life."

"I love you too," Nicole replied, "with all my heart."

There was a knock at the door and everyone jumped reflexively, "It's probably my father," Giselle stated.

Dr. Montreau set his black bag on the coffee table. He said hello to everyone and sat next to Nicole on the sofa, preparing for her examination. To give them privacy, Giselle and Falcon went into the kitchen to make tea. Twenty minutes later Dr. Montreau walked into the kitchen and announced, "I've cleaned the wound and closed the bite marks, and given Nicole a tetanus shot." Looking at Colin he stated, "Please bring her to Good Faith hospital as soon as possible. She'll be on watch for twenty-four hours. I want to make sure she didn't contract any bacterium or virus from the Keeper. Being bitten by a Keeper is like being bitten by a rabid dog."

"I'll come tonight," Nicole said. "I'm feeling better, and I'd really like to get this over with."

"Marvelous," Dr. Montreau agreed. "Colin, see that she rests quietly here two hours, until the pain medicine gives her some relief. I'll call ahead and make sure her room is prepared."

"We'll be there," Colin replied.

"Is there any family history I should know about?" Dr. Montreau asked as he placed his medical supplies back in his bag.

"My biological father was a vampire," Nicole commented, "Other than that I don't think so. My mother died giving birth to me, but I've never had any physical abnormalities, other than the obvious ones we all have."

"We'll run few tests, just to make sure," Dr. Montreau replied. "In the meantime, rest easy, have a cup of tea, and lean red meat."

"If Nicole is a hybrid, perhaps that explains Raven's sudden departure," Dr. Montreau suggested to Falcon as they walked outside.

"Perhaps he realized she didn't fit the profile," Falcon suggested.

"Even Keepers, rarely feed on other vampires, unless they're starving," Dr. Montreau explained.

"Then what stopped him from killing Nicole," Falcon wondered aloud.

"It had to be something else," Dr. Montreau responded. "He was ravenous. He couldn't have been thinking clearly, yet a primal instinct told him not to feed on the girl. There's only one other possibility for Nicole's escape."

"They're related?" Falcon asked.

"It's a possibility," Dr. Montreau answered.

"We have to tell her," Falcon stated.

"Not now," Dr. Montreau advised. "After the blood tests, I'll be certain then. In the meantime, let's allow her a peaceful recovery."

"Can I tell Colin to prepare him?" Falcon asked.

"Of Course," the doctor agreed. "She'll need his support to get over the shock."

"Nicole is a smart woman," Falcon stated. "I wouldn't be surprised if she figures all this out before we tell her."

"I don't doubt that for a moment," Dr. Montreau acknowledged. "She has intuition that is far above heightened, vampire ability."

Chapter 25

As Raven fled, leaving Nicole unharmed, his mind was spinning in horror. He had almost killed his own daughter. Without a doubt she was his child. His wife, Angelica, had the mark of the rose on her side. Uncomfortable emotions flooded the vampire's senses, emotions he had kept repressed for a quarter of a century. As a Keeper he lived for survival, not love, yet he could not forget the tiny infant he had held in his arms so long ago. Memories of her mother still haunted his dreams.

Nicole's mother, Angelica, was on the run when they met twenty-five years ago. She had fled her abusive husband. Court mandates had failed to stop his violent and terrifying behavior.

One night, twenty-six years ago, Raven had been prowling the city for warm blood. He had heard Angelica's terrified screams of pain. Her raging husband had found her once again, and was beating her.

To this day, Raven couldn't fathom why he intervened. The domestic violence of Ordinaries wasn't his problem. It was no more relevant to his existence than hearing a couple of cats fighting in an alley. Perhaps the high-pitched sound had unleashed some primal male need to come to her rescue. More than likely, it was the incessant noise, no one else in the neighborhood seemed to notice, which had vexed him. Whatever the reason, Raven had climbed the backstairs of her building using the fire escape ladder, punched through a closed window, and pulled the brute off the bruised and bleeding woman.

After nearly splitting the man's skull with his bare fist, he had picked up the semi-conscious woman and carried her out of the building. He was living in a respectable little cottage outside of town, playing the role of groundskeeper to a local bank president. The estate was isolated by fifty acres of land. His cottage was a half-mile from the main house in the middle of the woods.

He had planned on taking the woman home, cleaning her up, and later that night, imbibing on her vibrant young blood. He had to be patient and care for her because blood in the turmoil of certain death, could not be consumed. Fear releases certain unpalatable enzymes into the bloodstream. For this reason, Keeper's render their prey unconscious before feeding. Romance rarely occurred before a vampire's repast, in spite of lingering myths. Occasionally, a vampire became attracted to his intended victim and a relationship developed. Usually the affair ended badly, for the Ordinary.

After he had cared for her, he discovered Angelica was an exotic beauty, in face, form and personality. How, he had wondered, had such a lovely woman been trapped in a run-down neighborhood with a lowlife reprobate of a husband? The woman sleeping on his couch was tall and willowy, with long flowing blonde hair. Her beauty was classic; high cheekbones and full lips. Everything about her was nearly perfect, from her narrow waist, soft round shoulders, long shapely legs, to her slim delicate feet. Those qualities would have been enough for him to linger, but when she came to and stared at him intently with large blue-violet eyes, he had melted. When she spoke for the first time, her voice was lilting, and curiously, unafraid.

"Who are you?" she had asked, meeting his cool dark eyes.

"My name is Chance, Chance Drakkor," He had lied. "I heard you screaming. I nearly killed that brute husband of yours and brought you here. He won't bother you anymore," Raven had answered.

"He's not my husband anymore," she had corrected him. Where am I?" was her next question.

"About thirty miles outside of town on the Chambers Estates," he had informed her,

"You mean the family who owns Chambers Bank?"

"The same," He had answered. "Don't start getting dollar signs in your eyes my dear. I'm the groundskeeper, not an heir."

"You saved my life," Angelica had stated, gazing at him softly, through long, dark lashes.

"Shucks it weren't nothing ma'am," Raven had answered, in his best cowboy imitation.

She had laughed saying, "You're a strange and wonderful man."

"Well let's agree for now that I am merely, strange," He had replied, his heart pounding.

The next few weeks they both slept during the day. Raven cared for "Angel" as he called her, all night long. Three weeks later she was well enough to move about the apartment, and had become quite comfortable with his unusual hours. She even enjoyed the rare steaks they dined on most nights. When she grew tired of the singularity of his diet, Angelica added fish and chicken to hers.

Raven realized he had fallen hopelessly in love one evening when she kissed him goodbye before his nightly prowl, and had dinner on the table when he returned. Angelica never questioned where he went, or what he did on his brief excursions. He treated her well, and she responded by letting him have his space.

Three months later Raven had braved the late afternoon sun and the couple drove to city hall, where he and Angelica were married. The newlyweds spent their honeymoon camping by Lake Luna, on the estate. Remembering the feel of her cheek, her sweet scent, her gentle hands, and her unyielding affection, Raven turned away, unaware that his eyes were glistening with tears.

All the perfection of their union had come crashing down on the day Angelica announced she was pregnant. He hadn't really thought about the possibility. Pregnancy was rare between Keepers and Ordinaries. To his relief, Angelica was radiant the first four months. Sadly, the half-Keeper child began growing rapidly, demanding more nourishment than she could provide, even though she was eating all day long.

Seven months later, the baby came. Raven's weakened and terrified wife had died in his arms. The birth had occurred so rapidly, there had been no time to get her to a vampire hospital that could deliver such a child. He held their child, a tiny beautiful dark-haired girl, for a few moments. Although stunned and weary, Raven had cleaned, diapered, and swaddled her. She looked up at him with large, trusting, violet eyes and fell asleep in his arms.

The next night Raven had buried Angelica at Lake Luna where they had spent their Honeymoon. He remembered howling miserably up at the silver moon, like a wolf that had just lost its mate.

Raven had explained to the landlord and their small group of friends that Angelica had left him. The stresses of motherhood and postpartum depression had driven her away. They had gathered around him offering help and support. As time went on, their incessant questions about Angelica began to irritate him.

Born on Christmas Eve, little Kikki, as he called her, was his pride and joy. To escape prying eyes and unwanted attention, he had taken the child and moved, without notice, late one night in January.

Raven had moved to a small town outside Topeka, and bought a large house with ten acres. He had hired a local girl, Mattie, to clean house, prepare dinner, and care for Kikki. She baby sat many an evening that he had gone on the prowl looking for food.

Mattie had grown to love Kikki, and had doted on her like a mother. The arrangement had worked out so well for an entire year that Raven had asked her to move in with them. She was a pretty young woman, with an infectious smile, and would have been a pleasant companion. Unfortunately, she had declined his offer, reminding him that she was engaged and was getting married in six months.

Enraged, Raven had let his temper get the better of him. He had grabbed the young woman, chloroformed her, and drained her blood while Kikki slept in the other room. After quickly burying Mattie in the woods, he had picked up his daughter, loaded her in his new Monte Carlo, and had left town that same night.

Raven tried again, buying a three-bedroom bungalow on eighty acres of farmland, in Salem, a small town in Southwestern Missouri. It was wine country and he had agreed to rent fifty acres of his land to two brothers who wanted to expand their vineyard. For a while he and Kikki had lived a quiet and peaceful existence.

In this town, Raven had hired Shannon, the teenage daughter of a tenant farmer, to take care of Kikki. This time, he had driven hundreds of miles, several times a month, to find the kind of nourishment he required. For those two years local newspapers in all the little towns he ravaged had been filled with headlines about him, "The Night Killer Strikes again", or "Police Unable To Apprehend The "Midnight Murderer."

When Kikki turned four and was the image of his dead wife, Raven's feelings for his daughter had changed. He had begun to resent the little girl, blaming her for his beloved Angel's death and his resultant loneliness. When resentment nearly grew into hatred, Raven feared he might snap and harm the child. Before he acted on his growing inner turmoil, Raven had driven to Canton Ohio, and dropped the sleeping girl off at the rectory of a catholic church. Anxious to put an ocean between him and his old life, Raven secretly boarded a vessel bound for Europe, hiding in the cargo hold.

When Raven saw the birthmark of the rose on Nicole, he knew that his little Kikki had lived after all. Her hair was dark and wavy like his, her dark violet eyes were like her mother's. The shape of her face and her classic beauty were from Angelica. She wasn't tall and willowy, but petite and perfect, like a porcelain doll. He was relieved that somehow, he had been able to pull himself away from Nicole, in the midst of his terrible hunger.

He wept uncontrollably for his lost love, and the beautiful family that could have redeemed his meaningless life. He had hoped to find this kind of love again with Valerie, but she had spurned him for Trey Hawkins. His large shoulders shook with a torrent of emotions, buried deep inside over the years. He cried out and shook his fist violently at the rising moon, cursing the gods for abandoning him.

"Ra!" he agonized. "Where are you now?"

Chapter 26

Pulling himself together, Raven raced along the snow-covered streets in his black sedan with its smoke-tinted windows. Feeling dejected and empty, he gave in to the gnawing persistent hunger that had to be satisfied. Grinding his teeth, he acknowledged to himself that there was no redemption for his kind. He was a Keeper, and would always be a Keeper. To be anything else would bring disaster and pain raining down on him again.

He drove the nearly vacant streets and pulled in front of Bailey's Chocolate Bar. His spirits were lifted by the presence of warm-blooded people filling the dining rooms at this late hour. There had been no murders in two weeks, and the curfew had been lifted. People were eager to put the finality of death behind them and celebrate life.

He sat at a small table in the back, waiting for the waitress to take his order for a drink. As he had hoped, it was the vivacious brown-eyed Antonia who walked up to his table. Apparently she hadn't heard of Nicole's abduction, because her smile was welcoming, though wary. The woman had a sixth-sense about her that would be difficult to override.

The hungry-eyed Raven ordered a Hot Toddy and waited patiently, gazing around the room, feeling less lonely among the noisy crowd. He had an affinity for observing Ordinaries, just as a hunter would quietly track a family of deer in the woods. Antonia, however, beautiful, only held his interest as nourishment. He would turn on the charm, put her at ease, and wait until the right moment to take what was rightfully his.

The Hot Toddy did its work and began warming the hungry vampire's insides making him more aware of the rich, warm blood coursing through Antonia's veins. Feeding off of her would be even more gratifying because she was seeing the disabled veteran who was part of Falcon's team. While he was hesitant to kill a Freeblood, he had no problem killing an Ordinary. It was what he was born to do as a Keeper.

When Antonia returned to take a second drink order, he requested huskily, "Will you hit me with another hot toddy, love?" When she reached for his tumbler, his hand touched hers briefly. He smiled up at her lazily. Turning on the charm he asked, "You work so hard, Senorita, what do you do for play?"

"I spend time with my little girl, Maria," Antonia replied, happily.

"How old is the little nina?" Raven returned, feigning interest.

"She just turned eight this month," the woman answered proudly.

"You were a child when you had her," Raven commented, softly.

"I was twenty years old," Antonia offered casually. "Maria's father was killed on 9/11."

"How tragic, my dear," Raven answered with a look of compassion. Antonia, not fooled by Raven's superficial demeanor, wondered why he was in the city, Alberto had told her he was safely locked in Dr. Montreau's hospital an hour away. Knowing he was a dangerous man, Antonia handled him with caution, displaying reserved civility. When Antonia went returned to the bar to get Raven's drink, she quickly sent a text message to Alberto to let him know he was in the restaurant. Fortunately, it was only fifteen minutes until the restaurant closed, and she would be rid of the frightening man and his uncomfortable stares.

Closing time came with Raven still sipping his fourth Toddy, the only customer left. Steve, the manager, finally went over to his table to remind him that the bar was closing. Raven smiled, thanked Steve and rose, gulping down the last of his drink. He waved to Antonia, and took out his wallet to pay the bill. He gave her a generous tip and left.

While Raven hid in the darkness of the gangway next to the restaurant. After twenty minutes, Antonia emerged from the building in a long hooded coat. She walked quickly down the street to her car. Raven followed, moving in the shadows. Silently he crept up behind her, towering over her as she opened her car door. When she pulled the door open, he fell on her. Gripping her with one arm, he savagely brushed her soft hair aside, seeking a tender spot near the nape of her neck. The terrified woman cried out as he shoved the chloroformed handkerchief near her face.

Suddenly, he was pulled from behind and spun around. Alberto Ramos stood glaring at him, the street light glinting on the tire iron he held in his hands.

Raven looked at the stocky, muscular man poised solidly on titanium legs and said, "No hice nada." (I have done nothing.)

"!Ya! Basta! (Enough!)" Alberto hurled at him angrily, swinging the tire iron back and forth.

!"Me Toca!"(My turn) Raven screamed, and lunged at the man. Unprepared for the quick dodge of the legless man on titanium springs, Raven stumbled past Alberto, nearly losing his balance.

Albert whirled around on one leg and sliced into Raven's two legs with his other prosthetic, knocking him to the ground, yelling, !"Tiempo!"(Times up!)

Alberto growled as he brought the tire iron down on Raven's head. His strike met only a whoosh of air as the vampire side stepped his move and streaked across the street in a blur. Alberto started to pursue him, but stopped when Antonia put her hand on his arm.

"!Dejaloir, mi amor,"(Let him go, my love), she uttered softly. "Lo atraparas otra dia." (You will catch him another day.)

Antonia nearly collapsed in Alberto's arms, the trauma of the vicious attack still visible on her lovely tear-stained face. Leaving her car parked on the street, Alberto drove her home.

When the couple arrived at Antonia's flat, Maria was already asleep. Alberto walked Rita, Antonia's mother, up to her apartment on the third floor, checking her rooms carefully to make sure she was safe. Hurrying back downstairs, he examined Antonia's neck and shoulder. Mercifully there were no punctures, only purple bruises in the shape of large fingerprints. He made an ice pack and handed it to Antonia, holding her in his arms while she calmed down.

"Can I make you a cup of tea, mi corizon?" Alberto asked softly.

"Gracias, tea would be nice," Antonia answered, smiling weakly.

Alberto returned with two cups, and a teapot full of steaming, black tea. Antonia gripped his arm and pleaded, "Don't leave me tonight."

"Do you think I would be so stupid as to leave my future wife alone on a night like this?" Alberto replied, a hurt look on his face.

"Your future wife?" Antonia asked. Through ebbing tears she added, "The couch is very comfortable and there are sheets, blankets and extra pillows in the linen closet."

"Sounds better than a military cot," Albert replied. "First, let's get you tucked into bed with a couple of aspirin to relieve the swelling on your neck."

Later that night, Alberto lay awake, gazing out the living room window. It seemed so quiet, so peaceful outside, yet somewhere on the city streets, a monster lurked, waiting to devour another unsuspecting young woman. He thanked God it hadn't been Antonia. Like Antonia had said, he and his friends would catch Raven another day. That was one promise he would be glad to keep.

Chapter 27

Hearing strange noises coming from the caretaker's apartment, Father Francis looked up from the Book of Psalms. He walked over to the window just as Victor's light went out. He went to his desk and opened the top drawer. Inside were five old issues of the Post Dispatch. Thumbing through them, the priest confirmed what he had already knew; in each issue was an article about one of the dead girl's slain by the Central West End Ripper. The priest had found them stuffed in the space between the caretaker's bed and wall, while searching the man's modest apartment for the extra banquet room key. He hadn't meant to pry, he valued his own privacy, and would never snoop, but the picture spilling over onto the bedcovers had been of Valerie.

After the Thanksgiving Holiday, he had urged Falcon to use his FBI source to research Victor. He told Falcon his full name was Victor, Vladimir Oransky. According to Victor his family had immigrated to America shortly before WWII.

He recalled Theodore's return call with growing anxiety.

"Father I got an e-mail from my FBI friend who contacted INTERPOL for me."

"What did you find out Theodore?" he had returned expectantly.

"There is no such person and no such family that came from Russia in the late thirties."

"I suspected as much," he had replied with a sigh.

"What are you going to do?" Falcon had asked with concern in his voice.

"The only thing I can do for the safety of my parish," he had replied. "I will confront him about his lies, and quietly send him away."

Finding the incriminating newspapers, spurred the priest to search the caretakers bureau. He started with the top drawer, carefully lifting the socks, handkerchiefs, and undershirts. Finding nothing suspicious there, he opened the second drawer, which held Victor's slacks. As he searched through the layers, he noticed the space in the drawer was five inches shallower than the depth of the drawer itself. He poked ad prodded, until a false bottom lifted up, exposing several strange instruments. One was a hand rake with three sharpened stainless Steel prongs. Even more frightening, was a wooden handle which held three sharp animal claws. When Father Francis turned the claws facing downward, his hand began shaking.

He now realized that Victor, his caretaker, was not just a liar, he was the notorious Central West End Ripper. The weapon he held in his hand had been used to kill the five women, including Valerie. The scope of Victor's evil hit the priest with such a blow, his knees nearly folded under him. Dropping both tools into the pockets of his robe, he carefully replaced the false bottom of the drawer.

Overcome with emotion, he stumbled to the bed and sat down. Feeling lightheaded, he took a few deep breaths and hastily checked the room, making sure he left it the way he had entered it.

Walking quickly across the courtyard, the priest sought the comfort and darkness of his own bedroom. He said a prayer for strength to confront the caretaker with the truth.

He jumped nervously when the phone by his bed rang. He picked it up asking, "Hello?"

"It's Dr. Montreau, Father," the cultured voice stated. "I didn't wake you did I?"

"No. I'm still reading," Father Francis reassured him. "How can I help you?" He asked calmly. The priest had never met the doctor, but his excellent reputation preceded him in the community of Ordinaries and Freebloods.

"Raven has escaped," The doctor informed him in a grave voice.

"I know. He is a very cunning adversary," Father Francis replied numbly.

"You know Beau, the homeless fellow Colin took in at the Redeemer Mission?" Dr. Montreau asked.

"Yes, I heard from Colin that he was in rehab at your center," The priest answered.

"He helped Raven escape," The doctor stated. "He must have stolen my keys when he came for his consultation earlier this evening."

"Beau, poor soul, is a notorious pick-pocket," The priest confirmed.

"He's dead, Father," The doctor answered in a somber voice.

"Dear God, how?" The priest asked, his voice trembling.

"After using my keys to release Raven, he jumped from the five-story roof of the rehab center," Dr. Montreau answered grimly.

"Why would he do such a thing?" The priest wondered aloud. "He was terrified of Raven. The man nearly killed his friend Damien."

"My guess is Raven made some empty promises to him in exchange for helping him escape," the doctor suggested.

"Yes, Beau might have believed him too," Father Francis replied, "He has always been fascinated with vampires. He would come in the shelter and watch any vampire movie he could find. Sometimes he had difficulty distinguishing between fantasy and reality. He suffers from dementia, caused by his alcoholism. Raven was willing to promise anything to Trey and Beau to get what he wanted. It is tragic that both men realized too late that the only thing he could give them was death."

"If that weren't horrible enough, he kidnapped Nicole this evening," Dr. Montreau added.

"I know. Giselle brought the children here." Father Francis stated. "Their parents just picked them up a while ago. Colin called me earlier to tell me she escaped and made her way to their apartment. I take it Nicole is at your hospital for twenty-four hour observation."

"She is sleeping peacefully," Dr. Montreau reassured him. "A blood test revealed there was no poison in her blood. I stitched the puncture wounds and gave her a sleep aid. It is fortunate that she escaped Raven relatively unscathed."

"I'm pleased, but not surprised," the priest responded. "Raven wouldn't harm Nicole, she's his daughter,"

"You knew?" Montreau asked in surprise.

"Yes I found out a few days ago," Father Francis answered. "Several years ago, Nicole wanted to find her biological parents. She and Colin want to have a child. I offered to use my connection in the Church to help. Months went by, and finally, a record of her parent's marriage was found. Raven called himself Drakkor in those days. I could find no evidence of what happened to her mother. After analyzing the research, I came to believe that the woman must have been an Ordinary. I have a feeling she died in childbirth.

After the incident last night, I decided it wasn't the right time to tell Nicole that Henri Raven could be her father."

"Do you have any idea where Raven would hide in this city?" Dr. Montreau asked hopefully.

"Raven would hide in the most unlikely place of all," Father Francis answered in a clipped voice.

"Where would that be?" Doctor Montreau asked.

"In the basement of this church," Father Francis answered, hanging up the phone.

Father Francis took the flashlight from his bureau drawer. The only way to deal with a vampire, who prowls all night, is to stop him by day. The priest pulled the hood of his robe over his face to block out the sunlight as he left the rectory. Crossing over to the church, he opened a side door, and calmly walked down the main aisle to the sanctuary. Kneeling down he whispered prayers. Taking hold of a Eucharist wafer, he consumed it, saying, "Body of Christ." He then took the communion wine and poured it into a silver chalice, holding it up saying, "Blood of Christ give me strength." He drank the wine and genuflected.

Father Francis walked silently down the stairs and made his way to Victor's room, flashlight in one hand, and newspaper clippings in the other. He rapped loudly on Victor's door calling his name. When there was no reply, he opened the unlocked door and peered inside. Victor was in his bed, snoring and seemingly asleep. Entering the room the priest called out. "Victor, wake up!"

The figure under the covers did not move. Father Francis knew that Keepers slept very soundly, but he also knew they had a sixth sense that alerted them when danger was near. He walked boldly into the room stating, "I know you're awake. Get up. We need to talk, now!"

The figure in the bed rose to a sitting position. "Turn off the light priest, and we'll talk." The voice was Victor's, but with more baritone and authority.

"What were these news clippings of the dead girls doing in your room?" The priest asked in an equally commanding tone.

"Do you always spy on your employees?" Raven asked, rising from the bed, standing over the priest.

"I was looking for the extra banquet room key," Father Francis explained. "Now, answer my question," the priest commanded in a deeper tone.

"Let's not play games, Francis," Raven replied. He walked forward, his black eyes boring into the priest's eyes.

"Your tricks won't work with me," The priest answered, standing his ground. "A higher authority than you controls my heart and soul."

Raven stopped and spread his two hands out defensively, saying, "I have no quarrel with you, priest. Step aside and I will leave this place. All this sanctity is getting on my nerves anyway. It's run by a bunch of sniveling, cowardly, Bible thumpers whose idea of fun is feeding a bunch of low-life bums a decent meal."

"Valerie was no low-life!" Father Francis exclaimed.

"Oh, you're right about that, priest," Raven agreed in a low voice. "She was going to be my beautiful queen, until she confessed her love for that weakling, Hawkins. She refused me! No Ordinary has ever refused me and lived!"

"Is that why you murdered her?" Father Francis asked. While he distracted Raven began texting Falcon with cell phone hidden in the pocket of his robe. His message read: Raven here. "You must get used to rejection," he continued. "You are incapable of living among civilized people."

"You don't understand." Raven stated. "All I wanted was Valerie's blood, until I got to know her as your caretaker," Raven replied. When he continued, his voice was softer, almost nostalgic, "How was I to know, that after all this time, I could still feel love?" Pounding his fist on the chest of drawers, he continued, bitterness hardening his voice, "Love is not for Keepers, it makes you weak."

"If you truly loved Valerie, how could you kill her?" The priest asked pointedly.

"I told you she didn't want me!" Raven replied, reaching tentatively into the second drawer of his bureau.

"Your weapons aren't there Keeper," Father Francis informed him coldly. "Killing me will not solve your problems," the priest added calmly. "Go back to the clinic, if you want to live. My friends will be here soon, and they won't be as forgiving as I."

"Don't you understand, priest," Raven replied, his eyes glinting in the darkness. "No one can stop me!"

"Raven, I think you are beginning to believe your own lies," Francis replied stonily.

Father Francis barred the vampire's way as he tried to race past him, spreading his arms in the doorway to block his escape. Raven pushed and shoved. Try as he might, he couldn't budge the wiry priest. As Raven's head lurched forward to bite the priest's jugular, he was thrown back with such force that his weight punched a hole through the drywall and he lay momentarily stunned. Raven shook his head, jumped to his feet, and charged like an enraged bull. Using his head as a ramrod, he attacked, but the determined priest was much stronger than he looked. The enraged vampire paced furiously around the room bellowing.

Outraged at being trapped, Raven began pounding on the wall creating a deeper and deeper hole until he broke through to the banquet room. Bounding up the stairs, and crashing through the oak door, he sprinted by the sanctuary and streaked down the main aisle of the church.

He pushed the front doors open and flew down the stairs. He rushed down the street in a blur of vampire speed. After six blocks, he was about to disappear around the corner when he spotted Giselle dressed in a dark raincoat and hood, heading across the street to her car.

Thinking quickly, he bent low walking with Victor's stilted movements. He pretended to stumble and sprain his ankle. Giselle saw him crumple to the sidewalk, and she hurriedly ran over.

"Victor, are you all right?" she asked with concern in her voice.

"I twisted my ankle and I can't walk," Raven complained in Victor's voice.

"I'll get my car," Giselle state. "Stay right there." He watched as the lovely woman briskly walked to her car. She made a quick turn in the street and pulled up right beside him. Putting the car in park she rushed around the side to open the passenger door, and helped Victor get in.

"I live right down the street," she told him. "We'll take the elevator and get some ice on that ankle.

"You are so kind," Victor said looking over at her.

As Giselle turned the corner, Falcon pulled up in front of the church. He ran into the building and heard Father Francis groaning in pain. The priest lay against one of the pews.

"I tried to stall him until you got here, but he panicked. He broke through the wall, knocked me down the stairs, and ran out into the street."

"Are you going to be okay?" Falcon asked helping him to his feet.

"Yes Theodore," Father Francis answered. "Go! Stop him!"

As he watched Falcon rush out the door he yelled to his retreating form, "He's my caretaker, Victor!"

Chapter 28

After helping Father Francis, Falcon quickly texted Ethan and Colin then drove down the street. He saw something lying on the sidewalk and pulled over to the curb with a screech. It was Giselle's scarf. It became clear to him in a flash that Giselle had seen Victor, and for some reason drove him away. Why? Where would she take him? He would try her apartment.

As he drove up to the Ash Apartments his cell phone rang. It was Giselle's number. "Gisele where are you? Is Victor with you?"

"Falcon what a clever Freeblood you are," Raven said. "I'm afraid Giselle is busy right now and can't speak to you."

"If you hurt her—" Falcon started.

"Don't bother coming in," Raven stated. "We aren't there."

"Where did you take her?" Falcon demanded.

"If you happen to drive by the Melrose Apartments you may find the two of us on the roof," Raven suggested.

"If you touch her I'll tear you apart with my bare hands," Falcon stated.

"*I* won't do a thing to her," Raven commented. "However the sun is up, and you know how intently it can beat down on a flat roof."

Falcon hung up and raced to the Melrose Apartments. Rufus was thrown from side to side as he careened around corners and sped through the side streets. He put his phone on speaker and called Ethan.

"What's up man?" Ethan asked.

"Raven kidnapped Giselle and tied her up on the roof of the Melrose Apartments," Falcon explained hastily. "Where is the stairway to the roof?"

"I got the building plans on my web site," Ethan stated his voice rising in fear. "The stairway actually is at the end of the top floor. That's the floor where Valerie's apartment was."

Falcon pulled into the parking lot behind the building and parked the Hummer. He climbed up the fire escape ladders until he was on the fifth floor. Standing on top of the rail to the fire escape

Landing, he propelled himself upward, grabbed onto the edge of the building and climbed over.

He could see Giselle standing in the middle of the roof, tied onto one of the air vent pipes. She wore a gag and her face was exposed to the sun. Falcon raced towards her in a blur of motion.

Giselle's bloodshot eyes were watering profusely as she struggled to avoid the direct rays of the morning sun that beat down on her. As he neared, she shook her head furiously, looking frantically past Falcon at someone right behind him.

In one swift movement Falcon whirled away to the left, missing the blade of the Keeper's dagger by millimeters.

"I've had enough of your meddling, Freeblood!" Raven screamed angrily. "I was willing to leave your and your Freeblood friends alone, but you couldn't stop butting into my business."

"Shut up!" Falcon yelled between clenched teeth. "Stop your belly aching, and let's see what you can do!"

Raven let out a blood curdling battle cry and lunged at Falcon again this time grazing him across the rib cage. Falcon did a back flip away from him. Raven charged him again until he retreated, falling backward over the side of the building. As he went over he heard Giselle's muffled scream.

On his way down, Falcon grabbed a flag pole holding a streamer printed with the words, Melrose Apts. He bent the metal pole and vaulted back onto the roof. Before he landed he snapped the iron pole off of its moorings. Falcon Landed on his feet as Raven charged, jabbing at him with his knife. Before the vampire could reach him, Falcon stepped out of the way. As Raven whirled around to confront him, Falcon raised the pointed end of the flag pole and threw it like a javelin.

The point of the pole entered Raven's chest and pierced his heart. He fell on his back and lay still. Falcon grabbed Raven's knife from the concrete and raced back to Giselle. He cut her bonds and she fell limply into his arms. As he headed down the stairway to Giselle's old apartment, Colin, Ethan and Zeke met him at the stairs. Rufus was right behind them barking and whining.

Colin had called the landlord and he was waiting to open the door to Valerie's apartment. Falcon hurried to the couch and lay Giselle down. Ethan was rattling around in the kitchen and ran in with ice. In minutes Giselle's exposed skin was swathed in ice water soaked gauze bandages. She smiled up at Falcon through a puffy face and blood-shot eyes.

"Don't try to talk sweetheart. Your dad's on the way," Falcon stated in a husky voice. He caressed her soft hair with his fingers, and held her swathed hand.

A few minutes later Dr. Montreau and his wife burst in. The doctor's eyes were moist as he gently took his daughter's vital signs. Her mother poured a glass of elixir over ice and held it to her cracked lips so she could drink it.

Rufus was beside himself with worry over Giselle. The sentient canine quietly walked over to the couch and sniffed her tender face. He curled up on the floor near her feet and remained there three days, until the crisis was over.

Falcon walked into the kitchen and got a cup of elixir. Colin Zeke and Ethan followed him in. "How is Father Francis?" Falcon asked.

"He's got an egg-sized bump on his head, but he'll be okay,"

Ethan explained. "I talked to Alberto, Raven tried to kidnap Antonia, but Al kicked his butt, and he took off."

"Al called me before I went after Raven," Falcon replied. "I told him to protect Antonia and her family, in case Raven shows up there."

Dr. Montreau walked into the room, "May I speak to you Theodore?"

"Excuse me, will you guys?" Falcon asked. When the other three men filed out into the living room Falcon looked over at Dr. Montreau.

"I'm sorry Raven had to be killed," he said remorsefully. "I know it was important that he live in order to continue the experiments with Alpha-T, but there was no other way to save Giselle."

"I'm glad you dispatched him swiftly," Dr. Montreau stated.

"I would have done the same thing! As for the Alpha-T trials, I had no more use for Raven. His stay at Renfield proved that the serum works on Keepers." He gave Falcon a fatherly pat on the arm and continued, "It's probably better this way. After what he did to Giselle, I couldn't stomach the thought of having to wait for the Freeblood court to send him to trial. They move agonizingly slow."

Two weeks later, Giselle had healed without any permanent skin damage, courtesy of her vampire ability to regenerate new cells. Raven's body had been taken back to Africa by Dr. Lugano who had fully recovered from his wounds. The Keeper vampire would be buried in and underground cavern in the Hill of the Ghosts, very near the pride of mountain lions that had given him sanctuary.

"I can't believe it's finally over," Giselle stated, as she and Falcon sat together drinking elixir in his apartment. Zeke, who had joined them for a drink earlier, had gone sleepily up to bed.

"It's not over for all of us," Falcon stated. "Fortunately the Ripper is dead and the city can sleep peacefully again. As for the Freebloods in this city, thanks to your father's new formula it's just the beginning."

Taking Giselle's hand Falcon lowered himself onto one knee saying, "By the way there's something I want to ask you."

"Falcon, you surprise me," Giselle stated. She looked down at him happily adding, "The answer is definitely yes!"

"Please allow me the honor of asking the question," Falcon insisted playfully. His voice was steady as he asked, "Will you marry me?"

"Yes!" Giselle answered again.

The couple walked over to the window and gazed at the St. Louis skyline. It was just before dawn, and they felt confident that their city was now a safer place to live. While Ordinaries were getting ready to begin their day, and Freebloods were preparing to sleep, the city remained a constant in all their lives. The Arch, a monument to the brave explorers that opened the West, was splashed with the brilliant red and orange hues of the rising sun. The dark blue Mississippi River, filled with white chunks of ice floating on its choppy surface, would snake and meander until the end of time.

Suddenly, Falcon's cell phone began ringing noisily, "What now?" he thought, as he flipped it open and stared at the tiny screen.

"Falcon, something awful has happened," Colin said mysteriously.

"You're kidding right?" Falcon asked wearily.

"A blog exposing vampires has been circulating on the internet," Colin explained.

"I wouldn't take it too seriously," Falcon replied. "Who would believe it anyway?"

"If it were in the tabloids, I would say you're probably right," Colin returned. "In this case, a vampire wants to turn himself into the authorities and be examined to prove he's the real thing."

"Let me do a little research, and I'll get back with you," Falcon said signing off.

"Well, my love," Giselle said with a smile. "You were right about one thing."

"Just one?" Falcon asked facetiously.

"It's not over," Giselle sighed. "We have to stop that crazy vampire before he ruins everything. As I said before—"

"No dusty old European catacombs for you," Falcon interjected, completing her sentence. Putting his arm around her, he waited for her response.

"You got that right," Giselle agreed, with a grin. "I'm a red-blooded American vampire, and I aim to stay right here with you."

"Now, that's what I'm talking about!" Falcon exclaimed, taking her into his arms.